Finding Myself

OLGA SUSHINSKY

Finding Myself

A NOVEL

bhc
press™

Livonia, Michigan

Edited by:
Amanda Lewis & Rebecca Fischer

Finding Myself
Copyright © 2020 Olga Sushinski

Published by BHC Press

Library of Congress Control Number:
2019954303

ISBN: 978-1-64397-067-7 (Hardcover)
ISBN: 978-1-64397-098-1 (Softcover)
ISBN: 978-1-64397-099-8 (Ebook)

For information, write:
BHC Press
885 Penniman #5505
Plymouth, MI 48170

Visit the publisher:
www.bhcpress.com

Acknowledgments

To my wonderful family, thank you for believing in me and encouraging me to follow my dreams.

To my beta readers who saw the earliest drafts of *Finding Myself*, thank you for taking time to read the story and to provide constructive feedback!

To my publisher, BHC Press, thank you for turning this book into such a wonderful product. Special thanks to my editors, Amanda Lewis and Rebecca Fischer for your invaluable advice and input.

Last but not least, to my husband, Nikita, thank you for walking this journey with me.

Finding
Myself

One

I told myself not to fret. After all, it was just a misplaced invoice and nothing more. *It will probably turn up at someone's desk on Monday*, I kept repeating to myself like a mantra while going through the filing cabinet for the hundredth time.

"Did you find it?" Dave, my manager, asked.

"Not yet. I'm sure it's somewhere." I started going through the files faster.

"Rebecca, you need to stop being reckless," he muttered. "It was a very important order for a client in Vancouver."

I'm not being reckless, you idiot! I wanted to yell. There was at least one other person responsible for filing, so it could've been her.

"Rebecca, can I see you for a moment?" Rosa asked.

"Coming..." I closed the cabinet and walked over to Rosa's desk, fully expecting trouble. When I reached her desk, she was typing something on her computer. "I'm here," I said, tapping lightly on her table. She stopped her work and gave me that look that confirmed all my suspicions about the trouble.

"So, yesterday, I asked you to bring my docket to the shipping department," she began after a prolonged pause.

"Yes, I remember that." I vaguely recalled carrying a large envelope with files on the latest client order.

"Why did it end up in the embroidery department?"

"What?" My memory must've been betraying me, for I clearly remembered handing it to Diego, the manager of the shipping and receiving department.

Sensing my shock, Rosa softened. "All right, next time, please remember to put it in the right place."

"Sure. No problem." I sighed. "Sorry for this mistake."

I started packing for the day as soon as I returned to my desk. Since it was already four twenty-five, there was no point in staying longer. Surely this Friday wasn't ending the way I had imagined it, but I was still feeling excited. That night, Jason and I were planning to go out and possibly discuss our summer plans. I smiled at the thought of escaping together to some tropical resort. I quickly grabbed my purse before anyone else could catch me and left the building.

On the subway, I took out my iPod and drowned in my favorite music, which mostly comprised of the latest Israeli hits. I closed my eyes and tried imagining what it would be like to return to the land of our honeymoon. The desert, the sea, and a myriad of unexplored places came into my mind. It was the place where Jason and I went right after the wedding for a ten-day bus tour. Although we'd seen quite a few sites, it wasn't enough. I longed to come back, to big deeper into the land of mystery and enigma.

At the university, I had majored in anthropology with a special focus on Near Eastern archaeology. I had taken survey courses in ancient ceramics along with Hebrew and Aramaic. Since I also listened to Israeli music, I could speak the language of the Bible almost fluently. Most people assumed I was Jewish or had lived in Israel in the past, but neither was true about me. I was simply a geek with unusual interests. The only problem was that my degree never paid off in real life.

After graduating with a GPA of 3.7, I hoped to secure a job at the Archaeological Services of Canada or the Royal Ontario Museum. Instead, I ended up working as an office assistant at Happy Apparel Inc., a company that sold uniforms and promotional products to large-scale customers, including major grocery stores and coffee shops. My duties mostly revolved around order entries, invoices, and customer calls. Although this job was a good source of moderate income, it was not what I had envisioned back at university.

I reached home in less than fifty minutes. Except for the times I was taking night classes, I usually came home earlier than Jason. His work hours ran until five while mine were until four-thirty. It was amazing that even after four years of marriage and nearly five years of being together, I was still thrilled to see him every day after work. I ran to the door as soon as I heard the key in the lock.

"Hi, honey! How was your day?" he asked, hanging his coat. I observed his profile as he moved across the living room. His dark skin stood against the white collar of his shirt. Despite his mix of Scottish and French background, he looked more like a southerner. I suspected it was also his Native Canadian ancestry from his mother's side that contributed to his dark looks. But mostly, I believed, it was because he had grown up on a farm, under lots of sunshine, before moving to Toronto.

"Not too bad, thanks," I replied. "How was yours?"

"Well, I've got some exciting news you might like."

"Bring it on." I wrapped my arms around him and looked directly into his brown eyes.

"Our company is expanding, which means that new servers will be built," he replied. A former informatics major, he now worked at a midsize company, providing IT support. "I will be working more hours and making a better salary."

"That's great," I said, secretly feeling a bit upset. Jason always looked for opportunities to work more, even if it meant compromising our time for each other.

"But don't worry. I promise not to work on nights or weekends."

"I hope not. Well, I'm really happy for you." And I truly was.

"At last, we can afford to take a vacation we've always dreamed about."

"True, Jason."

We both loved traveling. We had never been to Europe but believed there was still enough time. Nevertheless, we had visited a lot of places in the United States and stopped by a few Caribbean resorts. Throughout the years, however, we were so busy with our jobs that vacations felt more like a necessity rather than a luxury.

"So, shall we get going?" he asked.

"Do you mind if I change first?"

"Sure! I'll wait for you here."

He plopped on a couch and took out his cell phone while I went to our bedroom and opened the closet doors. Feeling weary of the boring office clothes, which were mostly black and gray, I quickly found a pair of blue jeans and a pink denim shirt. Although I wasn't a high-maintenance type, I loved wearing bright colors. Having fixed my makeup, I emerged from the bedroom ready to go.

"What do you think?" I asked, making a twirl.

"You look great, as always." He got up from the couch and quickly retrieved jackets from our closet. "Here you go." He offered me mine.

Soon, we were walking toward the Firkin Pub, inhaling the flavors of grill mixed with smells of spicy food. The weather was quite cold for early May, and most trees were still bare of new growth. That year, we had had the longest winter in history, and everyone was fed up with the ruthless wind, rain, and snow. Just a few weeks ago, there had been the worst spring storm I could ever remember. An exception would probably be one ice rain that had happened in April when I was still in high school. Weary of the endless winter, many had already started ditching winter coats for shorts and sandals.

We quickly reached the pub, where a waitress escorted us to a table for two and asked if we would like something to drink. Jason ordered two light beers. As soon as the lady reappeared with our drinks, I requested a shepherd's pie while Jason asked for smoked salmon with baked potatoes.

"So, where do you want to go this summer?" I asked after the waitress left.

"Hmm, I was thinking about California." He took a sip from his glass of beer.

"Sounds nice. I'd love to see Sequoia National Park."

"Me too."

"We could drive there from San Francisco and stay in a lodge overnight."

"We could also try parasailing over the ocean," he suggested.

"No way, Jason! Just thinking about it gives me chills." I playfully slapped his hand.

"That comes from someone who wanted to go to Syria." He gave me a wicked grin.

"Why are you using past tense? I still want to go there."

"Here is your order," a waitress said, passing two sizable plates. Judging from the look on her face, she overheard parts of our conversation. For a moment, I felt a bit uncomfortable. My desire to see the entire world, particularly the Middle Eastern region, got a bit too much sometimes. "I went there back in 2009," the lady added, smiling. "It was beautiful." Immediately, any feeling of discomfort disappeared. I wanted to ask her more about the places she'd visited, but Jason quickly thanked her and took the plates. Before I had the chance to say anything, she made a usual spiel about letting her know if we needed anything and went off to another table.

"I just want to be sure I'm not going to Israel this summer," I said halfway through our meal.

"When will you find out?" he asked, forking his salmon.

"I don't know yet. But even if I win the scholarship, I still can't be gone for three weeks. I only booked off one this year."

Earlier that spring, I had applied for a scholarship through my favorite magazine, *BAR*—short for *Biblical Archaeology Review*. I had also sent an application to the Kiryat Adar Expedition to volunteer for a dig in southern Israel, positive that both applications would be turned down. Seriously, what chance did an average anthropology graduate have at winning an international competition? Students from across the North American continent routinely applied for such programs and scholarships in hopes of winning a summer adventure. I only filled out the application because I was supposed to be working on the copywriting assignment for my continuing studies program, but I became too bored and distracted. I did not truly expect any positive answer.

"But if, for some reason, you end up going," he added, "I'm thinking about spending a week together in Tel Aviv after the dig is over."

"Ah, that would be so nice." I sighed. "I miss that city so much!"

"Then we should go for it." He smiled.

"I'm sure my boss will fire me if he finds out."

"Well, I'm just making a suggestion."

We spent the rest of the evening fantasizing about other places we could visit this summer. I suggested Crow Canyon Archaeological Center in Colorado or Canyonlands National Park in Utah as alternatives to California. Jason, in turn, told me he really wanted to visit Florida, which wasn't very surprising to me considering how much he loved beaches and swimming. Soon enough, the dinner was over, and we were headed back home. With the night approaching, the temperature was getting close to zero.

"I'm so done with this stupid winter!" I exclaimed, my hands shivering from cold.

"I'm sure the summer will be nice," Jason said while trying to warm up my hands with his.

When we got home, I noticed an email notification at the top corner of my phone screen. I wasn't expecting anything serious on a Friday night, but decided to check it anyway. When I discovered the letter, I wasn't sure how to react.

Dear Rebecca O'Connor-Smith,

Congratulations! You have been selected for the Annual Archaeological Dig Scholarship by the Biblical Archaeological Society. We will fund your proposed project with a grant of $1,500. In order to receive funds for this fellowship, we require you to fill out the attached acceptance form and liability waiver and return both to our office as soon as possible.

By accepting this award, you are agreeing to submit a report by the end of the season. The report should be 250–350 words in length and include an appropriate photo that illustrates your participation in the project for which you received funding.

Best,

Biblical Archaeology Review Team

"Jason, I won it!" I jumped up, still holding the phone.

"What?" he asked.

"I won the scholarship. I'm going to Israel this summer."

He moved toward me. "Does it mean we get to spend a week in Tel Aviv?"

"Well, I still have to talk to my supervisor." The tiny feeling of dread crept inside, only to be pushed away with happy thoughts.

"I'm sure he'll be cool about that," Jason reassured me. "Haven't you accumulated four weeks already?"

"Yes, but we were booking off vacations a long time ago. I don't think he'll be happy to hear about our summer plans."

"Let's not think about the bad stuff. I think we need to celebrate." With these words, he strode to the kitchen and opened a bottle of champagne. I walked behind him and found two glasses inside our cupboard.

"If only we could go there this year!" I sighed, taking a sip. "Then we could revisit all the sites again."

"Or just lie on the beach. We hadn't done too much of it the last time."

"Okay, let's deal with one thing at a time. I'm going to try getting clearance at work."

"Please do so as soon as you can. I really want to find a good flight and a hotel."

"I'll try."

"In the meantime, I want to spend some quality time with my wife."

"Let's do that!" We put down our glasses of wine and went straight to our bedroom.

I loved being close to him, especially after such a busy week. Even after so many years, he could still ignite passion in me like no one else. I loved everything about him—the shape of his jaw, his facial features, and, most importantly, the way he held me during our most tender moments.

"I've missed you so much!" I whispered between the kisses and all.

"Me too, Becky."

Afterward, we took a long, lazy shower, allowing water to wash away all the stress and uncertainties of daily life. Then he declared he was tired and climbed under the bed covers.

Feeling jittery from the news, I walked back to the living room, where I sat on a couch, sipping my glass of wine and browsing through the latest issue of the *BAR* magazine. It featured a long article about the true location of the Mt. Sinai. Some claim the actual site is located in Saudi Arabia, believe it or not. Unable to concentrate on the text, I flipped through the pages, which contained lists of newly released books, images of antique jewellery, and ads of products for elderly people. Then I tiptoed to our bedroom and lay beside Jason, who was already soundly asleep.

Two

I phoned my sister, Erin, as soon as I got a chance the next morning. Jason left in the wee hours to run some errands while I was left with little to do but marvel at my luck.

"That's so exciting!" she exclaimed as soon as I relayed the news. "Now you get to have a summer adventure plus a second honeymoon."

"I can't wait already. I just have one more issue to take care of."

"What issue?" She sounded a bit annoyed.

"I still haven't booked my vacation at work, and I'm not sure if I have enough time before July."

"Wow, what a great planner you are!"

As the younger sister, I was often perceived as the least organized one. Although it wasn't completely true, Erin liked perpetuating this misconception about me.

"Come on, I didn't even know if I was going in the first place!"

"Well, they'll have to let you go," she tried reassuring me. "They've got no choice."

"I really hope they will."

"By the way, can you please bring me one of those Dead Sea products? I absolutely loved that Ahava lotion you brought me from your last trip."

"Definitely! Maybe your company should order some as well."

"We'd love to, but their products are so expensive."

As an aesthetician, Erin got to work with some of the best beauty products, but she had never managed to use anything from the Dead Sea collections.

"So, how did your date go?" I finally asked. Last night, she had gone on a date with a guy she had met online. The entire week, she had been feeling terribly excited and couldn't talk about anything else. Never mind it was probably her tenth date in the month.

"Alex is okay, and he seems to like me a lot," she began. "But honestly, I think we are too different from each other."

"How so?" I walked to the kitchen to turn on the coffee machine.

"I feel intimidated by him. He's finishing business school while I'm a college graduate."

"So what?"

"He looks so refined, Becky. When I'm with him, I feel out of place."

"Yesterday, you sounded quite optimistic."

"I was until he started talking about politics and global warming, and I didn't even know what to say."

"I bet you would rather talk to him about the latest fashion trends."

"Becky, don't laugh at me! You know how I feel about those heavy topics."

"Maybe you should give it some time. I mean, Jason and I are different in so many ways, but we get along very well."

"I'm so afraid of failing again! I know I'm only twenty-eight, but I'm so exhausted from searching for Mr. Right. I often wish I had your life."

I hated to hear my girl sound so pessimistic. On the outside, she always looked strong, almost invincible. However, I knew her better. Erin had a lot of insecurities others knew nothing about.

"Don't worry, Erin. You still have plenty of time. All I'm saying is you shouldn't jump to any conclusions just yet. Also, you shouldn't be ashamed of your education. Career-wise, you've achieved much more than I have."

The latter statement was completely true. While I held a boring nine-to-five office job I hated, Erin worked at a glamorous spa center in downtown and loved every minute of it. On the relationship front, however, I was the lucky one. At twenty-six, I had been happily married for nearly four years. Erin, although two years older than me, was still single and going on random dates in hopes of finding her man.

"Well, thanks for the reassurance," she said. "I'll see how it goes. It might work, or it might not. Anyway, I'm happy for you."

"We should go shopping someday," I suggested.

"Let's do that!" Her voice lightened up immediately.

"How about meeting sometime after my vacation days are sorted out?"

"Well, I hope it will happen soon."

"Me too."

After our conversation, I grabbed my jacket and stepped onto the balcony to get some fresh air. Although our condo was located right on Yonge and Finch, our windows faced the inner courtyard which had a small fountain surrounded by trees. I observed the green grass on a nearby field, marvelling at all the ways in which Erin and I were different from each other.

WE GREW up in the quiet town of Oakville, located only thirty minutes away from Toronto. Our parents, Isabel and Anthony O'Connor, owned an antique bookstore, which still brought out many happy memories. My father also worked at a restaurant on a side. The smell of old books, the feel of yellowy paper under my fingers, and, most importantly, the hours spent reading a vintage encyclopaedia about the ancient civilizations were enough for me to forget all about the world outside.

I became infatuated with ancient Israel at the age of twelve. It happened when I was walking home from school and decided to stop at my mother's bookstore. As soon as I entered the shop, my attention got caught by a large vintage book titled *Encyclopaedia of the Ancient Civilizations*. I picked it up and quickly skimmed through the table of contents. The book had chapters on Egypt, Mesopotamia, and the biblical land of Canaan. The latter immediately captivated me. Since we had already studied the first two at school, I was a bit familiar with these civilizations. However, I knew very little about ancient Israel. The next day, I went back to the store, found the book resting on its shelf, and sat with it for two hours straight. The pattern continued for the next few months. I read about the origins of the ancient Israelites, King David's reign, and the temple built by King Solomon. Then I moved on to other chapters. My mother noted my interest in the book but didn't say anything. The following winter, I was thrilled to discover the book under the Christmas tree.

During the times I wasn't reading, I was a normal teenager, who had a few good friends and enjoyed playing sports. I also loved singing and was a soloist in our school's choir. However, next to my sister, I was a complete nerd and a weirdo.

Like most girls our age, Erin was an avid follower of everything related to Britney Spears and Justin Timberlake, whose romance was a hot topic at the time. She kept a stack of *People* magazines under her bed, and her walls were plastered with posters of pop artists and movie stars. I, on the contrary, didn't care about that stuff and preferred encyclopaedias to celebrity gossip. Amazingly, our differences almost never interfered with our friendship.

We hardly ever experienced sibling rivalry and always had each other's backs during difficult times.

We left Oakville when I was fourteen, which was the time of some unpleasant changes. My parents' bookstore—and my afternoon respite from school—went bankrupt. I knew something wasn't quite right when I noticed fewer customers coming in. I began eavesdropping on my parents' conversations and found out about increasing expenses and declining profits. Eventually, they were forced to close down the store. A few weeks later, another calamity arrived. The restaurant where my father worked part time was having financial issues. As a result, several workers, including himself, were laid off.

They tried shielding us from the troubles, but it was pointless. We were old enough to understand what was happening. One day, I noticed a large "For Sale" sign placed in front of our house. Next to it was a picture of some man in a suit with big letters saying "Real Estate Agent." I couldn't remember his name, for I didn't care.

When my father announced over dinner that we were moving to Toronto, I wanted to protest every possible way. Not only were my parents closing my favorite bookstore, but they were also selling our house, which meant that I would no longer have my childhood room I had cherished for so long. However, I managed to hold it together for the sake of our family. Deep inside, I knew this bookstore meant just as much to them as it meant to me.

Things didn't get any better in Toronto. For the first few months, our reserve money was running out fast, and we were scrambling for every penny while trying to survive. Once a restaurant chef, my father was now flipping burgers at McDonald's. It took him several attempts and a few night courses on business management to find a better job. My mother became a cashier at Chapters Indigo. Although she was later promoted to a floor supervisor, this job was not the same as ownership of a bookstore.

As for myself, I did not like this big, gray city at all, and I absolutely hated our new school. We attended Evergreens Collegiate Institute, which was one of the best schools in the city. The level of education there was far higher than in most schools across Ontario, and in the beginning, my grades were terrible. While all my classmates were putting forth minimal effort to get As and Bs, I was barely passing my courses.

On the friendship front, the situation was even worse. No matter how hard I tried, I couldn't fit into the high school culture that was characterized by gray sweatpants, UGGs, and classic rock. I was way too different from everyone else, for I preferred Zohar Argov over Elvis Presley. So I would spend most of the breaks standing by a wall, headphones plugged in my ears, trying to obliterate all the stress and disappointment that was happening in my life by cranking up Putumayo series on my iPod.

Erin, by contrast, fell in love with Toronto and became the popular girl right from the start. Her grades weren't high either, but it didn't seem to bother her. She already had her mind set on the college for aestheticians and was doing well enough to get accepted. Besides, she was always the life of the party, and everyone adored her. During her high school years, she became a glamorous cheerleader, built a circle of girlfriends with similar pursuits, and attended countless house parties, where she met her first boyfriend, Jake. Together, they became the hottest couple in the entire school.

For the next year and a half, our yearbooks were filled with their photos from various events. Their relationship, however, didn't last beyond the prom date. The summer after their graduation, he moved to Montreal to study at McGill, and Erin never saw him again. She was a bit sad, but there were other exciting things happening in her life. She got accepted to Seneca College for the aesthetician program and was incredibly happy about having achieved her dream.

In the meantime, I studied hard for history tests, wrote long English essays, and did everything to make it to university. Slowly, my grades picked up. One beautiful spring day, I found an admission letter in our mailbox and became overwhelmed with pride. I had been admitted to the University of Toronto, one of the few universities in our province that offered a program in anthropology with a focus on ancient Near East. My efforts finally paid off.

To some extent, winning this scholarship reminded me of the day I had learned about my acceptance to the U of T. After being let down at work so many times, I began to yearn for a small accomplishment that would remind me of my capabilities.

HAVING STEPPED from the balcony, I went to the kitchen and made a cup of coffee. Jason came in a few minutes later carrying handfuls of grocery bags.

"Here. Let me help." I hurried to his side and took some of the bags from him.

"It's okay. I'll manage," he said in response.

"So, what are our plans for today?" I asked while unpacking the groceries.

"We could go for a walk and check out some stuff for your trip."

"That sounds nice. I'm sure we have more than enough time for shopping." I had to be 100 percent sure I was going in the first place.

"Whatever works for you, Becky," he replied before moving to the living room and turning on the TV.

MY MOTHER called in the evening and asked if there was anything new with us.

"Nothing much," I replied, feeling my stomach tighten. I had to disclose the truth to my parents too, and I wasn't sure how they would react. My parents read the news too much to think of Israel as anything more than a danger zone.

"I hope you didn't forget Dad's birthday is this weekend," she reminded me.

"Of course not! How could I?" I made a mental note to search for a present this week.

"Then you and Jason are invited to our dinner on Saturday. Will you come?"

"For sure! What time should we arrive?" I asked.

"Around six o'clock, I think."

"See you then."

For the rest of the weekend, I couldn't stop stressing out over the possibility of not getting the time off or even losing my job. I tried working on an assignment for my copywriting course, but I simply couldn't concentrate. Every time I sat down and opened the Blackboard, my mind would trail off to something else. In a few minutes, I would be checking Facebook, getting up for a cup of coffee, and doing everything else besides studying. After a gazillion futile attempts at studying, I finally gave up. The stubborn jitters refused to leave me alone. I had to know if the trip to Kiryat Adar was happening.

Three

Asking for four weeks off less than two months before my trip wouldn't be easy. Yet I had to stay positive to remain sane. So I woke up the following Monday feeling as cheerful as ever. Having put on my favorite fluffy robe over a nightgown, I went to the kitchen and turned on the coffee machine. Then I went straight to the washroom and began rehearsing my speech in front of a mirror. I would tell my supervisor about my unexpected trip and apologize for the late notice. Quite possibly, his reaction would not be so bad, and he would grant me my time off right away. Jason came in and greeted me with a warm embrace.

"May I use the sink?" he asked.

"No," I replied jokingly.

By the time we got out of the bathroom, the coffee was already boiling. If we'd come out a minute later, it would've already made a huge mess on our countertop. After a quick breakfast, we slipped into our jackets, packed our lunch bags, and walked out.

"See you later, honey," I told Jason downstairs while exiting the elevator.

"Have a great day and take it easy."

"I'll try." Once again, I wanted to be optimistic.

Our condo was located right on the subway line, making it very easy to commute. Every morning, I had around forty or fifty minutes of free time before starting work. Unless the train was extremely crowded or there were delays, riding on the subway was quite enjoyable. I spent this ride fantasizing about Kiryat Adar and its hidden treasures. One of my former university classmates discovered a three-thousand-year-old statue while excavating in Turkey, and I hoped something similar would turn up during my trip. My daydreaming was over as soon as the train operator announced my station, which was Warden. I quickly got out of the train and ran to the bus platform. Two stops later, I was already at my workplace.

"Good morning," I said to Dave, my supervisor. "Can I speak to you for a second?"

"Not now," he replied, looking a little annoyed.

Probably the traffic, I thought to myself.

Dave commuted from Oshawa to Scarborough every day. Sometimes, he would get stuck on the highway and arrive thirty minutes late because of some stupid accident or construction. For this exact reason, I did not want to buy a house in the suburbs even though Jason occasionally browsed listings in Brampton and Richmond Hill. For me, it would only mean too much trouble with traffic.

I sat down in my cubicle peering at the Outlook screen. I had three customer complaints to resolve and forty orders to enter into the system. Dave showed up at my desk a few hours later and asked if I had something to discuss. To my relief, he looked a bit more relaxed than in the morning. I asked him if I could schedule some vacation time.

"For which dates?" he asked, tension palpable in his voice.

"From June thirtieth until July twenty-fifth," I said, heart thumping.

"Four weeks?" He looked surprised. "That's quite a long time to be gone during one of our busiest times."

"I believe I have accrued enough days over the past few years."

"Why didn't you schedule these weeks ahead of time?"

For a split second, I wondered if disclosing the truth about my scholarship and the excavation dig was a good idea. People at my work knew almost nothing about my interests. However, lying about some made-up emergency was out of question. So I chose to go with the truth.

"I won a scholarship that will allow me to participate in an excavation dig," I said. "It will take place in Israel. I only found out this weekend."

He listened quietly, making me feel even tenser.

"If those dates are a problem for the company, I will cancel the trip and stay here," I added, trying to salvage the situation. "I just wanted to check if there was the slightest chance I could still go."

"I'm afraid I'll have to speak to our senior manager," he muttered.

"When can I expect the answer?"

"Sometime today." He gave me a faint smile.

"Thanks, Dave."

Although I felt a bit relieved, my ordeal didn't stop. More orders kept coming, and more phone calls had to be answered. I did find the invoice from last Friday—on the receptionist's desk—but it did little to alleviate the stress.

Dave showed up at my desk again at around three in the afternoon and informed me that we needed to talk. He didn't look upset, which I took as a good sign.

"I spoke with the senior manager," he said matter-of-factly.

Chills went down my spine. Maybe that was it, and I was going to be fired.

"She said those four weeks shouldn't be a problem."

The moment these words came out, I became overwhelmed with relief.

"Thank you!" I exclaimed, unable to hide my excitement.

"But next time, please let us know ahead of time," he added.

"Definitely." At this moment, I was ready to promise almost anything.

"And by the way, congratulations on your scholarship!" He smiled.

"Thanks."

As soon as Dave left, I sent text messages to Jason and Erin. Both replied with smiles. I later received a message from Erin who suggested meeting at the Eaton Center for shopping. We still had to find a present for our father. I agreed wholeheartedly, and we arranged to meet at five-thirty.

In the meantime, I started getting restless. The day was almost over, and in about an hour, I would be having fun with my sister. At four twenty-five, my phone rang.

It was Glenn, one of the sales representatives, with whom I had never managed to get along. The moment I picked up the phone, she started accusing me of entering an invoice incorrectly, which meant she wouldn't get her commission. It was frustrating that no matter how hard I tried to avoid those mistakes, they would still turn up and always at the very last minute. Instead of running to the door at four-thirty, I had to stay a few minutes late and redo the invoice.

"Why aren't you going home?" Ashley, a fellow office assistant, asked me while passing my cubicle.

"Something urgent came up," I replied while nervously retyping the invoice. "Have to stay."

"Just go. We aren't even getting paid for the extra time."

"I'll go in a few minutes," I mumbled, trying to concentrate.

Suddenly, the system froze. "Dammit!" I sighed.

"What?" She turned around.

"The system isn't working."

"It only means you should go home."

I looked at my watch and noticed it was already quarter to five. "Maybe you're right. I'll just go home," I said in frustration. The invoice could surely wait until the next day. Thus, I left feeling dissatisfied with my day again. The feeling of accomplishment simply didn't exist at my job.

Forty minutes later, I was at the Eaton Center, waiting for Erin to arrive. Soon, I spotted her walking toward me with a huge Starbucks cup in her hand. She was wearing a short Danier jacket over a cashmere sweater and a pair of skinny jeans. He black, shiny hair was tied into a sleek ponytail, and her dark blue eyes were accentuated by a black eyeliner she applied so effortlessly every morning. Her usual five-inch pumps, however, had been replaced with running shoes. She always kept a spare pair in her car just in case she decided to go on a spontaneous shopping spree.

"Hello, stranger!" I said.

"Hi, Becky." She gave me a hug.

We decided to check out the latest products at Future Shop and to look for summer clothes. Since the electronics store was open until later, we agreed to hit the mall first. Erin went straight to designer stores hunting for sales. Somehow, she always managed to find Armani tops and Gucci bags for half price. I opted for Gap and Old Navy, as I didn't need anything fancy. So I picked a few pairs of shorts, cargo pants, and a bunch of long-sleeved shirts that would protect me from the sun.

"You should try this." She showed me a leopard-print shirt by Marciano. "You want to look good for your man."

"Are you kidding me? It's $200!"

"It's 70 percent off, and it will look great on you."

"Where am I going to wear it? To the field?" I laughed.

"Think of what you'll wear when your hubby arrives."

"I'm sure after three weeks, he'll be happy to see me in almost anything." We giggled. "We'll probably go shopping in Tel Aviv," I added.

"Eh, lucky you! I wish I were in the faculty of archaeology." She stared dreamily at one of the clothing racks.

"I'm no longer a part of any faculty. I'm just an ordinary office worker trying to take some time off."

"I'm still jealous."

After our first round of purchases, Erin suggested going to Bikini Village, where we tried on a dozen bathing suits. She picked two pink bikinis while I landed on a traditional one-piece bathing suit, which she deemed "old fashioned."

"I don't need too much attention in a foreign place."

"Well, I guess you are right," she said. "We don't want you to get abducted by the Bedouins."

"Stop it, Erin! Israel is the safest place in the Middle East, and the Bedouins are friendly." I recalled a few stories from my ex-classmates from school about their Birthright trips, which often included spending a night in a Bedouin tent, smoking shisha, and sleeping under the stars.

"As you say, Becky." She rolled her eyes.

Erin only used her TV for Netflix and Popcorn Time, so I didn't have to try hard to convince her.

After shopping, we stopped at the food court and ordered chicken souvlaki from Jimmy the Greek. We talked about the impending dinner with our parents, and for the first time, I began to wonder how they would feel about my trip.

"Mom will probably be unhappy," I admitted. "She wasn't thrilled the last time we went."

"Ah, don't worry. It will pass. If you are too nervous, I can always help you."

"But how?" I took a bite from a baked potato.

"I can call her and tell her everything myself," she replied casually.

"Oh, please don't do that!" I didn't want my parents to learn the news from someone else.

"Okay, I won't. I just wanted to offer my help."

"Thanks, Erin. I'll sort it out by myself."

"Anyway, let's hurry up. We still have to buy a present for Dad."

After a careful inventory of the newest products at Future Shop, we decided to buy a new GPS, which our parents could use on their next road trip. Then we went straight to Erin's car. I was willing to take the subway home, but she insisted on giving me a ride.

"You are not going on the subway with all those bags," she said in her bossy tone.

When we arrived at my place, Jason was already at home, idling on the couch.

"Hey, Erin! Good to see you." He offered my sister a friendly hug.

"Hey, how was your day?" I asked my husband.

"It was great, thanks. Look what I got for you!" He showed me a brimmed hat and pair of gardening gloves. "You'll need these on your dig."

"Oh, how nice!" Erin exclaimed. "You've got such a great husband."

"I know." I couldn't help but smile. I could bet she no longer thought I had made a mistake. She used to disapprove of my decision to marry at twenty-two, but surely, this must've changed with time.

"Want some tea?" Jason asked.

"Sure," Erin and I replied in unison.

The three of us spent a few minutes in the living room chatting about random stuff. After Erin left, I tried reading my *BAR* magazine in our bedroom, but Jason took it away from me.

"What are you doing?" I asked, pretending to be angry.

"You will have ten hours on a plane to read your magazines," he said while unbuttoning my blouse. "We need to use our time more constructively."

I couldn't agree with him more.

Four

On Saturday morning, I woke up feeling happy. Our flight tickets were finally booked, and my doctor's appointment was scheduled for the following Monday. I had to undergo a physical evaluation to be deemed fit for archaeological work. Such was the requirement of the program. To me, it was more of a formality because I already knew my health was good enough to endure several hours under the sun.

"Hungry?" I asked Jason, as he came out of the shower.

"Yes, as always," he replied, lying down beside me and pulling me to his side.

A few minutes later, he offered to fix us some breakfast, to which I gladly agreed. I was really tired after a long week and didn't mind a little downtime. He made coffee and served it with a cup of strawberries and Greek yogurt.

"I'm a bit nervous about tonight," I admitted while loading the dishwasher. Tonight, I was planning to tell my parents about the upcoming trip.

"Don't worry about anything," he said.

"I'll try. After all, we are adults now."

"Exactly!"

I tried doing my homework after breakfast. Since I hadn't accomplished much during the work week, I had more catching up to do. Readings and exercises about writing for the web were downright boring, but I managed to finish all of them in less than an hour. My next assignment required me to write compelling copy for an imaginary website selling computers. The deadline was only a few days away. Normally, I didn't have any problems with getting work done on time, especially for my continuing education courses. This time, however, my mind simply refused to come up with any ideas.

"How is everything?" Jason asked me after an hour had passed. The entire time, he was sitting beside me and browsing the Internet.

"Not so good," I replied candidly.

"Any progress at all?"

"Jason, I don't even know what I'm doing!"

"All right, let me see." He moved closer and started reading off the screen. "Our store is the best...Good quality for low prices... Look no further. Goodness, is that all you wrote in the last hour?"

"I know! This is horrible! I'll never become a good copywriter." I put my hands over my face.

"It's okay, Becky." He gave me a hug. "Maybe we should take a break and go for a walk."

"Oh, that would be nice. I'm dying for some fresh air."

"Let's go then."

We walked slowly on the busy street, savoring the spring air mixed with smells from restaurants and coffee shops. Even at thirteen degrees over zero, the spring weather felt like a respite after the fierce winter. At the end of the walk, we decided to stop at Second Cup and grab two hot chocolates. Once we returned home, I tried working on my assignment but got stuck again. Finally, I gave it up for good.

"BECKY, I think it's time to go now," Jason said, pointing at the clock hanging in the living room. He was flipping through

TV channels, while I was reading Kiryat Adar: Figurines and Pottery from Iron Age II. I had ordered this book on Amazon a couple of days ago, and it arrived in our mailbox yesterday. Every time I picked it up, I became overwhelmed with euphoria and excitement.

"Yeah, you're right," I said, my eyes still fixed on the images platter showcasing the top artifacts from the site.

"Don't worry about your assignment," he added. "I'm pretty sure you'll come up with great ideas later."

I quickly signed the card and packed the GPS into a gift bag I had bought at Hallmark on our way home. Then we started getting dressed. I chose to wear a simple Gap T-shirt, jeans, and a hoodie, while Jason put on a beige shirt I had given him last Christmas.

"That beige color really suits you," I told him while checking myself in the mirror.

"Thanks, darling! You look great too."

A few minutes later, we were parked on the side of the road right across from my parents' home. Ever since our family had gotten out of debt, my parents had been living in a small house in the Annex area. It had also been my home until Jason and I had gotten married.

By the time we reached their house, my mother was already waiting for us at the door. While we were exchanging our hellos, I eyed Erin, who looked absolutely gorgeous in her floral print dress and denim jacket. She was standing next to the kitchen, winking at me.

"It'll be all right," she whispered to me as we were giving our present to Dad.

My mother served a fine selection of Japanese dishes that she had learned from cookbooks she had gotten from Chapters on discount. I had a bowl of rice with shrimps and scallops, while Jason had teriyaki chicken and pasta. The main course was followed by a homemade cake with strawberries and cream.

As the dinner progressed, we talked about different topics, including our holiday plans. My parents were planning on traveling to the United States on the Queen Victoria weekend, which was only a week away, and were also considering flying to Europe at the end of August.

When it was our turn to talk about summer plans, I couldn't muster the courage to tell my parents the truth. I knew they wouldn't take the news very well. So I kept on steering our conversation in other directions to avoid the topic as much as possible until it was almost time to go home.

"Becky, can I have a word with you in private?" Erin asked me as we were getting ready to take off.

"Sure," I replied reluctantly. She took my hand and led me to what used to be my room.

"When are you going to tell them?" she whispered.

"I don't know. I'm afraid they won't be thrilled about the news."

"Come on, Becky! Grow up at last!"

"I am a grown-up. Stop bossing me!"

"Then why don't you just tell them?" Her whispering was now louder than any normal speaking.

"It's not easy, Erin."

"What isn't easy?" My mother appeared at the doorway.

"Eh, nothing much." I shrugged.

"Come on, just tell her." Erin nudged me. "Okay, I will, then."

"What! No! You can't do this!" For a second, I became oblivious to whoever was watching us.

"What's going on in here?" our father asked, walking in. Jason followed him.

"Do you want to tell?" Jason asked, winking at me.

"Fine, I will." I sighed. Everyone looked at me.

"I'm going to Israel this summer. I won a scholarship through an archaeological magazine. I'll be excavating in Kiryat Adar in the south, and my trip will be partially funded. Jason will join me at the end of the dig, and we'll be staying in Tel Aviv for a week." My sudden announcement was followed by silence.

"Wait, you are flying to another country alone?" My mother looked baffled.

"Yes, but I'll be with a group most of the time." I tried acting as if it wasn't a big deal, but deep inside, I was feeling tense.

"Well, have a safe drive home, kids," my mother said after a prolonged pause. Even though she acted cool and composed, I could tell she wasn't happy. Maybe she would need more time to process the news. For now, all I could do was play along.

"Goodnight, Mom! Thanks for the dinner."

"You didn't have to act like you've done something wrong," Jason told me on our way home.

"I know. I should've told them right away."

"Even if you didn't, it would be okay. It's our life now, our plans."

"You are right. At least it's over now."

Just as I was about to go to bed, Erin phoned me. She asked me if I was okay and even apologized for pushing me into telling my parents the truth. I told her it was okay. They would've found out eventually. She even suggested going for a cup of coffee the next day, but I refused. Not because I was angry at her at this point, but because I still had a lot of work to accomplish for my copywriting course. In the end, we wished each other good night, and she reassured me that I had every right to pursue my hobbies. Despite the initial anger, it still felt good to talk to my sister and end this evening on a friendly note.

For most of Sunday, I worked fiercely on my copywriting project. I finally managed to come up with a few ideas. Studying always helped me to put my mind at ease.

Five

Following my father's birthday, I kept in touch my parents regularly. Although we appeared to be on friendly terms, I could tell they weren't happy about the trip. In the meantime, I was still very busy with monotonous order entries, invoices, and customer calls. Half the time, our clients' misfortunes had nothing to do with me, but I was always held responsible. The next few weeks flew by because I had my trip to look forward to.

For starters, I couldn't wait to finish the copywriting course, which I often found mind-numbing. Luckily, I had only one more course to complete before I couple apply for a program certificate.

Finally, the day before my departure arrived. The coursework was done, phone calls answered, and invoices filed away. Shortly before I left, Dave and a few others wished me a safe trip, and a couple of people from the shipping department made jokes about bringing a bulletproof vest on the trip. Although I felt tempted to tell these guys stop watching TV too much, I thanked everyone for their wishes.

That night, Jason and I decided to order pizza as a way of celebrating summer's promises. While discussing our plans over delicious pepperoni slices, we promised each other to keep in touch during my stay in Kiryat Adar and discussed my plan to buy a local phone card. Then we talked about the places we hoped to visit. The Old Cities of Jerusalem and Jaffa were definitely on the list.

I couldn't stop looking at him as he sat across from me, nibbling at his pizza. Every time his eyes met mine, I was reminded of the first time we met at a library cafeteria all those five years ago. I was standing in a long line, waiting for a microwave to become available, and he was standing in front of me. When his turn came, he looked at me with his deep brown eyes and told me to go ahead. I felt something special as soon as I saw him. Somehow, we ended up sitting together and striking up a conversation. Little did I know that this simple conversation would lead to a full-blown romance and ultimately marriage.

We tied the knot after a little over a year of dating. Naturally, everyone thought we were too young for such a big step. I had just turned twenty-two, while he was twenty-seven. By then, I was still fresh out of university, while he had just begun his first real job in information technology. Before that, he was working at a U of T library, providing computer support. Every single piece of relationship advice I found online or in books told me that we were supposed to date for a few years before even thinking about commitment. However, I could not say "no" to his proposal, which came one beautiful autumn afternoon when we were out in a park, enjoying sunshine. I was madly in love with him and could not wait to begin our life together.

That last evening before the trip made me relive all those memories. For the first time since that letter, I began worrying about how I would make it without him for the entire three weeks. When I casually voiced my concern, he reminded me that we would have an entire week for us after the dig.

We made love several times through the night. Since we wouldn't be seeing each other for three weeks, we had to make the best of our last moments together. Exhausted and happy all at once, we finally fell asleep.

The next day, I was standing at Pearson Airport, saying last-minute goodbyes to my husband and my family.

"Have a safe trip and don't forget to send us emails and text messages," my mother said.

"And bring me some Israeli wine," my father joked.

"Best of luck," Erin said, hugging me.

Soon, I was standing alone on my way to the security check. I looked back one more time and waved to everyone. For a moment, I felt my throat tighten. I was on my way to the dream journey, and yet I couldn't shake off the feeling of sadness over leaving everyone for so long. I knew I would miss Jason, and he would miss me. However, I quickly reminded myself that these three weeks were probably nothing in the grand scheme of things. We would be reunited in no time, and he would be the first person to find out about all my adventures on the dig. That made me feel a bit better. I waved at everyone for the last time before moving forward with the security check.

The feeling of sadness evaporated as soon as I reached the duty free. After passing through a chain of overpriced shops and checking out a few items just for fun, I went looking for my boarding gate, which was located in a separate room, at the very end of the duty free. As soon as I approached it, a stern-looking officer asked me to present my passport and boarding pass. I obliged. Then he demanded I open my backpack.

"You have a very long name, ma'am," he mumbled, going through my things.

"Can I go now?" I asked.

He nodded without saying a word.

I often wondered what it was about my last name that made people frown. I chose to be O'Connor-Smith because I wanted both to preserve my identity and to carry my husband's name. Many women did the same. Besides, many people from other cultures had multiple and oftentimes far more complicated names.

The room was full of passengers waiting for their departures. I caught a glimpse of families with kids reading travel guides. I also saw a girl who strongly reminded me of a U of T student. She was around my age and wore jeans, running shoes, a polo T-shirt, and a pair of black-rimmed glasses. The girl was reading something on her laptop.

As soon as the boarding time was announced, I wanted to jump from excitement. This was really happening! I was going to Israel on an archaeological dig. I joined the lineup, anticipation rising with every second.

I slept through most of the flight, waking up only for meals and drinks. As one can imagine, I was very tired from the last night but also happy. I had a lot of dreams. I dreamed about small towns on hills with flat-roofed houses and winding roads. I dreamed about the blue sea and yellow caves storing ancient scrolls. I dreamed about the glorious city that had been destroyed and rebuilt multiple times.

I woke up dazzled by the bright light. Outside my tiny window, I saw the outline of the Mediterranean coast along with the aerial view of Tel Aviv. I felt a surge of excitement again. My long-awaited adventure was about to begin.

"Passengers, please return to your seats and fasten your seatbelts," the captain announced. "We kindly ask you to turn off all your electronic devices during the landing."

Thirty minutes later, I was standing in the waiting zone, the same place Jason and I had been welcomed by our tour guide four years ago. Despite the fully functioning air conditioner, I was still sweating because of the hot and humid air coming from the outside. It would probably take me a few days to get used to the local climate. In the meantime, I saw representatives from various touring agencies holding signs. There were also a lot of people who looked like family members and friends waiting for their loved ones to arrive. Many signs were written in the Cyrillic alphabet I could recognize as Russian. The outside part of the airport was filled with tourist buses and taxis. A few Arab-looking taxi drivers tried to offer me a ride, but I politely declined by saying, "*Lan, shukran kathiran,*" which meant "no, thank you." It was one of the few Arabic phrases I knew, and in situations like this, it was a real lifesaver.

Since the Kiryat Adar team was getting picked up a bit later, I had some free time. First, I bought a local phone card from a booth located right across from the arrival zone and let everyone in Toronto know I'd arrived safely. I roamed around the airport's area for a while until I decided to find something to eat. Following the signs, I headed upstairs to the food court. Right at the top of the escalators was a journalist interviewing a passerby.

What if I get on the local TV? I thought to myself while walking past them and inadvertently appearing in front of the camera.

After passing a chain of boutiques and convenience stores, I finally spotted a small food court. To my disappointment, it only offered American-style fast foods, like burgers and fries. Feeling hungry and jetlagged, I had no choice but to grab a hamburger and Pepsi from the closest counter. Quite honestly, the spongy bread and soft fries garnished with old ketchup tasted horrible, and I would rather have had a tasty falafel wrap with a plate of hummus. I definitely had to catch up with local food later.

Having finished my not-so-great meal, I headed downstairs, where the Kiryat Adar group was already waiting for the bus. Among them, I saw a middle-aged black lady wearing a T-shirt saying "Kiryat Adar Expedition" over a long dress and holding a notepad. She asked me whether I was here for the Kiryat Adar dig. After I replied "yes," she asked my name and marked me off the list.

"Nice to meet you!" she said, offering a handshake. "My name is Olivia."

I proceeded to join the rest of the group and meet other volunteers. Among them was the girl I had seen back in Toronto's airport. Her name was Claire, and she had flown all the way from Missouri to participate in the dig. When I told her she looked like a typical U of T student, she laughed and said it was probably because of the glasses. I also got to know Jocelyn, a retired teacher from Billings, Montana. In spite of her loud voice and stern demeanour, I could tell she was very friendly. I learned that it was her fifth time in Kiryat Adar, and she was hoping to return next year. I also met Carol, a fifty-something-year-old social worker from Florida. Both of them already had adult children in college. At some point, a group of young people in Kiryat Adar T-shirts joined us. These were the students from Harvard University taking a summer abroad course.

As soon as everyone was marked off the list, we were headed to the bus. The moment I breathed in the humid air filled with scents of exotic plants, memories of our honeymoon flooded back. I briefly recalled the first night when Jason and I went for a walk along HaYarkon Street and ended up listening to the sound of the Mediterranean Sea lapping against the shore. We sang, laughed, and talked about our future. We even made a few jokes about retiring in central Tel Aviv. I felt a sudden pang for this beautiful evening as I hauled my suitcase to the bus compartment designed specifically for heavy bags.

The drive took no longer than fifty minutes, equal to a commute from Toronto to Oakville. After a transcontinental flight, however, it seemed endless. All I wanted was to get to our hotel in Kiryat Adar and collapse on a bed. Nevertheless, I would lie if I said I didn't enjoy the scenery. The winding road took us through a desert landscape graced by small, reddish hills and yellow plains marked by small shrubs here and there. I even managed to snap a few photos with my cell phone camera.

By the time our team arrived at the hotel, it was already close to the evening. After sorting through paperwork, we got our keys and were directed to our rooms. I was supposed to share mine with three other girls, which was a typical living arrangement for an archaeological dig.

"Hi, I'm Madeline," one of my roommates said while hauling her baggage to the room. She had long blonde hair and was wearing a T-shirt and blue jeans.

"Hi, I'm Janice," a girl with black hair said. She was wearing a pair of shorts and a T-shirt with the Harvard University insignia. Erin always insisted that wearing shirts with university logos was a hallmark of snobbishness and never wore her Humber T-shirt in public. I vehemently disagreed with her. To me, my University of Toronto T-shirt was more linked to the sense of pride and accomplishment, and I planned to wear it to the dig every day.

"I'm Rachel," the third girl said. She had curly red hair and was wearing a graphic T-shirt over yoga pants and a pair of flats.

"Nice to meet you all! I'm Rebecca."

We all lined up at the bathroom door to take a shower. Although my turn came last, I didn't mind because I wanted to spend some time by myself.

"See you downstairs," Janice told me as I was unpacking my shampoo and a change of clothes.

I COULDN'T find the cafeteria. I checked out all the rooms, but to no avail. I began to worry I would stay dinnerless for the night. Then I spotted Rachel talking to some guy I'd seen briefly on the bus. He was rather tall—much taller than me or Jason—and was wearing a simple polo shirt and jean shorts. Rachel was giggling like a schoolgirl, probably in an attempt to get his attention.

"Sorry, do you know where the cafeteria is?" I asked, desperate for some good food.

"Oh, yes. Let me show you," the guy replied. "See you later," he said to Rachel.

"Is it your first time in Kiryat Adar?" he asked me as we were walking down a long, wide corridor leading into the cafeteria. I noticed his eyes were of a dark blue color which stood perfectly against the dark complexion of his face.

"Yes," I replied.

"I've been here before, so I know the place quite well." He winked.

"That's lovely," I replied, feeling slightly inadequate. After all, it was probably my one and only time in Kiryat Adar.

"Here it is." He pointed at the entrance to a large buffet room.

"Thank you so much!"

"No problem." He grinned.

"By the way, my name is Rebecca." I offered a handshake.

"Nice to meet you. I'm George." I felt something at the touch of his hand—a tiny sizzle maybe. I chalked it up to the jitters associated with the arrival at a new place.

"Are you another volunteer?" I asked as we went on to line up for the buffet table.

"Oh, I'm actually here for my PhD dissertation. I'm working with one of the directors as his assistant."

"How nice!" I exclaimed dreamily. "I always wanted to be an archaeologist."

"How about yourself?" he asked. "What brings you over here?"

"Just taking a break from work and traveling." I felt it was the best answer I could give. "I imagine there're lots of archaeology majors on this dig."

"You'll actually be surprised tomorrow when you learn there aren't too many. Most students are taking this course as an elective credit."

"Still exciting." In truth, this dig would probably be the closest thing to my dream study abroad program I always wanted to attend.

Although we went separate ways after getting food, something made me want to talk to him a bit longer. Could it be because of our similar fields? Or was it because he seemed easygoing and approachable. I decided to ignore this feeling. For now.

THE FOOD did not betray my expectations. As soon as we entered the buffet, all I could see was a countless number of salads, fruits, and vegetables, as well as several hot meals. There was also a huge counter with desserts.

I got to sit with Jocelyn and Carol, both of whom were very excited about the dig.

"So your husband is staying home and working, right?" Jocelyn asked jokingly. "Like a good husband," she added before I had a chance to reply. To tell the truth, her comment caught me a bit off guard, but I didn't mind it the least.

"He'll be flying over by the end of the dig," I replied.

"That's nice," Carol commented. "Where do you plan to stay?"

"Mostly in Tel Aviv. But we plan on going to Jerusalem too."

Our conversation continued through dinner. The two ladies told me they were planning to return home right after the dig, but they would use the two weekends for travel and sightseeing.

"Make sure you get to see the Rockefeller Museum," Jocelyn said. "It's totally worth it."

"Israel Museum is better," Carol interjected.

"We might run out of time since we only have one week," I admitted. "However, we'll definitely visit the Old City."

After dinner, one of the field directors made an announcement about a meeting that would take place the next morning at the site. It would give us a chance to get to know each other better and to become familiar with the program's routine.

Before going to bed, I decided to take a brief walk around the hotel and explore the vicinity. My natural curiosity made me forget all about the fatigue I had been experiencing half an hour earlier. The hotel had a large flower garden and a swimming pool. Halfway through my walk, I decided to call Jason and to see how he was doing. With my new, amazing phone plan I had bought at the airport, I no longer had to worry about roaming rates.

"Hey, Becky. How are you doing over there?" he asked.

"I'm great. Walking around the hotel and thinking about you."

"Nice. I've been thinking about you too. What time is it over there?"

"Close to nine o'clock. I should probably go to bed soon, but I decided to take time and call you."

"Glad to hear that! I've been wanting to call you too. How was the flight?"

"Not too bad. Although I do feel a bit jetlagged at the moment."

"You bet. I'd be feeling jetlagged too."

"Remember the time we walked down HaYarkon Street and joked about retiring in Tel Aviv?" I said.

Jason laughed. "Yeah, I remember that evening. It was nice to allow ourselves to get carried away for a bit."

"I know. Today, when we were outside on the way to the bus, I wished we could actually do it."

"You mean retire in Tel Aviv?" I heard a sense of sarcasm in his voice.

"Why not? We could escape winter for the rest of our lives and just enjoy the sunshine." I also wanted to add that I would spend my last years on earth visiting every single museum in the city.

"I heard Israeli winters can get just as nasty as ours."

"It's mostly rain and cool breeze. Nothing like our snow blizzards."

"Nah, I'd rather stay in Toronto when we're older. Maybe find a bigger place in Brampton or Aurora."

Immediately, I felt my chest tighten. The truth was, I always wanted to live in a foreign country. I believed this experience would enrich me as a person, but my parents were too cautious to even let me go on a summer abroad program. And Jason... Well, he was too attached to his family and his job to even think of living anywhere outside the Greater Toronto Area. I set aside this pang for something more and carried on with the conversation.

We talked a bit about his impending audit at work and his planned visit to his parents who owned a farm at the north of Richmond Hill. I told him to drive carefully and be safe. We mentioned a few places we hoped to see together. At the end of the call, we wished each other a great week and promised to stay in touch.

The darkness arrived very fast. In southern countries, twilight is almost nonexistent. That's just the beauty of the Mediterranean region. When I returned to the hotel, the room was empty. Having changed into comfortable pajamas, I dropped down on my bed and immediately fell asleep.

I woke up around midnight when I heard my roommates walk in.

"Do you think I have a chance?" one of them asked in a whispering voice.

"Well, you'll have to try extra hard. Like, show him how much you love archaeology and stuff."

"I'm trying, but he doesn't seem to notice."

"Give it some time, Rach," the third voice replied.

"Anyway, what do you think about our new roommate?" the second voice asked.

"Oh, I hate her already," Rachel said. "You should've seen how she charged at me when I was talking to him. I bet she came here to steal guys and have fun with them."

"Hey, are you sure she won't hear?" the third voice whispered.

"No, she's asleep."

I had an urge to get up and let everyone know that I'd heard everything. Instead, I lay with my eyes closed, pretending to be asleep. I couldn't believe I was already having issues with people on the dig.

I had encountered many difficult people in the past. One of them was Sandra from work. She constantly picked on me and occasionally drove me to tears. One time, she noticed a tiny mistake in my order entry and sent an email to the entire department, copying everyone, including my boss. I bet she felt like a hero while I felt like a total loser. Sandra didn't stop at one incident. She began spreading rumors about me and my supervisor, and within a month, my coworkers lost all respect for me. Fortunately, she was now on a maternity leave, thus making my life much easier.

If Rachel wanted to spread false rumors and make my life miserable, I had to move away. The last thing I needed was an enemy on a vacation. So I came up with a plan to talk to the receptionist tomorrow and ask for a different room.

Six

The next morning, we all hopped on a big bus that took us straight to the ruins. The moment we got out, I was welcomed by the morning sun and a lovely sea breeze. As we proceeded to the site, I found granite and marble capitals gracing the entrance. However, this part of the site wasn't the one I wanted to explore. I was more curious about areas from the Bronze and Iron Ages.

"Good morning, everyone." Andrew Logan, one of the directors, started the orientation. He was probably in his late thirties or early forties, and he had short black hair and brown eyes. "Thank you all for participating in the Kiryat Adar Expedition. Before we begin, I would like to introduce our team and give you a chance to introduce each other."

Andrew Logan taught at Wheaton College while Jayden Williams, the other director, taught at Harvard. The latter of the two looked much older and was probably around seventy. He had gray hair at the back of his balding head and a white beard. Both were wearing shorts and T-shirts with Kiryat Adar logo. There were also a few other staff members, including Vivian Aubrey, from the University of Chicago, and Keith Mason, from Boston University.

During the volunteers' introductions, I heard almost every major mentioned. Janice and Madeline were studying psychology at Harvard while Rachel had recently graduated from New York

University with a major in English. Ironically, there were only two archaeology majors on the dig. One was me and the other was George, a PhD student from Wheaton College, whom I met yesterday while frantically looking for the cafeteria. There was also a girl named Karen who had studied marine archaeology at the University of California but decided to switch to medicine. She was now a registered nurse.

"Do you know Evan Harris from the U of T?" Jayden Williams asked me after I finished my introduction.

"Of course," I replied, feeling cheerful. "He was one of my university instructors."

"Well, nice to meet you, Rebecca. Maybe you'll help us to identify some of the finds."

As introductions continued, I learned more about the older volunteers. Barry was a pastor from Los Angeles, and together with his wife, Theresa, they were organizing Holy Land tours. Olivia, who had taken our attendance last night, turned out to be a teacher from Kansas, not a staff member as I had initially thought. She had been part of the Kiryat Adar team for many years and was willing to take on more responsibilities. She took care of the attendance, drew site plans, and recorded levels.

I was surprised to learn that many older participants came from well-respected fields, and some were even capable of saving a life. Among them was James, a family doctor from Texas.

"Well, we have a doctor, a nurse, and a social worker in the field. We should survive," Andrew joked. The rest of the group laughed.

After the introductions, the directors briefly touched upon safety at the site. The top tips included drinking plenty of water to avoid dehydration, wearing hats for sun protection, and not sticking hands under stones, which could conceal crabs and vipers. They also reassured us that animal-related accidents were extremely rare. Not a word was said about the political tensions.

However, we already knew the site had a bomb shelter in case anything bad was to happen.

At some point, I saw a bus park next to ours, and a group of tourists exited. The guide took them straight to the site. For a second, I wondered if I could become a tour guide someday. I would take tourists through archaeological parks and entertain them with stories. At the back of my mind, I already knew it was just a dream.

The meeting was concluded with a brief tour of the site. We were taken around the classical and medieval areas, as well as the part of the site dating to the Iron Age. We got to see the famous marketplace, the mud brick towers mentioned in the Bible, and what was presumably the world's earliest arch, which dated to the nineteenth century BC. I could already tell the season would be exciting. Once the meeting was over, we were free until the next morning when the dig would officially start.

I spotted Rachel several times during the meeting and at lunchtime but tried to avoid her as much as possible. If I wanted a drama-free stay, I had to get my act together. So I went to the lobby immediately after lunch and asked a receptionist to put me in a different room. I hoped the process would be quick and painless. The lady was quite surprised by my request.

"Why do you want to change your room?" she asked me in a strong Israeli accent.

"Um, personal reasons," I quickly replied, not knowing what else to say.

"Well, we would need to get the other person's consent. We can't just move people around. It's against our hotel policy." She sounded a bit angry.

"No chance at all?" I still wanted to believe there was a slight possibility.

"Sorry, *motek*." She smiled a second after raising her voice.

I walked back to the room feeling disappointed. My best choice was to ignore the situation altogether and to enjoy my stay as much as possible. So I decided to check out the beach.

"Hey, where are you going?" Madeline asked me as I was exiting the room, carrying a bag stuffed with towels and sunscreen. She and Janice were returning from a short meeting with Jayden Williams, their instructor.

"To the beach," I replied matter-of-factly.

"Really? Janice and I are also going to the beach!" she exclaimed.

"Then maybe we should all go together," Janice suggested.

"Sure." Although I wanted to spend time at the sea by myself, I couldn't exclude them. I had to get along at least with someone.

"Let's do that," Madeline said, beaming.

"Let's wait for Rachel," Janice suggested. "She'll be back in a second."

"By the way, don't pay attention to her," Madeline remarked. "She's been grumpy since her arrival."

"Do you, by chance, know why?" I asked.

"I heard she had a hard time at the airport yesterday. You know how tough the customs can be."

"Oh, yes! Last time, my husband and I traveled to Israel, someone at the airport flatly asked us if we were carrying a bomb."

"Wait! Are you married?" Madeline asked, looking surprised.

"Four years," I replied, showcasing my plain golden band. I knew many brides preferred elaborate, diamond-laden rings (rightfully dubbed as eternity bands), but Jason and I decided to go for plain, old-fashioned yellow bands, and I was happy of this decision, especially now. I could safely take my ring anywhere I traveled without worrying about unwanted attention or possible damage. My solitaire diamond was now tucked safely in the upper cupboard of our bedroom.

Every time someone noticed my ring, I would receive comments like, "Oh, you are so young!" or "That's so great!" or "When is the baby coming?" With time, I became immune to these remarks. Instead, Janice simply shrugged and said, "Cool."

The waiting was a drag, especially since I was feeling so jumpy. At last, Rachel entered the room.

"We are heading to the beach," I announced, unable to contain my excitement.

She didn't say a word.

"Let's hurry up," Madeline said. "You don't want to miss out on the afternoon sunshine!"

"Are you kidding me? It's blazing hot outside!" Rachel exclaimed.

"Well, you don't have to go if you don't feel like it," I said.

"Okay, I'm going." She sounded more annoyed than ever.

It took around twenty minutes for everyone to get ready. When we finally exited the hotel, Janice realized that she had forgotten her water bottle.

"I'm sure you can buy one at the beach," Madeline said.

"No! I can't. It's expensive."

"Maybe we could keep on walking to save time," I suggested. "You could catch up with us."

"Please wait for me. I promise to be quick." She disappeared for another ten minutes.

As much as I wanted to be friends with everyone, I was feeling beyond annoyed. Living with three other people for the entire three weeks would definitely be a big challenge.

"I HEARD there's a cool party happening tonight," Madeline told us while laying her towel down on the sand.

"We should all go out and meet cool boys!" Janice exclaimed while applying her sunscreen. "Oh, look at that guy! He's so hot!" She pointed at a tall, muscular guy walking out from the sea.

"Go talk to him." Madeline nudged her. "Maybe he'll be at the party."

"I'm going for a swim," I announced, unable to hold off my simultaneous irritation and excitement any longer. I couldn't care less about the boys or their damn party.

As I entered the sea, warm, salty waves enveloped me and carried me back to four years ago. Last time we were in Israel, Jason and I got to swim in the Mediterranean only once. We arrived in Tel Aviv for an overnight stay and were taken to a kibbutz in the north the very next morning. It was already close to evening, so we didn't have much time. Oblivious to sleep deprivation and jetlag, we grabbed our towels, ran to the beach, and later went for a walk as well.

Although I wasn't a very good swimmer, I could float in the water quite well. With the sun shining brightly on my face, I swam around, feeling happy and carefree. The entire time I was swimming, the girls were on the beach, talking to a group of guys they met shortly after I left. For them, this trip was probably an opportunity to escape home and meet new people. I could bet that some of the participants would meet new partners by the end of the dig. I was sure it wouldn't happen to me as I was completely happy with Jason and was already missing him.

DURING DINNERTIME, I sat with a random group of young people. Luke, one of the Harvard students, was sharing stories about his early university years with the rest.

"So one time, I handed in my paper and went straight to the bar," he began. "Then I got so drunk that I fell asleep on the floor. They had to kick me out next morning. This was some crazy shit."

The rest of us laughed.

"You bet," Karen noted.

I tried to come up with a similar story but couldn't think of anything impressive. I was a good girl through my high school and university years, and I hardly ever got into trouble. The only time something similar happened to me was when Jason and I went to a dance party, and I decided to try my first shot. I fell asleep on a couch reserved for bottle service, and Jason had to carry me on our way home.

"I had even worse incidents," Vincent, another summer abroad student, said. "I'm not sure you want to hear my story."

"Tell them." Luke nudged him.

"Okay. One time, me and my buddy decided to go for a drink after an exam. We were still new to the city, so we went to the first club we found."

"So what?" Karen asked.

"It turned out to be a gay club."

We laughed again, and this time even louder. More crazy stories were passed around the table. This group was definitely fun to talk to. With them, I could loosen up and laugh a little, even if I had nothing to say.

After dinner, I spent a few hours browsing the Internet on my laptop in the lobby. Then I went back to the room, ready to fall asleep. I couldn't imagine anyone going out after such a long and exhausting day.

"Hey, are you coming along?" Madeline asked. She was wearing a bathrobe and drying her long hair with a towel.

"You don't have to go with us," Rachel said while flattening her black dress with an iron.

I gave it a thought. Perhaps I could go just to annoy this chick and teach her a lesson. I could even practice my Hebrew with bartenders and enjoy music. After all, I was the only one familiar with the local entertainment scene. But then, I remembered we would have to be ready by five o'clock tomorrow morning and decided against going. I would still have plenty of chances to go out on Friday and Saturday nights.

"It's okay. I'll probably just go to sleep. You all have fun."

"Have a good night then," Madeline said.

"Don't forget to put your alarm on for four o'clock," Rachel commanded. "I don't want to wake you up."

We'll see who will wake up whom, I thought to myself, wondering how they were planning to survive through the dig tomorrow.

After the girls had left, I took out my pajamas and went straight to the shower. Then I arranged my clothes for the next day, filled my water bottle, and plopped on the bed, ready for some good sleep. This time, I didn't wake up when they returned. I decided that as long as I didn't hear any gossip about me, I would be fine.

Seven

When I rose at four-thirty sharp, my roommates were still asleep, and I couldn't blame them. Had I gone out last night, I would be sleeping too. Having looked around, I saw evening dresses and shoes scattered all over the room. I tiptoed to the bathroom, tripping on a stiletto, and splashed cold water on my face. My eyes felt crusty, but my mind was sharp. Then I quickly got ready for a new day, double-checking I had water and a sun hat—the two essentials.

"Good morning," I said.

The girls moved a little.

"What time is it?" Madeline asked, stretching.

"Almost five," I replied.

"Shoot, we're late for the first breakfast!" Janice bolted up.

"Should I wait for you downstairs?" I asked, unable to hide my smile.

"Wow, you're ready!" Madeline exclaimed, staring at my backpack in disbelief.

"Yes, I am," I said, hoping that Rachel heard me too.

"Okay, we'll meet at the cafeteria. Please tell the bus driver not to leave without us."

"Twenty-five cents," I joked before leaving the room.

To be honest, I wasn't hungry at all. I never ate at such an early hour, except for a few times when I absolutely needed a cup of coffee while crunching in some last-minute paper. But I had no choice but to follow everyone's schedule. The breakfast was quick and quiet, as many volunteers were still too sleepy. To my surprise, I wasn't feeling tired in the least. Having finished my bowl of cereal, I went straight to the bus.

At the site, we were directed toward the storage room to fetch our tools. After loading our wheelbarrows with shovels and axes, we proceeded to the inner parts of the site, which were shaded by tents. All volunteers were asked to choose from different excavation grids, each of which was loosely connected to a particular historical period—Persian, Islamic, Hellenistic, and Philistine. I chose the latter.

My best memory of university all-nighters was linked to the Sea Peoples. I was studying for the archaeology final, trying to memorize all the names. The Philistines weren't the only group I had to remember. *Weshesh, Djekker, Sherden, Pelest...* My mind went on. It was in the middle of spring, and the sun had just started rising earlier. Just as I finished preparing for the exam, birds started singing outside, and the sun came up. The morning sun that was shining above our tent reminded me of this final.

We were asked to fill up our buckets with as much earth as possible, to carry them to the sifter, and then slowly empty them out. Anything that resembled an artifact had to be collected into a bucket labeled with the grid's name. Having emptied my first bucket, I slowly began to sift through the sand in hopes of finding something extraordinary. However, all I could see for the first three hours was plain rocks and undecorated potsherds. I began to feel frustrated. My constant crouching wasn't producing the results I expected.

Around nine o'clock, we had our second breakfast, and by that time, I was definitely hungry. Some volunteers helped to set up the table and lay out different foods, which included traditional pita, *labaneh* cheese, some cold cuts, cereals, and fruits.

I sat with Claire and a few Harvard girls with whom I hadn't talked earlier. We chatted for a while about our studies and our plans for the future. I was surprised to discover that most of them still had no idea what they were planning to do after graduation. You'd think that Harvard students would have it all figured out.

"Mind if I join you?" George asked, carrying a huge sandwich and a cup of coffee. From the corner of my eye, I saw Rachel standing by the buffet table, looking longingly at him.

"Sure, come in." Claire offered him an empty seat next to her.

"How do you like it so far?" he asked us.

"Well, it's not too bad at all," I replied. "Except for the fact that I haven't found any gold yet."

We all laughed. No one really expected to find anything tremendously exciting on the first day. However, I was hoping for at least a Byzantine coin or an Egyptian scarab seal.

"Don't expect to find any, or you'll set yourself up for a major disappointment," George said. "Trust me. I know what I'm talking about."

"So what is your area of focus?" I asked. Although I already knew he was in archaeology, I wanted to learn more about his field.

"I'm working with Dr. Logan, researching about the Philistine houses during the Late Bronze Age and Iron I."

"Sounds exciting!" I exclaimed, secretly wishing I could do something that fascinating in my life.

"I'm also teaching a course on ancient Israel this year," he added. "How about yourself? What do you do?"

"I finished the University of Toronto a few years ago. Now I'm working in marketing." This wasn't completely true. Even though Happy Apparel did specialize in marketing, I wasn't really part of the department.

"Oh, it must be fun to work in that industry. I heard it pays really good money."

"Not exactly," I replied, instantly regretting my small lie. "I actually don't do the advertising part," I admitted. "It's mostly secretarial work and some client service. I kind of wish my job was closely related to my degree, but you can't expect that when you're a humanities major."

"I see. So what did you study?" He looked genuinely interested.

"I majored in anthropology with a special focus on the ancient Near East. I took a course in ancient Israel once. It was amazing."

"Oh, nice! We're in the same field."

Whenever I talked about my major to strangers, I would be bombarded with questions on what I was planning to do with my degree. At some point in time, I decided to avoid the topic altogether, and it saved me a lot of hassle during interviews. It was nice to talk to my fellow humanities majors without worrying what they would think.

Our breakfast was followed by lab work done in a small barrack off the site. It mostly involved organizing pottery and labeling it according to different archaeological periods. I must admit that making chronological distinctions between different sets of sherds was a daunting task. It took time and skill to learn how to differentiate between different shapes, clay composition, and color. However, I had some background in the subject and could easily tell the difference between, say, Cypriot Monochrome and Bichrome wares. I enjoyed every single minute of this activity, and whenever a familiar term came up, I couldn't stop myself from smiling.

Time went by fast, and by eleven, we had our fruit break. As we were munching our strawberries, grapes, and pieces of watermelon, I heard a heavy sound coming from above.

"I'll be back in a second," I told the rest of the group and ran outside. Two menacing-looking airplanes were circling around the site.

What is it? I asked myself, trying to remember anything similar from my last trip to Israel. Suddenly, I recalled our tour guide telling us about special planes that patrol the country to make sure nothing bad is happening. I took a deep breath and stepped back into the lab.

"Is everything okay?" Olivia asked, smoothing out the folds of her skirt.

"Yeah, I just saw a very loud plane. It sounded like a military one. That's all."

"Get used to it. You'll see them very often here. It doesn't mean anything is wrong."

"I know. I was told about those planes during our last visit. It's just unusual to hear such loud noises."

"Believe me, it's normal in Kiryat Adar."

We worked in the lab for a few more hours after the break, and at one o'clock, we headed back to the hotel. On my way to the room, I met Janice and Madeline, who were talking about boys.

"Vince is really cute," Janice said.

"I like Luke better. He's so darn funny," Madeline argued.

"I liked the one we met at the beach yesterday. I think he's from New Jersey."

"The one who's studying MBA?"

"Yep. He's gorgeous. I mean, look at those biceps!"

Rachel was standing next to them looking sulky. I began to wonder if she was having some personal issues and needed help. Well, I was not the one to talk to, especially after everything she had said about me.

"HAMAS IS firing rockets again," I heard someone say in the cafeteria.

"They might start a war in Gaza," another voice said.

I looked around and saw an elderly couple sitting at one of the tables. I didn't exactly like the content of their conversation, and I had no idea how this purported war would impact our dig. After all, we were only forty kilometers or so away from the Gaza border. However, from what I had heard, the Iron Dome was highly effective in protecting cities, and half the time, the rockets fell into open areas. Perhaps there was a chance we wouldn't even notice the conflict.

I chose to sit with Karen, Madeline, and another girl named Lara. We chatted about our first impressions of the digging session.

"I excavated before," Karen said.

"Where?" I asked, feeling my curiosity rise.

"Many places. Costa Rica, for example. I even swam underwater."

"What made you switch into nursing?" Lara asked.

"Better money," Karen admitted. "I don't regret my decision in the least because I like being a nurse."

"That's great. I wish I could say the same thing about my job," I admitted.

"You don't like your job?" Lara asked.

"Not really." I sighed.

"How come?"

"Well, I get to work long hours, do monotonous stuff, and my pay is crap." I was surprised by my own sincerity. Although I normally didn't talk about my problems to strangers, the environment around me was so friendly that I felt free to speak my mind.

After lunch, we were free until four-thirty, and then it was pottery washing time. My roommates and I crept back to our hotel room and collapsed on our beds. For the first time in the day, I felt tired.

Unable to fall asleep right away, I took out my cell phone and checked messages. I was happy to discover a few from Jason.

"Hey, Becky, how is your dig so far? Found anything cool yet? Miss you."

Despite the fatigue, I forced myself to type back a reply. "Other than a bunch rocks, I haven't found anything exciting yet. But I'm still having an amazing time here. I met so many people from Harvard today. You won't believe it."

"Aww. Jealous." The message came back almost instantly.

"You've got nothing to worry about. I'm only thinking about you."

"Have fun over there. Don't forget to text me when you have your first big find."

"Bye-bye." I smiled at the idea of Jason being interested in my finds. He hardly ever showed interest in my glossy archaeology magazines, so his new attitude was a welcoming change.

I also got a few messages from my parents and Erin probing me for details about my first dig session. I told everyone that I was doing great and that the first morning in the field was quite enjoyable. I also attached a few photos I had snapped during the dig, including a photo of me in a U of T T-shirt and white gloves holding a shovel. For a moment, I considered sending it to the Summer of the Selfie contest that was being constantly advertised on Virgin Radio in Toronto. No one probably expected an entry from an amateur archaeologist.

I dozed off for about forty minutes. When I woke up, everyone was still asleep. I could imagine their level of fatigue after the whole night of partying and several hours of toiling under the sun. Since there was another free hour, I decided to check out the swimming pool. I quickly prepared my beach bag, put on my bathing suit, slipped into flip-flops, and crept downstairs. I truly hoped none of my roommates would wake up and follow me. Otherwise, we would not make it to the pottery washing session on time.

It was very quiet downstairs. I saw a few tourists check in at the reception desk and a young couple lounging in the lobby. As for the swimming area, I could see only one person lying on a sun bed and drinking beer. It was George.

"Hey, what's up?" he asked. Somehow, everything about him exuded confidence. I wondered if he was a self-absorbed type. I placed my beach bag on the farthest sun bed, removed my dress, and started applying the tanning lotion.

"Nice legs!" I heard him say.

"Excuse me?" I turned around and met his penetrating gaze.

"What?" He shrugged.

"Would you please leave me alone?"

"Okay, I'm sorry! I didn't mean it that way! May I join you in swimming?" He got up and walked toward the pool.

"Whatever," I replied in disdain. I couldn't believe we had such a nice conversation this morning. He was, indeed, self-absorbed.

After five laps, I decided to get something to drink, so I wrapped a towel around my waist and walked to the bar.

"*Shalom, mitz tapuchim bevakasha,*" I said, ordering a cup of apple juice.

"*Beseder,*" the waiter replied.

I loved giving food and drink orders in Hebrew. Sometimes, waiters would answer back in English, but I always tried my best not to give in. Never mind I could forget a word or two and get stuck for a few seconds. I was confident enough to take the risk, and showcasing language skills always paid off. During our last visit, a few Israelis even asked us where we were living, mistaking us for locals. I found such a mistake quite flattering.

George joined me a few seconds later and ordered another beer.

"Why don't you use Hebrew?" I asked him, hoping to score at least one point over this snob.

"I only know Biblical and Phoenician. I don't think they would be useful here."

"That's true." I laughed. "I studied both Biblical and modern, but I like the modern one more," I added.

"Do you plan on moving here?"

"I don't think so. My husband wouldn't be very fond of the idea."

"Wait! You're married?" he asked, eyeing my band.

"Yes, I am." I couldn't help but smile. A small part of me wondered if he was fancying me in one way or another.

"Oh, I'm sorry. I didn't know that." George looked a bit embarrassed.

"That's okay."

"I just assumed everyone here was single."

"Some may be in committed relationships."

"True."

"How about yourself? Are you seeing someone?" I found myself asking.

"I just broke up with my girlfriend."

"Oh, what happened?" I asked.

"She thought I spent too much time at school," he replied candidly. "We hardly ever had any time for each other with my crazy schedule."

"That's why I'm never doing a PhD," I declared. Deep inside, I knew my steady job and the mortgage were the true culprits.

"Well, it has many other rewards. It's not just sleep-deprived nights and cold pizza, you know."

We talked for a bit longer before I realized it was almost time for the pottery washing session.

"See you later, Becky," he said as I was about to take off.

Even after I took a shower and changed, the girls were still sleeping. I took a few steps toward their beds and told them that it was almost time to go. There was no answer. I repeated myself.

Madeline opened her eyes, looked around, and asked, "What happened?"

"Sorry to disturb you, but it's time for the lab work," I affirmed.

"I'm so tired," she said, yawning. "Can't we just skip it?"

"I'm not skipping the lab work!" Janice exclaimed, jumping out of the bed.

They all crawled out of their beds and stumbled to the bathroom.

"I'll wait for you downstairs." I felt content to be ahead of everyone else again.

"See you, Rebecca," Madeline replied.

The pottery wash lasted for two hours. At times, it was monotonous and even boring. Just like any other work, archaeology involved some not-so-glamorous tasks, and scrubbing dirt from colorless sherds was one of them. Half the finds were so small that they could be tossed away immediately, for they were impossible to identify.

I began to worry I would never find anything worthy. I still had a report to write upon my return, so I absolutely had to find something fascinating. It didn't have to be a three-thousand-year-old statue or a Byzantine mosaic. Neither did it have to be made of gold. A coin or a figurine, however, would certainly do.

At dinner, I heard more rumors about the looming conflict in Gaza. I decided not to panic and to check the facts myself. So I Googled "Israel" on my cell phone and discovered some unpleasant news. A rocket had been fired at Jerusalem, and a few more were coming toward Tel Aviv.

"What are you reading?" Madeline asked, putting a bowl of hummus in front of her.

"Look what happened!" I showed her my phone screen. She took it from me and started reading the article quietly.

"Oh, jeez! That doesn't look good."

"That's what I'm saying."

"Don't worry. We're safe," Janice reassured me. "Otherwise, this program wouldn't be happening."

"I hope so," I said, wanting to believe her.

The last thing I needed was for this dig to become interrupted. Then I would fly back to Toronto before having a long-awaited vacation with Jason. Such a possibility was out of question.

In spite of the worrying news, I slept very well through the night. I heard a few planes above but couldn't care less what they were. All that mattered to me was discovering a treasure.

Eight

I had more luck on the second day. As I was sifting through rocks and dirt, I came across a few small sherds with faded lines. It was hard to tell whether or not they represented the famous Red Slip ware, as the color was barely visible to the naked eye. Yet it was definitely a possibility.

After several rounds of emptying dirt buckets, I noticed a small object of an irregular shape. Having examined it closely, I realized it remotely resembled a woman. Just as I was about to put it together with the rest of the findings, I saw Jayden Williams approach our area.

"Hey, Rebecca! *Ma nishma?*" He waved at me.

"Hi, Dr. Williams."

"You can call me Jayden."

"I think I found something."

"Can I see it?"

"Here it is. It looks like a woman to me."

He removed some of the dirt with a small bristle brush and looked more closely at the object. Without excessive dirt, it looked like a woman even more. The figurine had pronounced facial features and curly hair perfectly chiseled on its top. Her hands were supporting the breasts, and the lower part looked like a skirt. "You're right," Dr. Williams said. "It is indeed a woman. In fact, it's a figurine of the

Canaanite goddess Asherah. Everyone, please pay attention for a moment." He lifted up my find. "Rebecca just discovered something unique. It's a goddess figurine very typical for the Iron II."

As soon as his words came out, I became consumed with pride. Everyone gazed at us in awe, and some even gave applause. We just had our first significant find of the season, and I finally had something to put on my report.

The rest of the morning went by easily. The burning sun and several hours of hard labor had little effect on my energy levels. I learned how to use my tools with more efficiency and with less physical effort. I also learned that taking small breaks every now and then made a huge difference. I could even imagine going out with my roommates in a few days from now. Quite possibly, it would happen earlier.

As soon as the second breakfast came, I took out my cell phone, which I was carrying everywhere, and texted the news to everyone in Toronto. "Hey, I just found a Canaanite goddess figurine," I wrote. I received four "wows" in response. I also uploaded the photo of the find on Facebook and earned a dozen likes. I was becoming popular—something that had never happened to me before. Although I wasn't an extrovert, being at the center of attention felt great, especially now that I was part of Harvard's research team.

During our lunch at the hotel, I met Madeline, who had been working in the Hellenistic area through the morning.

"Hey, I heard you found something special today," she said.

"Really? I wonder who told you that." I smiled at her knowledge of my find.

"News spreads here very quickly."

"Hmm, that appears to be true."

"Was it gold?" she asked, eyes blazing.

"Not yet," I laughed. "It was a female figurine from the Iron II."

"Wow, I can't believe you know all of that stuff."

"Me too," said Jocelyn, who was sitting at the next table. "And I also heard you speak Hebrew."

"That's true." I smiled.

"You must have a natural talent for languages."

"Thanks." I felt proud of myself in spite of her patronizing tone. I didn't hear such comments very often. In Toronto, I was simply a recent graduate with a useless major and a crap job. Here, everything was different.

Having finished my lunch, I returned to our room. Janice and Madeline decided to stay at the lobby to catch up with readings while Rachel was nowhere in sight. So I decided to go to the beach alone like I always wanted.

I walked down an alley surrounded by palm and cypress trees. Under one of them were three stray cats idling in the shade. A few bicycle riders passed me by. As I approached the beach, I became overwhelmed with a feeling of freedom. I was completely alone in a foreign city, and this aloneness was empowering. It was then I realized that I was in charge of my own destiny. I could turn my life in any direction I wanted. All I needed was a little courage.

At the same moment, I also realized how lucky I was to have so many wonderful people in my life. I had loving parents, who were wishing the best for me, a sister, who was also my best friend, and a wonderful husband. Even though he was miles away from me, we were still together. And finally, I was in the most beautiful place on the planet—a place so exotic and yet so familiar.

I quickly removed my upper clothes, lay down a towel, placed my bag on the ground, and ran straight to the sea. I made a couple of attempts to swim, and then a huge wave splashed right across my face. I laughed and kicked the wave, oblivious to anyone seeing me. I swam for a little bit before hearing a Hebrew song coming from a lifeguard's booth. Curious to hear it more closely, I walked back to the beach and sat down on my towel.

The song had a nice melody and a good beat, but most importantly, its lyrics were appealing to me on a personal level. It was about a woman living in a big city and trying to fulfill her dreams. According to the song, she often felt out of place, but nevertheless always smiled, knowing that one day, she would succeed. As soon as I managed to discern the words, I wanted to cry. The song reminded me of my first years in Toronto, when I was struggling like crazy and yet always staying optimistic that someday, things would change for the better. And they did eventually.

My life completely changed once I entered university, especially after not-so-great years in high school. I finally got to study what I always loved and to spend time in some of the most beautiful libraries. I even began to appreciate the special, funky vibe of downtown Toronto. But above all, I loved the challenge that came with learning something new every day. And now I was taking my love of learning to the next level by excavating in Kiryat Adar.

On my way to the hotel, I found a booth where I could buy a freshly made juice.

"Hi, can I please have some orange juice?" I asked a waiter in Hebrew.

"No problem." He picked a handful of oranges and squeezed them in a blender.

"I'm Rebecca, by the way." Something made me want to introduce myself by name.

"I'm Shlomo." He smiled. "How long have you been here?"

"Three days."

"So you just arrived."

"I guess so. I'm staying at the Shimoni Hotel."

"Nice. Do you plan on living at a kibbutz or an apartment?"

"What do you mean? I'll be at the same hotel for the entire time."

"I thought you just moved here."

"No, I'm only visiting." I chuckled.

"Do you have a family here?"

"No, I'm a tourist."

"Oh, sorry!"

We laughed. Once again, I'd been mistaken for a local.

"How come your Hebrew is so good?" he asked. "Have you lived here before?"

"Maybe in another life," I replied. "As for my Hebrew, I took courses at my university."

"Wow, I'm impressed. So, what brings you to Kiryat Adar?"

"I'm with the Kiryat Adar Expedition."

"Oh, I see. I have many customers from this dig."

Our conversation lasted for almost an hour. We talked about the places in Israel we liked the most. He said he truly loved visiting the Golan Heights because of their lush greenery and cooler temperatures. I told him about our last visit to the Banias Springs and the Druze villages. Then we talked about our favorite artists, and I admitted my dream of attending a concert in Caesarea. The conversation had to stop when another customer came.

By the time I returned to the room, it was already four-thirty, and everyone was gone to the pottery washing session. Realizing that I had completely lost track of time, I ran downstairs in the same clothes I had worn to the beach and quietly snuck into the room. Andrew Logan was making an announcement. I tiptoed to the closest spot available and sat down, trying to make as little noise as possible. The chair made a loud, squeaking sound, causing several people look in my direction.

"Sorry," I said, trying to look nonchalant. Inside, I was burning from embarrassment.

I decided not to ask about the announcements until later. Instead, I grabbed a few findings and began cleaning them. It turned out that the student group from Harvard was planning a tour to the southern sites, and everyone else was welcome to join for a small fee. The stops would include the Ramon Crater, the Timna Valley Park, and ultimately, Eilat. I was definitely in.

"Please don't forget about the lecture tonight," Andrew said before we dispersed.

"What lecture?" I asked Lara, who was sitting next to me.

"Something about the Palestinians." She shrugged.

"No, silly," George interjected. "It's about the Philistines, the Sea People."

I suppressed a laugh.

THE LECTURE was incredibly engaging. The presenting scholars briefly provided an overview of the group's Aegean origins (most scholars believe they came from the Greek islands), their migration patterns at the end of the Late Bronze Age, and their settlements in the Southern Levant at the beginning of the Iron Age. They also went over the Philistine Pentapolis, which consisted of Gaza, Ashdod, Ekron, Gath, and Ashkelon. Kiryat Adar was among the smaller Philistine sites.

Over the course of my time at the U of T, I came to realize the Philistines were not as bad as the Bible portrayed them. It is true that they settled in the land of the Israelites, and their kingdom posed some form of external threat. However, in the Near East, both ancient and modern, settlements simply existed on a first come, first serve basis. Everyone was eager to settle in the narrow passage that existed between Egypt and Mesopotamia and to take advantage of its valuable trade resources. The Bible simply retold the story from the Israelites' point of view. If Philistine texts existed, they would probably depict everything differently. As for me,

I was equally drawn to all the civilizations that had existed in the Holy Land.

Halfway through this lecture, we got to hold a piece of a Philistine stirrup jar, which got passed around the table. It was rather bulbous and smooth to touch, and its surface was covered with dark-red lines and geometric patterns. I took time to trace the shape, the clay texture, and the artistic pattern with my hands.

"Can I have it, please?" I heard George say.

"Oh, yes, sure." I passed the jar to him.

"Do you know it was inspired by the Mycenaean tradition?"

"No, I thought it resembled the Cypriot style."

"Well, the Cypriot and Mycenaean are fundamentally different."

"I'm sorry." I felt my face become hot. I couldn't believe I'd mixed up something that obvious.

"It's okay. A lot of people confuse them. If you are interested, we could meet up afterward, and I could tell you more about their differences." He winked.

"Well, thanks for the invitation, but I would rather go sleep after the lecture." For some reason, going out with this guy, even for an innocent talk, felt wrong.

"Are you sure? We are planning to go to the bar. You could join us."

"Everyone, please be quiet," one of the lecturers said.

"Oh, we are sorry," I said, my face getting hot again. "We were talking about the pottery styles," I added. I probably sounded like a grade nine student who got caught chatting about some new, popular movie.

"Okay, let's wrap up today's lecture." He went on and on talking about different samples of the Philistine material culture, passing more artifacts around the table.

"YOU SHOULD join us," Janice urged me as I was unpacking my pajamas. "You can't stay in the room all the time."

"I'm worried we'll be late for the dig tomorrow."

"We won't be out for too long. We all need to be up early," Madeline insisted. "Come on, you should come."

"Okay, I'll go with you." I gave in.

I was lucky not to have Rachel with us in the room. She would surely say something about my lateness to the pottery washing session or my decision to go to the pub. I later spotted her sitting in the lobby talking to George.

"Becky, you are going!" he exclaimed as soon as he eyed me.

"Yep! I decided to get a drink in the end."

"Okay, let's go." He rose up. "See you tomorrow, Rach."

"Are you coming with us?" I asked her casually.

"Nah, you go."

She sounded defeated. According to my theory, she was trying to get George's attention but was perpetually unsuccessful.

Among the goers were also Luke, Vince, and Karen. As we were walking down the street, enjoying the fresh air, we talked about everything and nothing. The topics included our favorite movies, late nights at university, and drunken sorority parties. Although I normally didn't enjoy small talk, I was having a good time. After passing by a few bars and coffee shops, we finally stopped at a small pub where Kiesza's "Hideaway" was playing.

"Hey, folks, can I get you something to drink?" a bartender asked as soon as he saw us.

"Sure, I'll take a glass of beer," I replied in Hebrew.

The bartender looked puzzled. "*At medaberet ivrit! Eize yofi!*" he exclaimed.

Everyone else looked at me in awe. They couldn't believe an average Canadian with zero ties to Israel could speak Hebrew so well. Part of me even wished Rachel was here to see me shine.

"I wish my Hebrew was that good," George said, as we were waiting for our drinks. "It would help me to find a postdoc opportunity here."

"You're already thinking about postdocs?"

"Well, I have to plan ahead. Have you considered going to a grad school yet?"

"Not really." I sighed.

"You seem to know a lot about ancient Israel."

"It's probably nothing compared to how much you know. Plus, I know neither French nor German."

"I thought French was mandatory in Canada."

"Yes, but I forgot it after Grade Ten. In fact, French was the least of my favorite subjects at school." I briefly recalled how much I dreaded those tests that involved memorizing all the *er* and *ir* verbs.

"Well, I doubt it will be a problem because you seem to have a knack for languages."

"That's what everyone says." I smiled, recalling Jocelyn's remark.

"By the way, I'll be presenting a paper on Beit Shean next week. I thought you might be interested."

"That must be exciting for you!"

"Well, I've presented at conferences before. You get used to it after a while."

"May I ask which part of the site you will be focusing on?"

"The one dating to the Late Bronze Age."

"The Egyptian one?"

"Yes."

"Are you going to mention the Mekal stele?"

"Only briefly. I'll be mainly talking about the pottery. Hey, why don't you wait and see?"

"Okay, no more questions, then. But you promised to enlighten me about the Cypriot and Mycenaean styles."

"Oh, yes. I nearly forgot."

We had a long conversation about Cypriot imports during the Late Bronze Age. George talked about different types of pottery and scholarly articles that had been published on that topic. I couldn't help but admire this guy—at least his intellectual abilities. He was so refined and educated, and he looked downright gorgeous in his polo T-shirt and gridded shorts. I told myself there was no attraction involved. We were just random people talking about something that interested us.

Halfway through the conversation, I realized how much I'd been missing challenging talks. While Jason was smart, his intelligence was rooted in a totally different field. Most of the time, we didn't talk about anything remotely intellectual, except for the latest news about economic crises and global warming. Our mundane conversations usually revolved around problems at work, plans for weekends, and food choices for dinners. It didn't really dawn on me until that evening.

"Should we wrap up and get going?" Madeline asked, looking pensively at her watch. For the whole time, she and the rest of the group had been discussing indie music.

"Oh, yes, definitely." I immediately jumped from my chair, spilling a few drops from my glass of beer.

"Let's go," Karen said.

Once we reached the rooms, I checked my cell phone. To my surprise, it had no messages. I wondered what Jason was doing. Was he happy at work? Was he at home or working overtime? Then George came into my mind. I recalled our conversation and the satisfaction I got from talking about something that truly fascinated me.

THE REST of the week was just as exciting as the beginning. I relentlessly dug in the mornings, enjoyed the sea and the sun after lunches, and diligently washed pottery in the afternoons. Never again did I show up late. I have to admit that not all days were terribly successful in terms of findings. Sometimes, I would spend several hours filling up buckets with dirt and carrying them over to the sifter just to find a bunch of pebbles. Nevertheless, the work was incredibly enjoyable.

During mealtimes, I became friends with Jocelyn, Carol, and Olivia. Our discussions involved many topics, including mortgages, furniture, and family life. They told me about their children, what they were studying, and some of the typical struggles associated with parenthood. To my surprise, I often found myself siding with them despite the fact that I was around the same age as their kids.

We also discussed our past trips and favorite places in the world. As real travel veterans, they had all visited Europe at least once and had seen most of the key places in the States. Although I had never been to Europe, I had done my fair share of travel on the American continent. The most memorable spot for me was probably the Grand Canyon, which I had visited with my parents as a child and later with Jason.

But what still bugged me all those days was the fact that I had been truly missing out on the intellectual fulfilment back at home. I knew I had no right to feel this way. Most girls would love to have my life with a loving husband, a condo by the subway, and a stable job. Yet something had been missing all this time, and I began to see more clearly, especially after my outing with George. I made a conscious effort not to overthink this feeling and to carry on with the fun of the dig.

Nine

"Are we ready yet?" Madeline asked while double-checking the contents of her bag. It was a Saturday morning, and we were packing for the trip. Since I had prepared my backpack the night before, I didn't have to worry too much about making it to the lobby on time.

"Most definitely," Janice replied while applying her sunscreen. "Did you guys remember to bring your cameras? They promised the scenery will be awesome."

"Oops, did I?" I immediately started double-checking everything in my backpack. The camera was missing. It was strange because I remembered putting it together with my water bottle and a sunscreen. For some reason, it was lying on my dresser.

"Thanks for reminding me!" I exclaimed with relief. "I can't believe I almost forgot the most important item!"

"Don't worry," Madeline said. "We will share pictures regardless. Besides, the most important thing you'll need is your water. It's supposed to be freaking hot outside."

"That's true," Rachel noted with a smirk on her face.

For a second, I wondered if she had snuck into my bag and taken out the camera. I instantly dismissed the thought. Despite our mutual dislike, it was highly unlikely that Rachel would do such thing.

"All right, let's go!" Janice said.

A minute later, we were standing at the hotel lobby, waiting for the fun to begin. It would be our first day trip, and I was sure there were more to come. At last, I saw a large vehicle with two horn-like mirrors approach in our direction. There was no mistaking it was our bus. I immediately felt a surge of excitement. I was going to see the south of Israel for the very first time! Since the last trip was about the sites of the Holy Land in the north, we didn't get to travel anywhere south of Tel Aviv and Qumran. Now was my chance.

As soon as we took off, I plugged in my earphones and closed my eyes. The music slowly faded in the background as I dozed off. I couldn't tell how much time passed before I was woken up by the deadly sound of a siren.

Someone must have forgotten to turn off an iron, I thought while rubbing my eyes. I expected our bus to pull over to the right side and to wait for the emergency vehicle to pass. However, there was no fire truck or ambulance car in sight.

"Everyone, please get out of the bus and lie face down," Kobi, the tour guide, commanded. Out of the corner of my eye, I noticed that he looked slightly distraught. Yet he was trying his hardest to keep it cool in front of our group.

"*Ma pitom!*" I exclaimed.

Our group quickly got up and moved toward the closest exit. What I saw next was unbelievable. The rest of the cars stopped on the open highway, and all the people ran outside to lay face down. Suddenly, I realized that whatever was happening was far more serious than a fire alarm. As I was lying on the ground, hands covering my head, I heard a strange whistling sound coming from a distance. A child from some other car started crying.

"You can go back to the bus," Kobi announced three minutes later.

Our trip resumed as usual, and the cars around us began to move as well. From my window, I caught a glimpse of the child, who was crying inconsolably just a few minutes ago, playing with his toys. His mother continued driving as if nothing had happened. Most likely, she was shaken by this event, but the car passed too quickly for me to discern her expression. In the meantime, everyone on the bus, including myself, was confused.

"What happened?" Madeline asked halfway through the ride.

"We had a rocket threat from Gaza," Luke said. His announcement was followed by the humming of different voices.

"Are you freaking kidding me?" someone asked loudly.

"Guys, please be quiet!" Kobi commanded.

"Can we go home?" one of the girls asked in a shrieking voice.

"Silence, please." Again, I could tell he was trying hard to play cool. "What happened is we had a missile threat," he began. "Ninety-nine percent of the time, they are nothing to worry about. But when you hear a siren, it means you have to either run to a bomb shelter or lie face down."

Expressions of shock and disbelief appeared on people's faces. I recalled all the news and rumors about the war. The threat was real. I wondered if this event would appear on the world news. If it would, I would have to come up with something to say to Jason and my parents the next time we spoke on the phone.

Although the trip continued, the mood was spoiled. Students looked gloomy, and some girls even approached the tour guide asking to be sent back to the hotel. He did everything in his power to convince them they were safe, but they were relentless. As soon as we stopped for the first break at a small town, they demanded to be put on a taxi and taken back to Kiryat Adar. I couldn't blame them. If I weren't so adamant about seeing the Timna Park and Eilat, I would've returned to the hotel too.

"WERE YOU scared this morning?" George asked me as we were sitting in a cafeteria and eating our falafel wraps.

"Of course, I was!" I replied defensively. "I mean half of the bus was scared too."

"That's because most people don't know this place too well. But as someone who's been here five times, I can tell you that it's nothing to worry about. In all the times I've done excavations, nothing serious ever happened."

"Good to hear." I took a bite from my wrap and washed it down with a gulp of orange juice. Although I was no longer deadly frightened, there was still some feeling of unease left. If anything, his words were reassuring to me. "So tell me more about your work here. You did excavations at another site, right?"

"Yes, I excavated in Tell es-Safi before joining the team in Kiryat Adar."

"The biblical Gath? The place where King David slayed Goliath?"

"Yes, if you believe the story. I mostly worked on the Philistine temple. Anyway, we spent around four weeks working at the site, and one day, a siren went off. Everyone got scared shitless, and it was a false alarm."

"What's a false alarm?" I had never heard of this term before and wanted to know more about it.

"Do you remember the Arab Spring?" he suddenly asked.

"Oh, yes." That was the year Jason and I moved from our ragged one-bedroom apartment on Jane and Sheppard to our new condo on Yonge and Finch. I could still recall seeing the news of Middle Eastern riots on television and subway screens.

"They were conducting a military drill across the country just to make sure people were prepared for the worst-case scenario."

"I see. That would make sense considering that Egypt and Syria were in upheaval."

"Egypt was okay by then, and Syria was too far from us. The thing is, Rebecca, this conflict has been around for a while, and so, most Israelis have become used to it. The media likes to blow everything out of proportion."

"That's what I tell everybody in Toronto, but people don't believe me. They think Israel is some kind of a warzone. When we came here last time, this place seemed so peaceful. I couldn't believe we were in one of the world's most troubled countries."

"You see? I wouldn't be too concerned." He finished his wrap and took our trays over to the garbage bin. I sincerely hoped this siren would be just a one-time event everyone would remember as an adventure.

In the meantime, I couldn't keep my eyes off George. While we were riding on the bus, he was sitting next to Rachel across from me and Karen. Rachel was wearing a pair of ripped mini shorts and a T-shirt with a plunging V neck. It was obvious to everyone including me that she was trying too hard to get his attention. I wondered how much time would pass before she would finally give up.

As soon as the bus stopped at our next destination, George turned to me and said, "Okay, Becky, let's go."

"Let's go." I smiled.

"Hey, are you enjoying some freedom from your husband?" Rachel asked poignantly as we were exiting.

"What are you talking about?"

"Oh, don't act so innocent! I saw you with George during the break."

"Ah, we were just talking about what happened this morning." I wasn't in the mood for a confrontation.

"Look how awesome it is over here!" Karen exclaimed, as if trying to dispel the rising tension. "I'm glad we didn't go back today."

"Me too," I replied, feeling heat on my skin. The weather was undeniably hot, and I knew well that we wouldn't be able to stay in one spot for too long.

What we saw was truly unforgettable. Before our eyes spread golden toffee plains and a chasm known as the Ramon Crater that lay in contrast with a cloudless, turquoise sky. According to the sources, it had been formed millions of years ago when the desert was still covered by the ocean.

"Look! What is this?" I exclaimed, eyeing a small creature standing nearby. It looked like a small goat with a pair of curvy horns.

"It's called an ibex!" George explained. "They're very common in this region."

"Let's take a photo. Quick!" I couldn't let the chance slip away.

My gaiety became contagious, and soon, the entire group was excited about seeing the exotic animal. I managed to snap a few photos before it ran off.

"Boy, these horns look scary," Janice remarked.

"Well, after what happened this morning, nothing seems scary anymore," Madeline said, rolling her eyes. After spending some time, roaming around, we headed back to the bus, ready for the next stop.

The Timna Valley Park was even more memorable than the Ramon Crater. This time, we were surrounded with hues of bright red and fiery orange. I had never seen anything similar, except for maybe one time when I went to the Valley of Fire State Park with Jason. It was also the time I nearly passed out after trying to hike in forty-five degrees Celsius heat. This time, I became so engaged in photographing pillars with Egyptian hieroglyphs and the famous Mushroom that I almost forgot how hot it was outside. Needless to say, my skin was glistening with perspiration, and my feet were burning inside my running shoes. I had to remind myself to take a few gulps of water to save myself from a heatstroke.

The sightseeing bliss came to a halt when my phone rang. For a split second, I considered ignoring it because the call could easily be a spam. Last time we were in Israel, I got a courtesy call from Rogers and had been stupid enough to pick up the phone. As a result, our phone bill skyrocketed by the end of the trip. This happened way before I figured out how to buy a local card instead of getting the Fido plan. Although I was unlikely to get into the same issue this time around, I wasn't in the mood to hear about some rip-off promotion. After a second ring, I gave in, realizing it could also be someone from my family.

"Hey, Rebecca! Is everything all right with you?" I heard Jason ask in an alarmed tone.

"Yes, baby, I'm fine. What happened?"

"The Hamas rocket fire is in the news!"

I was busted. Our morning incident did indeed reach the media, which meant my parents would be worried too.

"What rocket fire?" I asked, pretending to be oblivious to what he was saying.

"They fired missiles at Eilat today, and from what I remember, you were supposed to go there with your group. Am I correct?"

"Yes, you are. In fact, I'm having the best time of my life here. I'm going to send you the photos as soon I can."

"You should text or call your parents," he said, ignoring my happy babbling. "Your mom is really worried."

"Okay, sure. But tell her not to worry. We are taking all the precautions."

"Please be careful, Becky. You don't know how scared I am."

"I promise to stay safe. Jason, I'm really sorry, but I have to keep up with my group. Talk to you later."

After hanging up, I noticed more unread messages. They were from Erin, Mom and Dad, and even Chantal and Brian, my in-laws. Everyone was asking me if I was safe, and my mother was even urging me to come back to Toronto. Feeling uneasy, I dialed my parents' number but was directed to their voicemail. So I sent them a few text messages along with my photos from the Ramon Crater.

By the time we reached Eilat, the memory of the morning siren was long forgotten. Some students even took the initiative to start singing. In Eilat, we had a bit of downtime to cool off in the Red Sea. While attempting a few laps, I eyed George watching me from the beach. I looked back at him, and he winked at me. Then I turned away and continued swimming.

After the beach time, we were escorted to the underwater observatory, from which we could see a myriad of colorful fish swimming around coral reefs. I made a mental note to come back here someday with kids. Eilat would make a great destination for a Christmas or a March Break getaway. A big part of me hoped that Jason and I would be able afford it in years to come.

The day trip was concluded by a stopover at a local restaurant where we got to enjoy the best selections of Israeli food. At some point, I excused myself to the washroom just to be interrupted by a ringing cell phone.

"Hello?" I tried to sound composed.

"Hey, Rebecca, you should come back as soon as possible!" my mother exclaimed. "Dad's been looking for a return flight for you."

"What? I'm not coming back after one week!" There was no way I would return without finishing my work in Kiryat Adar.

"The Gaza conflict is in the news! They fired several rockets today, including a few to the south. This doesn't look good at all."

"Mom, I'm sorry, but I'm not going anywhere," I repeated. "The security is very tough here, and we are well-protected by the Iron Dome. If anything serious happens, we'll be evacuated."

"Do you really need to be evacuated? And what if the Iron Dome fails?" I could clearly sense panic in her voice.

"It won't." I tried to sound as persuasive as possible.

"Okay, but please be careful. And don't go anywhere alone. Remember those kids who got kidnapped?"

"Mom, that was in the West Bank, and we are in Kiryat Adar. But fine, I won't walk alone anymore." My statement was partly untrue because I still hoped to continue my solo walks to the beach. However, I was willing to say anything to prevent my parents from buying me a ticket to Toronto.

"I'm so worried about you, Becky. If only you knew!"

"I understand, Mom. I'm sorry."

"Becky, love, please be careful."

"Love you, Mom."

I hung up the phone and walked back to the table feeling a bit sad. If the stupid missiles hadn't been fired, this day would have been perfect.

"Is everything okay?" Karen asked, sensing my worry.

"The news of the missiles reached my parents," I replied, staring blankly at my spicy fish.

"Don't worry. It's been like this for many years," Janice said. "If it were that bad, none of us would be here. I mean, we are taking a credit course. What university would send its students to a place that isn't safe?"

"Tell that to my Mom." I sighed.

"Hey, I heard Eilat has a great party scene," she added later, when we were already finishing our main courses. "Maybe we should come back here during our next weekend."

"Unless they plan some other tour," Madeline said.

The idea sounded quite appealing. We could all hop into one big car we would rent at a local dealership and drive to Eilat at sunset. Then we would spend a night grooving to "Az Yalla" by Lior Narkis and other Oriental hits.

"We should also go to Beit Guvrin," Karen suggested. "It's only a few minutes' drive from Kiryat Adar, and I heard it's impressive."

"What is it?" Madeline asked curiously.

"It's a Roman site famous for its colorful mosaics and tunnels," Karen replied. "I'm sure you all will love it."

"Are you referring to the Maresha caves?" I asked, recalling an article from the *BAR* magazine.

"I think so," Karen replied.

"Excuse me. Did I hear something about the Maresha caves?" George asked as he approached our table. Up until now, he had been sitting with Luke and Vincent, completely oblivious to our conversation.

"Yes, you did," I said, staring directly into his eyes.

"We should do it during one of the breaks," Karen said. "Just rent a car and drive there."

"Hmm, it sounds like a cool idea," he said pensively.

"How about Eilat?" Janice chimed in. "We were also thinking about driving to Eilat next weekend or the one after."

"And party 'til sunrise," I added.

"Hmm, I'll have to think about that," George replied.

"Cheers." Janice raised a glass of wine.

ON OUR way back, I ended up sitting with George, and I couldn't deny he was good company. Every time his elbow brushed against mine, I felt the same sizzle from the first time we met at the cafeteria. I wanted to ignore it, but it kept coming back with every exchanged glance and every conversation. We chatted about his studies and his previous trips to Israel. It turned out that at Tell es-Safi, he'd even supervised a small group of students. Then he moved on to Kiryat Adar to continue his research.

"Have a great night," he told me at the hotel entrance.

"You too," I replied and walked away, feeling butterflies flutter in my stomach. In the room, I ran into Rachel, who gave me a dirty look.

"Want to use the shower first?" I asked.

She didn't say anything but simply grabbed a towel and went to the bathroom. Janice and Madeline entered the room a few minutes later. They were discussing some report they had to submit on Monday.

"We should try completing it tomorrow afternoon," Madeline suggested.

"That's a good idea," Janice said. "We could finish it after lunch and hand it in right away. Maybe we'll even have time for the beach." The thought of the Mediterranean Sea made me smile.

"Lucky you! You don't have to study for this dig," Madeline said to me.

I wanted to tell them how lucky they were not to have my job. Unless they were working somewhere part time, they weren't dealing with angry customers on a regular basis. Nor were they overwhelmed with boring orders and invoices.

Soon, Rachel stepped out of the shower, and I was allowed to go next. As I was standing under a warm stream of water, I thought about the events of the day. I thought about the unexpected siren and the fear, which were followed by memorable stops at colorful sites and mind-provoking conversations with George. I wondered what it would feel like to attend the dig for two or three consecutive years. People like George were truly committed to the field, while I and most other volunteers were spending less than a month helping out with the dirty work.

I also wondered about the future of my own expedition. It was highly unlikely that I would come back the following summer. Instead, I was destined to finish the dig and to go back to my ordinary life. I definitely had to enjoy this opportunity while it lasted. And maybe, just maybe, there was still a slight chance that things would go back to normal before the end of the dig.

The next day, I couldn't stop myself from thinking about him. I hoped to run into him at the site or during mealtimes, but he was nowhere to be seen. I hoped to bump into him at the hotel or on a street. Even my solo walk to the beach in the afternoon failed to provide me with the sense of calm I had enjoyed a few days earlier.

My jitters were mixed with feelings of guilt and confusion. I knew it was wrong to have this feeling, and yet here it was—the feeling I hadn't experienced in a long time—the thrill of meeting someone new. For the first time in my life, I began to wonder if getting married at twenty-two had been the right choice. I tried not to dwell on this thought.

During dinner, I sat with Jocelyn and Carol, as I often did. In spite of our age difference, I really enjoyed talking to them. One thing led to another, and we started discussing our personal lives. Carol had been married for thirty-five years; Jocelyn, for twenty. At the back of my mind, I wondered if they had ever encountered the same issue. Had they ever had a crush at some point? If so, how did they handle it? Of course, I wouldn't dare to ask such a question.

"My first marriage failed after ten years, and I was single through my thirties," Jocelyn began. "Then I met my current husband and couldn't be happier."

"What happened?" I asked.

"I was too young when I got married the first time," she replied. "Only twenty-two."

I felt chills run down my spine. I had been exactly the same age as her, and to top it off, everyone had been warning me against making a potential mistake.

"Did you grow apart with time?" I dared to ask.

"Yes. We were too different from each other."

"But how?" I knew it was none of my business, but I couldn't stop myself from asking.

"He was a computer programmer who worked long hours and preferred staying home most of the time, and I am a teacher and a very outgoing person, as you've probably already noticed."

Jason and I also came from different occupations. Although it never bothered me before, I started to worry that it could create issues down the road. I was already craving conversations he couldn't provide and getting them on the side.

"Did you notice differences right away?" I asked, hoping that she would, at least, say yes. It would give me some peace of mind, knowing that Jason and I hadn't noticed any issues yet.

"No, it wasn't until our fifth anniversary when we started having problems."

"I also married young, and your story makes me feel worried," I admitted.

I had never been that open with anyone, not even with Erin. Yet I was admitting my fears to someone I'd known for a little longer than a week.

"Does your husband allow you to have friends and a life outside of home?" Jocelyn asked.

"Of course!" I exclaimed. "In fact, this whole trip is proof of how much independence I get to have."

"My first husband wasn't like that at all," she said. "He was too jealous. I could have never gone on this trip if he were still around."

"Do you come from the same background?" Carol continued.

"More or less," I replied. "My family is Irish, and my husband is a mix of British, French, and Native. We both grew up in the suburbs."

"Are you from the same faith?" Jocelyn asked.

"We're not religious. We celebrate Christmas and Easter, and we believe in the Higher Power, but that's pretty much it."

"Look, I think you've got a strong marriage," Jocelyn reassured me.

I felt relieved. Maybe I was just obsessing over the whole thing. Sure, George and I had a few interests in common, and I liked him on the outside. However, it didn't have to mean anything. Besides, who said that having friends outside of marriage was a crime?

My self-convincing only worked until the night when I saw him in a dream. We were walking on a beach and discussing something related to archaeology when suddenly I felt his body pressed against mine. As the sweet desire coursed through my veins, the earth started shaking under us. Then I found myself standing alone in some dark, foreign place feeling frightened and lonely. I woke up breathing hard.

"What happened?" Janice asked, stretching. "You just screamed in your sleep."

"Did I?" I hoped I didn't give them any other clues about my dream.

"Yes."

"Nothing. Just a bad dream," I replied briskly.

"Can we have some quiet sleep, please?" Rachel grumbled.

"I didn't sleep well, either." Madeline came to my defense. "And it's time to go."

I turned my head toward the window and saw the first rays of sun shining at us.

During the first part of the morning, I was plagued by different thoughts. Did I truly have feelings for George? If so, would they go away in time? I exchanged a few text messages with Jason during breakfast just to feel better. The heavy thoughts disappeared during the second part of the fieldwork, when sorting through potsherds and trying to discern bases from handles made me forget all about the world outside. My fascination with the lab work was stronger than any worry on earth.

Ten

The following week, the excavation project continued as usual. We had digging and lab work in the early mornings, free time and pottery washing in the afternoons, and occasional trips to the bar in the evenings. I became so involved in archaeology and the social life of the dig that I almost forgot about my doubts. My fears about the war were also gone. I caught the news about the Operation Protective Edge on TV at one of the city's cafés, but everyone around me seemed aloof.

I met Shlomo a few times during my walks from the beach, and we exchanged a few words in Hebrew. He asked me about my archaeological work and whether I was enjoying my stay in Kiryat Adar. I told him about our trip to Eilat and even showed him the photos I'd taken of the ibex at the Ramon Crater. No missiles were mentioned, not even once. People were simply going about their businesses as if nothing wrong was happening.

I kept receiving messages from Jason, who wanted to know everything about my whereabouts. He was constantly telling me how worried he was, and sometimes, I even found his attention smothering—something that never happened in our marriage. I kept reassuring him that I was perfectly safe, and if anything were to happen, we had bomb shelters and the Iron Dome. After all, the atmosphere around the town was so relaxed, and half the TV channels were broadcasting local concerts and soap operas.

EVERYTHING CHANGED on the night of George's lecture.

"Good evening, everyone," he began after everyone gathered in one of the conference rooms of our hotel. "Tonight, I'm going to talk about one of the most important sites from the Late Bronze Age. Has anyone heard about Beit Shean?"

I raised my hand.

"Good. Rebecca, can you please tell us a bit about it?"

"Well, it was occupied by the Egyptians for nearly five hundred years. As a result, some Egyptian-style buildings and small artifacts have been unearthed at the site."

"Thank you!" He smiled at me. "Among those artifacts were beer jars and flowerpots, which I'm going to discuss tonight."

George pointed at images of plain vase-like objects.

"It's commonly believed they were used as part of an Egyptian food ritual that involved bread and beer. By the way, did you know the Egyptians were big drinkers?"

Ripples of laughter passed through the room. Jokes like this one were not uncommon in the academic world. In fact, lecturers with the greatest number of jokes always received the highest points on professor ranking websites. As a future course instructor, George was definitely showing a lot of promise in that area.

"The question is whether the Egyptian-style pottery was produced by the local population or if it was imported from Egypt," he continued. "I am planning to discuss the two theories: the emulation model and the direct rule."

Bzzzz! The siren rang, interrupting the flow of the lecture. Everyone got up from their seats and started running toward the bomb shelter. For a few seconds, I sat in my chair motionless. I felt scared, of course, but a huge part of me was also disappointed about the interruption.

George ran to me, grabbed my arm, and screamed, "Run!"

"But your presentation!" I protested a few seconds later, when we were already inside.

"Don't you realize that staying alive is the most important thing right now?" he nearly screamed.

"Well, I hope the rocket doesn't hit your computer, 'cause those images are priceless."

"Thanks, Becky." He laughed. "I hope it doesn't even reach the town."

We stayed inside the shelter for a while. By the time the situation was cleared, it was already quarter to eleven, time to go to sleep.

"Unfortunately, due to unforeseeable circumstances, the lecture has been canceled," Jayden Williams announced as soon as we returned to the conference room. He looked rather tense. "We hope to resume it another time."

It was then that the reality of the conflict hit me hard. We were in the midst of a war. Any one of us could die or get seriously injured at any moment.

Before going to bed, I stepped outside into the pool area, hoping that fresh air would help me calm my nerves. Without thinking twice, I took out my cell phone and dialed Erin's number.

"Hey, girl! How are you?" she asked, cheerful as usual.

"I'm great. Love it here. Yourself?"

"Eh, nothing much. Except that Alex and I broke up."

"Oh, sorry to hear about that. What happened?"

"It's been three months now, and I still haven't felt anything," Erin replied. "No butterflies, no nothing."

"Really? Maybe you could give it some time."

"How much more time, Becky? It's clear we're not meant to be. I know that giddy in-love feeling isn't everything, but it must mean something, right?"

"Definitely!" I recalled how much in love I used to be when I first met Jason. Back then, he was providing IT support to one of the university libraries, so we would often sneak in some time for each other between my lectures and his work hours. We could never get enough of each other, no matter how often we went out. It was not until the last few days that his phone calls and messages began to get on my nerves—and even that was something minor.

"And since I don't feel anything, I decided to call it quits," Erin concluded.

"You've made the right choice, Erin. I wouldn't want to go out with someone just for the sake of having a boyfriend."

"Exactly! So, yesterday, I told him exactly how I feel. He asked me for another chance, but I already know it has nothing to do with him. It's me, Becky."

"Well, I hope it all works out well in the end."

"Me too. I'm so exhausted from the dating scene. I'm ready to take a break." She sighed profoundly.

"Maybe it's a good idea. Just focus on yourself. Take a solo vacation or something."

"Maybe. Anyway, why are we talking about my problems? How's everything with you?"

"Well, as I said, I've been enjoying the dig. I'm sure you've already seen the photo of the figurine I discovered on the second day."

"I did indeed, and it looks fantastic."

"But I have an issue, and I need your advice."

"What is it? Tell me, Becky."

I took a deep breath, thinking about everything that happened in the past few days.

"Do you think I should stay here 'til the end of our excavation season?"

"What do you mean? Aren't you supposed to be there for two more weeks or so?"

"Yes, but I'm starting to worry about the situation here. It looks like Israel is going into a war with Gaza. Mom is constantly worried about me, and so is Jason."

"Oh, yeah, I can see that. Becky, we are all worried about you. But I personally think you should stay."

"Really?" Her opinion made me feel a bit relieved.

"The truth is, I've never heard you sound so happy. Not even on your wedding day! Every time you call or leave a text message, I can almost see your sweet smile."

"Wow, I didn't know that!" At the back of my mind, I wondered if this trip was making me feel even happier than the wedding itself, which, until now, I considered as the happiest day of my life.

"I know Mom will try to persuade you to come back and stuff, but if this place makes you happy, then you should stay."

"Thanks, Erin. I'm glad you said so."

I looked around and made sure no one was nearby to hear me. The pool area was completely deserted. Then I climbed on a sun bed and looked up at the sky. The missiles could appear at any moment, but so far, all I could see was the stars and the moon.

"There is another thing I need to tell you," I started. "But you must promise not to judge me and not to tell anyone."

"What is it? Please don't tell me you've met someone new on your dig."

I took a deep breath. "Well, sort of. His name is George, and he is studying at Wheaton College in the States. He's really good-looking. We started out as friends, but now I'm finding myself attracted to him, and I can't help it. We seem to have so much in common! I know it all sounds terrible, but—"

"I definitely saw it coming!" she exclaimed without letting me finish.

"What do you mean?" I asked in fear. Maybe she was judging me.

"Remember when you were getting married, and I kept telling you to wait?"

"Erin, please! That's the most annoying thing anyone can say to me in my situation."

"I'm not saying anything, Becky. All I want to say is this attraction was almost inevitable."

"I try not to dwell on this feeling too much, but it always haunts me. Besides, he's so nice. He helped me to get to the bomb shelter today when the siren went off."

"Wait, what bomb shelter? What siren?" I could sense a bit of shock in her voice.

"Didn't you know? I thought you heard the news."

"I hardly ever watch TV. You have to tell me."

"We had several rockets coming toward our city, and—"

"Holy shit! I had no idea it was that bad! No wonder Mom has been so worried lately. I visited our parents yesterday, and they both looked distressed. I thought maybe it was just the middle of the week or something."

I was overcome with a feeling of sadness. Why did this war have to start when I was living my dream? Now everyone I cared about was worried about me.

"Okay, tell them I'm really sorry. I don't know what to do. I can't just leave."

"Well, I hope your group comes up with some plan before the situation gets worse."

"Me too. So do you still think I should stay?"

"It's up to you, Becky. I'm in no position to tell you."

At this moment, I really wanted her to tell me to stay, but she was right. I would have to decide for myself.

"I'm so sorry for causing all the distress!"

"Just remember to keep us posted if you choose to stay."

"I will try. In the meantime, I hope you finally meet someone special."

"Thanks. Me too, Becky. Anyway, please stay safe. And best of luck with finding gold."

"Thanks. I need it."

I hung up the phone and let my thoughts unravel. Finding a reasonable solution, which would allow us to stay without being in any danger, would be amazing. However, I couldn't see anything viable on the horizon except for interrupting the dig and sending everyone home.

By the time I returned to the room, everyone was already asleep. I tiptoed to my bed and lay down without even changing my clothes.

THE FOLLOWING morning, I tried my best not to think about the events of the last night. In the meantime, I became paranoid of the airplanes that continued circling around our site. At some point, I became so scared that I dropped my bucket right next to the sifter and began to run.

"Where are you going?" George asked me as I was trying to find the bomb shelter.

"To the shelter."

"Why? There isn't any threat at the moment."

"Look, there's a plane!" I pointed to the sky.

He looked up quietly and laughed.

"What's so funny?" I asked, feeling slightly annoyed. He always seemed to make a big deal of my natural fear of danger.

"It's the United Airlines."

I breathed with relief, and we both laughed out loud. I hoped he didn't think of me as someone silly.

After lunch, I considered my options of what I could do during my spare time. I no longer felt safe enough to walk to the beach, so I decided to check out the pool instead. At the lobby, I ran into Karen, who was wearing a floral sundress and a pair of flip-flops.

"Hey, Rebecca. Want to join us at the pool?"

"Oh, yes. I'm actually heading in that direction."

When we reached the area, Janice and Madeline were already relaxing on the sun beds, drinking cocktails. I decided to order one as well.

"I heard they're going to move us to the north," Janice said, running fingers through her hair.

"Really?" I asked, unsure if that was good or bad news.

"It's totally true," Madeline said. "It's becoming unsafe in Kiryat Adar. To be honest, I'm getting sick of these alarms constantly going off."

"Me too," Janice said, nodding.

"What about Eilat and Beit Guvrin?" Karen asked. "Weren't we supposed to check out car rentals tomorrow?"

"Do you honestly think we would want to do that after yesterday?" Madeline sounded slightly annoyed. If there was anyone in greater denial than me, it was Karen.

"Well, I was hoping for a safe window perhaps," Karen replied.

"No way!" Madeline protested. "I no longer want to leave our hotel, let alone drive somewhere. Like, what if we get lost and end up in Gaza?"

"Hey, ladies, may we join you?" I heard someone ask. I looked to the side and saw George and Luke standing with cans of beer in their hands.

"Go ahead," Karen replied.

The guys took two adjacent sun beds.

"We were just talking about the possibility of our dig being moved," Janice began.

Suddenly, the alarm went off.

"What the—!" Luke bolted up and spilled his beer.

Then everything happened in less than a minute. Everyone started running toward the shelter. I dropped my drink and ran after the rest. From the corner of my eye, I caught a glimpse of all the hotel personnel, from receptionists to bartenders, drop their work and run for their lives.

As soon as we reached the shelter, I heard an explosion from the outside. It wasn't too loud, more like a whistle, but it was loud enough to shake everyone up. Several people gasped. Some began crying and shaking. Relieved to still be alive, I hugged the closest person standing next to me, who happened to be George. He held me tight in response. Perhaps he, too, was experiencing this rare moment of gratitude and was eager to come into contact with another human being. It was during this moment of despair that I realized we were all in this together.

THE RUMORS about the evacuation were confirmed during the pottery washing session, when nobody could concentrate on anything other than the last alarm. Most of us were fiddling with sherds and discussing news. Many volunteers were still trying to recuperate from the aftershock of the afternoon siren. Before the session ended, the directors declared they had an important announcement to make.

"Recent events have forced us to reconsider the Kiryat Adar program," Jayden Williams began.

Whispers passed around the room. I heard someone say something about getting a university credit.

"Kiryat Adar is under direct fire from Gaza," he continued.

Everyone, including myself, gasped. We all knew the truth, but hearing it from someone else had a stronger impact.

"However, our team is still committed to teaching its student volunteers about the archaeology of Israel. Therefore, we are moving our dig to the north."

Madeline and Janice sighed with relief. I could imagine what this course meant for them, especially since I'd heard that tuition fees for American universities were insanely high. I was relieved too. Moving to a different location would be the solution I needed to keep my parents' and Jason's worries at bay.

"We are leaving tomorrow morning at seven sharp. Please be ready," he continued.

"What are we going to do?" Carol asked.

"We will take a mini tour in the Galilean region and excavate in Megiddo. By the way, those who are not getting a course credit are welcome to stay but aren't obliged to."

"Does it mean we can return home?" Jocelyn asked.

"Yes, if you wish," Jayden replied, smiling. "The rest of you are staying in Megiddo." He looked directly at the Harvard students. "Does anyone know anything about the site?"

"I do!" I instinctively raised my hand.

"Can you please tell us what you know?"

I cleared my throat and began speaking. "Megiddo was a very important site in the ancient times, as it was a trade route connecting Egypt and Assyria. Several historic battles happened there."

Everyone looked at me in amazement, making me feel proud of my spiel.

"Thank you, Rebecca. We'll talk more about the site once we get there. Does anyone have questions?"

"What are some other sites we are going to visit?" I asked, unable to hide my curiosity. Several people, including Rachel, looked in my direction. I knew it was the wrong time to discuss sightseeing, but I couldn't help myself. Every time someone mentioned a new day trip, I felt like a child hearing a rustling candy wrap.

"You will get more information about the itinerary tomorrow. For now, all I can say is there'll be some interesting stops along the way."

"All right, thanks."

As soon as the pottery washing was over, I decided to share the exciting news with my family. First, I dialed Jason's number.

"Hi, Rebecca! I'm so happy to hear from you," he said as soon as he heard my voice.

"How is everything?"

"Busy as always. Only a week and a half left before our vacation. Can't wait."

"How do you feel about coming here after everything that's been happening recently?"

A few days ago, a rocket landed near Ben Gurion Airport, causing all flights to get canceled. Even though they resumed twenty-four hours later, I started doubting our vacation plans.

"It's too late for me to do anything. Besides, I can't wait to see you, Becky!"

"Aren't you worried about the news?"

"Of course, I am. But like I said, it's way too late to cancel the tickets."

"So far, most of the rockets have been repelled by the Iron Dome, but it's still so scary when the alarm goes off."

"Tell me about it. I don't even want to watch TV anymore, knowing that the love of my life is in a warzone."

"Guess what? I'm calling you to let you know that I won't be living in a warzone anymore."

"What do you mean? Did they cancel your dig?" He sounded a bit dazed.

"Nope. Our team is departing north tomorrow. We will be working on a different site for the last week."

"Really? Which site?"

"Megiddo. Do you remember it?"

"Of course, I do! Wasn't it the one with a long staircase leading to a dark tunnel?"

"Yes, it was." I smiled at this memory.

"It was also where you regretted wearing flip-flops."

"Uh-huh."

"Then we went to Haifa to see the Baha'i Gardens, and they wouldn't let us in because of your sleeveless T-shirt."

"Come on, Jason. We were on our honeymoon! What was I supposed to wear? An old lady's gown?"

"You are funny." He laughed.

"Anyway, I'll text you tomorrow as soon as we arrive in Megiddo."

"Have a safe ride, Becky."

"And you have a nice last week of work."

"Goodnight."

I wanted to dial my mother's number but decided to send a brief email explaining our change of plans. I also copied my father and Erin to keep them posted about our group's whereabouts. Then I proceeded with packing my suitcase. Rachel walked in and started packing her stuff without saying a word to me. Janice and Madeline joined us a few minutes later.

"I hope there won't be any alarms tonight." Janice finally broke the silence. "I'm getting sick of constantly running to the bomb shelter. What if I'm washing my hair at the moment?"

"I agree. Soon, we'll be away from all this craziness," Rachel said.

It was the first time in the longest while that I'd heard her speak.

"Maybe we should sleep with our clothes and makeup on," Janice suggested, "just in case an alarm goes off."

"No need to be crazy," Madeline said. "If it goes off, everyone will be wearing pajamas, and no one will care."

"I agree," I said, picturing George in his boxers. "I'll be back in a minute."

I grabbed my towel and my pajamas and proceeded to the bathroom. As I was removing my black mascara and eye shadow, all I could hope was that I wouldn't have to run for my life at this precise moment. Perhaps running in pajamas in the middle of the night was acceptable. Having mascara smudged all over one's face mixed up with makeup remover would be a bit too extreme.

"I'm not going to the shower," Janice protested after I stepped out. "I don't want everyone to see me in a bathrobe."

"Come on, just do it!" Madeline nudged her.

"Nope, I'm scared."

"Come on. It won't ring this time," I found myself saying.

We ended up laughing and pushing each other under the cold shower. Rachel slowly joined us, for our gaiety was contagious. We fooled around with the shampoo and the toothpaste, challenging each other to take the risk. At last, we were too exhausted to continue on and were soon sleeping soundly, oblivious to all the danger that was surrounding us.

Eleven

S taying in bed past four-thirty began to feel like sleeping in. When I woke up around six the next morning, I was feeling better than ever. I quietly proceeded to the bathroom, where I splashed cold water on my face. In the mirror, I saw a girl in her mid-twenties with shiny chestnut hair and glowing skin kissed by the Mediterranean sun. I put on the first thing I found in the suitcase, which was a bright orange dress decorated with funky beads. Then I slipped into my sandals and quietly walked out the door.

I knew that going outside alone wasn't the wisest thing to do in light of the recent threat, but I had to walk the streets of Kiryat Adar for the very last time. The moment I stepped into my favorite alley, I saw the outlines of flowers and trees basking in the rays of the morning sun. The air was still chilly from the night, but that morning breeze from the sea felt welcoming.

As I walked down the street, I felt both happy and sad. I was sad about being forced to leave Kiryat Adar so early but also happy because the journey wasn't over yet. The evacuation turned our project in a new direction, and I had a strange feeling that something good would come out of it.

Having removed my sandals, I entered the sandy area and walked straight to the sea. The waves were still strong after the night. As I stepped into the salty water, a sense of calmness and peace overcame me. Who could tell I stood all alone in a city threatened by rocket fire?

Suddenly, I realized I didn't need anyone to find happiness. Surely, I loved my soul mate, Jason, and looked forward to seeing him after the dig. I had a loving family who cared about me. Yet I felt perfectly complete on my own. This realization was frightening and yet empowering.

I walked back to the hotel slowly, hoping to stop at Shlomo's booth and order a last drink. However, it wasn't open yet. I said a quick prayer for his safety. Over the last week and a half, I became so attached to the city and its people that I couldn't imagine anything bad happening to anyone. I could only hope the Iron Dome would continue repelling rockets until the conflict was over.

By the time I returned to the hotel, my roommates were already up and getting ready for breakfast. Madeline and Janice were discussing their final course project while Rachel was quietly applying her makeup in the bathroom.

"Good morning," I said, walking into the room.

"Hey, Becky. Where have you have you been?" Madeline asked.

"Just walked outside to get some fresh air," I replied. "Cannot sleep past six anymore."

Janice laughed. "I'm starting to have the same issue," she said. "Maybe I'll finally transform into an early bird."

"Well, there isn't much of a choice when you are in archaeology," I remarked. "Anyway, should we get going?"

"Definitely," Madeline replied.

During breakfast, I learned that Olivia, Jocelyn, and Carol were planning to return to the States. Because of all the threats, they could no longer enjoy the program. I asked them if they regretted the turn of the events, but all of them told me the evacuation was for the best.

"I can't wait to see my husband and my kids," Jocelyn admitted.

"Me too," Carol added. "Better to go home before it gets worse."

"I agree," Olivia said.

"Well, I'm going to miss you all," I said.

By the time we finished our coffees, the airport shuttle was already waiting for them outside. We shared our last group hug in the lobby and wished each other the best.

"Goodbye and have a safe stay in Megiddo," Carol said.

"And remember that you've got a brilliant future," Jocelyn added.

"Thanks, Jocelyn. I'm flattered."

"No kidding. We all heard you speak about Megiddo last night."

"I wish my boss would appreciate it." I thought of how little my knowledge meant in the real world.

"If you are not happy with your job, then change it," Olivia advised, making me wonder if she'd overheard my conversation with Karen the other day.

"Easier said than done." I sighed. "Anyway, all the best to you." We went through another round of hugs.

It didn't take long for our bus to arrive. As we were taking off, I looked outside the window and said my silent goodbye to Kiryat Adar. Soon, the city faded in the distance.

I hoped that the rest of my adventure would be free from sirens and evacuations. Fortunately, the bus ride went uninterrupted except for one bathroom break in the middle of the journey, during which we got ten minutes to roam around a gas station and buy snacks. I decided to get a pack of Bissli.

"How was your night?" George asked me as I was paying the cashier.

"It was okay. Thanks for asking."

"I could barely sleep," he admitted, stretching.

"Fear of the missile threat?" I asked while opening the pack.

"Yep. Too much adrenaline rush every day. The war is sick."

"Want some?" I offered him a few Bissli.

"Sure. I think we should get going."

We walked back into the half-empty bus talking about the dig. I told him about my hopes to come back to Kiryat Adar another year and to finish the fieldwork I had started earlier. He, in turn, told me more about his research project with Andrew Logan. Up until now, he had been hoping to gather more information about the sites from the Iron Age so that he could finish his thesis back home. It appeared that he would have to focus on something else until things became calmer in southern Israel.

Soon enough, we arrived at our kibbutz near the new site. As I stepped outside, the air felt quite hot but much milder than in Kiryat Adar. Having looked around, I saw a nice, cozy village surrounded by small houses. While we were registering for our rooms at the reception, I was pleased to learn that I no longer had to share a room with Rachel. Instead, I would be placed with two local volunteers, whom I had yet to meet.

"Hi, I'm Michelle," one of the girls said as we were trying to open our door.

"Nice to meet you. I'm Rebecca. You can call me Becky."

"I'm Katie." Another girl joined us.

Not unlike at the Shimoni Hotel, the lunch at this kibbutz was organized in a buffet style and had an excellent selection of Mediterranean salads, hot plates, and desserts.

We had a brief orientation after lunch. I learned that the kibbutz was housing at least two more groups from different excavation digs. One was from Jaffa, and similarly to the Kiryat Adar team, it had to be moved away from the conflict zone. Another group was from Megiddo proper, and my new roommates were part of it. I got to meet the prominent scholars from the two sites. Our own directors told us more about the upcoming tour, which was to take place the next day in the Golan Heights. They also informed us they would be leaving the kibbutz for Jerusalem in a couple of days.

After the orientation, I briefly checked out the pool and spent some time at the lobby texting Jason and my parents. Everyone urged me to be careful and to stay safe. In reality, I was only a couple of hours away from Kiryat Adar. Yet somehow, I felt secluded from the danger.

MY NEW roommates and I decided to go out during the evening. I hoped that George would come too. I just couldn't get enough of our long conversations and his brilliant insight into everything we discussed. At the bar, I met Karen, Janice, Madeline, and some other volunteers from Kiryat Adar. Quite surprisingly, George was not among them. Maybe he would show later, or so I hoped as our group took seats at the biggest table available and began ordering drinks. One of the volunteers laid cards on the table and suggested playing them for a while. The group began playing while I kept looking at the entrance, hoping that he would walk in any minute. After an hour, it became clear that he was not coming. I sighed with disappointment and maybe a tiny bit of relief. After all, we weren't supposed to be hanging out on purpose.

"Rebecca, you look a bit sad," Karen remarked.

"No, I'm fine. Just a bit tired after the road."

"Do you want to play with us?" Madeline suggested.

"Sure."

I was never good at card games, so I followed blindly whatever everyone was doing. To my surprise, I won a couple of times. Our group played another game, during which each person had to say, "Never ever did I..." and make a statement. The rest had to listen and fold their fingers if the opposite applied to them.

"Never ever did I live in Canada," Karen started. I folded one finger.

"Never ever did I smoke pot," Madeline continued. Two thirds of the group folded their fingers.

The statements went on. The drunker we got, the funnier and rowdier our statements became. When my turn came, I quickly thought of what I could say and decided to go with something simple. So I said that I'd never lived in the United States. In the meantime, I thought about all the things I had never done in my life. I had never skipped a class, smoked a cigarette, or had a one-night stand. The list could go on forever. At the back of my mind, I began to wonder if I had missed out on all the fun people often had in their early twenties. I chucked this thought and went on with the game.

A few games and drinks later, we all dispersed to our rooms. Although no one was terribly drunk, we were collectively worried about missing the morning alarm.

"I hope we can wake up on time tomorrow," I said, entering our room.

"Are you going away?" Michelle asked.

"Yes. We're going on a tour for two days."

"Nice."

"I think we had a great time," Katie said cheerfully, taking out her blanket.

"I agree." I smiled. Despite George's absence, I could say it was a great time in the end.

I RAN into George at the lobby in the morning.

"Hey, where were you last night?" I dared to ask. "We missed you at the bar." I turned around to check if anyone from our team was eavesdropping. Neither Janice nor Madeline were in sight. Rachel was still in the cafeteria, finishing her breakfast.

"I had an important meeting with Andrew," he replied. "By the time we were done, I was too pooped to go out."

"I see."

"By the way, I forgot to mention that I'm leaving tomorrow."

"Really?" I asked, feeling a mixture of sadness and relief. Although I enjoyed George's company, his leaving would certainly be for the best.

"Yes. We're going to work at the Albright Institute. You know where it is, right?"

Of course, I knew everything about the Albright Institute, the oldest research center for archaeology in the Middle East. Throughout my undergraduate years, I'd been dreaming of visiting it someday. I even tried to go there during our stay in Jerusalem four years ago, but the tour schedule got in the way and we never made it.

"What are you planning to do?" I asked.

"Lots of things. We've got tons of findings to enter into the system, reports to write, articles to publish. It will be a busy week."

"I wish I could be part of it," I found myself saying wistfully.

"Maybe someday you will," he said.

Out of the corner of my eye, I saw Madeline, Janice, and the rest of our group walk into the lobby. Rachel came out last. The moment she saw me and George together, I felt a vibe of disapproval and judgement coming from her side. Seriously, how long would it take for her to calm down?

"Let's go," one of the tour guides urged us. "The bus is waiting."

Thus, we embarked on our journey to the Golan Heights.

Twelve

Our first stop was at Gamla, the ancient Jewish site famous for its role in the Great Revolt. During the first century CE, the town's dwellers rebelled against the Romans and fought against Vespasian's legions. In spite of an initial victory, Gamla eventually lost the final battle. As sad as the history can be, Gamla is a great site to visit.

The moment we received our maps, I became alarmed from seeing an area marked with mines.

"What is it?" I asked, pointing at the map segment that looked menacing.

"Don't worry; we won't be there," George tried reassuring me.

"How do you know?" I was still unconvinced.

"Look, this is where we are now, and this is the mined area. We won't even have time to reach it. Even if we did, we'd recognize the signs."

"All right, kids, you should get going," the bus driver told us. "Please be back in forty minutes."

Having looked around, we realized we were the only people still standing at the entrance. Everyone else was already making a way through the site.

"Have you been to Golan Heights before?" I asked, while entering the hiking area.

"Only once, when I was still working at Tell es-Safi."

"I see. So which places have you seen?"

"This one, Banias, Katzrin, and a couple more. Anyway, let's get going. We only have forty minutes to reach the Hasmonean quarter and come back."

The hike through the site was a bit strenuous but totally worth it. We passed through a narrow trail that lay between lush, green hills. From afar, I could hear a faint sound of a waterfall hidden between the hills. The scenery hardly looked like the Israel presented in tourist commercials that always show desert and camels. It was so green, so peaceful, and almost surreal.

"Boy, it looks more like Scotland," I remarked, looking at the hills.

"Except in Scotland, you hardly ever wear shorts," George commented.

We laughed and continued walking. By the time we reached the ruins, I was close to fainting. Even excavating in Kiryat Adar was easier. After all, the hike was mostly climbing up under the scorching sun while the archaeological work was done under a tent. I was glad I didn't forget water, for without it, I probably wouldn't be able to survive.

"Sometimes, I wonder why no one has written a paper about life in the antiquity without air conditioners," I joked. That question had been bugging me since our trip to Eilat.

"Well, maybe it will be the topic for your paper." George looked dead serious.

"I've been done with school for quite a while."

"Never say never." He smirked.

A few photos and another trail later, we were back to the bus. On our way out of the park, I saw a few prehistoric structures known as megaliths, which looked like miniature versions of Stonehenge.

Our next stop was at the Nimrod Fortress, which was built in the thirteenth century by one of Saladin's sons. Historians believe it played a strategic role during the Sixth Crusade. Although this site also involved a lot of walking, the walk was much easier because the road was paved. Besides, the narrow stairs and corridors of the fortress provided everyone with a good respite from the afternoon heat.

As we were emerging from the fortress, I saw my three former roommates walking together with Luke and Karen.

"Hey, George! Where have you been?" Rachel exclaimed, running toward him.

"Hi!" he replied briskly.

"What's wrong with you, honey?" she asked. I rolled my eyes.

"Want to take a group picture?" Karen suggested.

"Sure," Janice replied.

We all gathered in front of a small fence with a castle in the background and looked at each other. My eyes met George's, and I immediately felt those stubborn butterflies again. At least, he would be gone tomorrow.

"You stand here," Rachel commanded, pushing me aside.

"I can take the photos," Madeline said. "Give me your cameras."

"Oh, that's so nice of you!" Karen exclaimed.

"Here, you can take mine," I said. The rest of us passed her our cameras.

"Let me take a photo of you with the rest of the group," I suggested after she finished.

"Thanks!"

"We should friend each other on Facebook," Janice suggested after I finished taking the last photo.

After the Nimrod Fortress, we stopped at the Banias Springs Park, an archaeological site, also known as Caesarea Philippi, located at the foot of Mount Hermon. According to the Christian tradition, it was the site where St. Peter received his ordination from Jesus to lead the church. It's also famous for a pagan shrine dedicated to the Greek god Pan. Today, one can still find small grottos carved out of rock that used to be mini altars. The actual park consists of small waterfalls and springs, one of which happens to be the source for the Jordan River. As soon as the grottos came into sight, I felt a twinge of excitement, for it was one of the places Jason and I had visited during our honeymoon.

Right next to the park entrance was a small picnic area where we had our lunch. It wasn't until I saw rows of salads and pita wraps that I realized how hungry I felt. Sometimes, sightseeing could make me forget about everything in the world, including food.

A group of Muslim women with kids sat at a table nearby and chatted happily in Arabic. One of them smiled at us and said, "Hello." I replied with *"Ahlan,"* another word I knew in their language. The scene reminded me of summer picnics in Toronto parks, where political conflicts existed only in newspapers.

At last, we proceeded to the park to explore the ruins and enjoy the natural wonders of the Banias Springs. Tired of my old sticky running shoes, I took them off and slipped on the flip-flops, which I had shoved into my backpack the last night. It felt quite refreshing not to have those boots on my feet. After taking a few photos of the shrines, I followed the road leading to the springs. For a few minutes, I was completely alone in a dark tunnel of trees. Then I saw a group of girls from our team walking together with Luke and George.

"Look, this is the starting point of the Jordan River," I announced. "We should all take a photo in it!"

"Let's do that!" George jumped in.

In front of us was a place that could be easily mistaken for a cave. A small area of water was surrounded by low-hanging branches that cast a shadow on anyone who entered it. Having removed his shoes, George walked into the water, and I followed him. The water felt pleasantly cold against my skin. So there I was, flip-flops off my feet, walking into the source of the Jordan River, holding onto the branches, and trying my best to maintain balance. All of a sudden, I lost my grip and fell into the water.

For a split second, everything went dark. Then I opened my eyes and saw George, who was splashing in the water, trying to help me out. My first thought was about the camera, which I had luckily entrusted to Karen before entering the stream.

"Are you okay?" George asked.

"Better than in Kiryat Adar's bomb shelters," I replied, trying to shake off streams of water flowing down my clothes.

Suddenly, hysterical laughter took over. Nothing could be more ridiculous than this incident. Karen, Madeline, and the rest picked up on my gaiety and also started to laugh. George tried to hold it in, but the laughter was contagious. We ended up fumbling toward the bus all wet and giggly.

The bus driver quietly drove us to Majdal al-Shams, a Druze town, and stopped by a small market.

"You have twenty minutes to find a change of clothes," he said.

"What are we going to buy here?" I asked, eyeing a row of *abayas* and *hijabs*.

"Whatever will prevent us from ruining the bus seats," George replied.

"Now he's trying to be funny." I playfully poked him.

Having looked around, I saw nothing that would fit. All the modern-looking clothes were either too big or small. Only one dress was my size, and it was a black *abaya* accessorized with a white scarf. There were more options for George, who ultimately bought a pair of sports pants and a T-shirt. Not having much of a choice, I bought the dress and immediately started looking for a bathroom to change in. Sensing my concern, the seller asked me if I needed help. After I told him I was looking for a ladies' room, he explained how to get to the closest coffee shop. George and I parted at the entrance, agreeing to meet in a minute.

"Please don't let the bus leave without me," I pleaded. "I have no idea how to get back to Megiddo alone."

"Of course, I won't leave you, Becky." The way he pronounced my name made my insides melt.

The entire time I was changing, my mind was focused on one thing—not to drop anything into the dirty toilet, which probably hadn't been cleaned up for ages. I still had a backpack full of things, such as running shoes, water, and, most importantly, the camera. If only I had packed extra clothes!

When I came out, George was waiting faithfully at the entrance, looking even better in his new clothes.

"You don't look that bad," he said, smiling.

"No comments, please. Let's go."

As soon as we boarded the bus, everyone clapped. I probably looked ridiculous in my long dress, but what choice did I have? So I tried to laugh with everyone else.

Our very last stop for the day was at Tel Dan, the site I'd been looking forward to seeing for the entire day. Despite feeling uncomfortable in my new, exotic clothes and having a few bruises from stones, I still enjoyed exploring the Israelite temple. I wondered what Jason and my Facebook friends would say about the dress I had to wear during the last photo session. I would probably have to write a note explaining what happened earlier.

In the meantime, George and I chatted about the structure of the temple and the Aramaic stela, which had been discovered in the area. It mentions the "House of David," which many scholars attribute to the rule of biblical King David.

"Do you think the stela gives enough evidence about King David's existence?" I asked.

"I don't think so," George answered frankly while snapping a few photos of the structure. "While I don't deny the possibility, I don't see enough evidence here."

"But the stela clearly mentions the 'House of David.'"

"So what? It could be anyone's name, not necessarily King David's."

"True." To be honest, I always had a hard time accepting the fact that most of the biblical narrative didn't always match with the actual evidence from the sites. With time, I learned to accept the facts and to acknowledge how little we knew about the past.

"I think the archaeologists are often too eager to find something related to the Bible," he said. "As a result, they get excited too quickly and start ignoring the facts."

"However, absence of evidence doesn't always mean nonexistence of a certain person or an event," I remarked.

"True. But like I said, I'm not denying anything. I'm just being critical."

I felt his gaze and wanted to move closer. Instead, I moved away and pretended to be photographing the sacrificial area. I could no longer deny my attraction to him. Somehow, the incident at the Banias Springs had brought us closer. We couldn't stop talking to each other on our way to the kibbutz.

"So, where do you think the Israelites came from?" he asked at some point.

"Well, I'm not sure, but there are many theories about their origins," I replied, trying to recall what I had learned in the biblical archaeology course back at the U of T.

"They were obviously the Canaanites!"

"You think they were the same group that existed in the Late Bronze Age?"

"Of course! The same language, material culture, and even the same religion."

"Well, I vaguely remember those theories, but, like you, I'm also being critical. You can't believe in everything the books say."

There was a moment of silence. Then he dropped a bomb. "I think you should seriously consider going to a grad school," he said.

"Maybe one day." I shrugged.

"You should consider it now before it's too late."

"Maybe you're right," I blurted out. "To be honest, I'd love to spend my life working with artifacts."

"Then what is stopping you?"

"I don't know." In truth, many things were stopping me. For one, I wanted to have kids someday, and I wasn't sure if long archaeological expeditions were compatible with parenthood. I knew there were many scholars who successfully balanced their work schedules and family lives, but I couldn't imagine being away from my children for most of the summer. I was also afraid of leaving my job and starting over as a student, especially in a field as narrow as Syro-Palestinian archaeology. However, I didn't admit any of these things to George.

He later took out his music and offered me one headphone. At the moment, "Zombie" by the Cranberries was playing. It was followed by a few songs from the Beatles, Queen, and Alanis Morissette. I suspected my taste in music wasn't as refined as his, but I felt like sharing a few of my favorite songs anyway. So I offered him my iPod and put on "Yafa Sheli" by Eyal Golan. We later listed to "Kmo Sinderela" by Sarit Hadad and "Halom Matok" by Moshik Afia.

"Wow, you know Hebrew music," he commented. "That's amazing!"

"That's all I've been listening to lately."

Jason had known my music preferences for a long time and was already used to them. We'd even gone to a few Israeli concerts in Toronto. To new people, my playlist still appeared a bit unusual. I hardly ever talked about my music to anyone, except for a few people I could trust. The moment I showed George my playlist, I felt like I had revealed a hidden part of me.

"Will I see you tomorrow?" I asked him as the bus was approaching the kibbutz.

"I believe so," he replied. "And maybe even after tomorrow."

"Aren't you going to the Albright Institute?" I asked, confused.

"Yep."

"So how will I see you then?"

"I said 'maybe.'" The mischievous glee on his face made me wonder if he was hiding something.

I decided to drop the subject. I was certain that his leaving would help me to put my mind back on track.

As soon as we reached the room, all I wanted was to remove that dress and to take a long shower. Being sticky for several hours straight was no fun. When I walked inside, all my roommates were still away. So I grabbed one of the new towels our cleaners had left for us, fished out some fresh clothes, and went straight to the bathroom.

I heard the door open a few minutes later when I was lying on my bed, relaxing. Katie and Michelle were chatting happily. I considered telling them about the incident, but decided against it. It was enough that the entire Kiryat Adar team had seen me drenched in the waters of the Jordan River.

"Hey, how was your day?" Katie asked me.

"It was great," I replied, getting up. "You won't believe how many sites we saw today."

"Did you go the Golan Heights?" Michelle asked.

"Yes, we did. Tons of hiking and sweating, but totally worth it."

"Our group went there last week," Michelle said.

"There is one place where you can actually set your foot on Lebanon," Katie added.

"No kidding!" I exclaimed. "I want to know where it is."

"Hmm, do you remember the name?" Katie turned to Michelle.

"Is it Tel Dan?" Michelle asked.

"I believe so," Katie said after a short pause.

"What? We just came from there! How come nobody told us?" I exclaimed furiously. I could have set my foot on the lands of Phoenicia and Aram without getting caught.

"We don't know if it's true," Michelle said. "I doubt the border between the two countries at war would be left unsupervised."

"I agree. It's probably a rumor," I said, trying to console myself.

"Let's go eat something," Katie suggested. "I'm hungry."

We quickly left the room and walked toward the cafeteria, where everything was already set up. The three of us dispersed, and I found myself sitting with two of my former roommates.

"So, do you like him?" Janice asked at some point.

"Who?" I said, pretending to be oblivious to her question.

"George, of course! I've noticed it from the very first day."

"I think he likes you too," Madeline added.

"Look, I'm married! Just because we talk doesn't mean something is going on between us."

"Not when you are spending every minute together," Janice remarked. "Besides, we all saw what happened at the Banias Springs today."

"It was just a crazy mishap. I felt so embarrassed later!"

"No need to be. It happened to almost all of us at some point."

"I know. We've all been in funny situations."

I was happy our conversation was steering in a different direction. If I felt anything for George, I didn't want to admit it to anyone, especially to Janice and Madeline.

"Now I've got a souvenir from Majdal al-Shams," I joked. "I doubt I'll ever wear it again unless I decide to visit Egypt or Jordan someday."

We had one more day of traveling before starting the Megiddo excavation. Although I would rather spend the next day relaxing at the kibbutz, I couldn't miss the opportunity to hike the Arbel cliffs and see Beit Alfa along with Beit Shean. I had to go, even if it meant putting forth extra effort. So I decided to head straight to the room after dinner and get ready for day two of sightseeing. This time, I was planning to throw in an extra T-shirt just to be on the safe side.

"Where are you going?" George asked me as I was walking from the cafeteria.

"To my room. I need to prepare for tomorrow's tour."

"I've got a surprise you might like." He winked at me.

"What do you mean?" I was truly confused.

"Would you like to join our team at the Albright?"

"Say that again?" I stopped walked and turned to face him.

"We want you to join us at the Albright Institute in Jerusalem," he repeated.

I couldn't believe my ears. "Isn't it the type of work meant only for qualified people?" I asked.

"Yes, it is. However, knowing how much you'd love to work in a lab, I convinced them to let you participate. Besides, your Hebrew could help us. We need some work translated into English, and everyone is overwhelmed right now."

"Okay," I said quietly, still trying to digest the news.

"Do you want to participate?" he pressed on. "You don't have to. It's only a suggestion."

"Are you sure you didn't misunderstand anything?" There was no way I was being invited to work at the research center of my dreams.

"Yes, I'm sure. If you really want to be part of our team, you're more than welcome to join us."

"I do!" I tried hard not to jump from excitement.

"Then you should get ready for tomorrow morning. We'll be leaving at seven-thirty."

"I will."

Suddenly, it all made sense. Before leaving Kiryat Adar, I knew something good would happen in the next few days, but I wasn't sure what it would be. When we first arrived at Megiddo, I had a strange feeling that I shouldn't completely unpack my suitcase. Now I knew where the feeling was coming from. No wonder George was so ambiguous when I asked if I would see him again.

I couldn't resist texting my entire family about the news and telling everyone about the new plan. Jason quickly replied with a congratulating message, while my parents an Erin replied with simples "wows." Nor could I resist updating my status on Facebook, which earned me a few likes from my former university classmates. The opportunity at the Albright Institute felt like a small victory after a chain of failures.

In my second year at university, I tried to get a campus job as an archaeology lab assistant. My application was rejected because, according to the lab director, I lacked proper experience. I later learned that the role was given to a graduate student and felt devastated. How was I supposed to get any experience without getting a chance? After graduation, I wanted to work with artifacts at a museum, but it never happened either.

Fast forward several years and many more miles, I was one step away from living my dream. Never mind I wasn't getting paid for the work. Never mind the opportunity would last for one week only. The thought of working side by side with scholars, handling ancient artifacts, could bring me nothing but a big smile.

Thirteen

"You don't understand! This bitch is winning!" I heard Rachel scream into her cell phone while walking to the cafeteria the next morning. "She's married, and she's trying hard to snatch him away. Oops, I think she heard me. Bye now." She put down her phone and started walking along.

"Good morning," I said casually.

She didn't say anything but looked at me with her red, puffy eyes. For a moment, I wondered if I should confront her about the situation. Perhaps I needed to tell her I was sorry about the way everything had turned out. However, I couldn't come up with anything that wouldn't sound awkward. So we continued walking side by side without exchanging a single word.

During breakfast, I bid farewell to everyone, including Lara, Claire, Luke, Karen, Janice, Madeline, and my new roommates, Katie and Michelle. I caught a glimpse of Rachel, who was sitting at a distant table by herself, looking defeated. I still couldn't believe we were practically competing against each other.

"Best of luck to everyone," I said while going around the circle and offering hugs.

"Let's keep in touch online." Katie handed me a paper with her Facebook email written on it.

"We'll see you at the reunion," Madeline added, referring to the final dinner the group was planning to have in Tel Aviv.

Over time, I had become attached to our group, and by now, I was able to imagine what living on a campus would be like. I would probably make tons of friends, and some friendships would go way past university years.

Having said my goodbyes, I grabbed my suitcase and boarded the bus. The most exciting part of the journey was about to begin.

The road to Jerusalem was quick and yet marvellous. At the beginning of the ride, I could only see plain, yellow fields and occasionally small towns. Then, all of a sudden, our bus became surrounded by valleys and hills covered with lush, green trees. No wonder this part of Israel is called the hill country, often believed to be the original place of the biblical Israelites. Who could imagine that the other side of the city was surrounded by desert? I tried taking as many photos as possible, but the angle would always shift, leaving me with a bunch of blurry images that failed to convey the beauty of the scenery.

As soon as we entered the city, I began looking for familiar places and spotted the tower of the Park Hotel, where Jason and I had stayed last time. The bus drove through a few busy streets and finally arrived at our destination, the Albright Institute. I was shocked to find it was located in East Jerusalem, which was easily recognizable by shops and houses with Arabic letters and hanging cords. Having opened the bus window, I smelled spices wafting through the air and heard sounds of *darbuka* coming from a shop nearby.

In theory, I had nothing against this part of the city. However, I somehow had to explain to my family where I was staying. My mother had asked me to send the address the night before, and I did so, assuming the Institute was located somewhere in the west end. I could only hope that no one would check it on the map.

As we stepped out, I saw a gate leading to a beautiful two-story building surrounded by a small garden. Having picked up our belongings, we proceeded to the Institute's guest hostel.

"Here is your key," the hotel owner said.

"*Toda rabbah*," I replied.

"*Bevaksha*." He looked a bit surprised. My language skills had a strange effect on the locals.

My room was small but clean and cozy. Although there were two beds, no roommates were in sight. The idea of having personal space was a welcoming change. After taking a quick shower, I proceeded to the basement where our group was supposed to meet.

"Do you know where we are going?" George asked me as we were walking down the stairs.

"No, I don't."

"Let me show you." He grabbed my hand and led me to a small room with dozens of boxes lying around and waiting to be opened. Some staff members were bringing in more.

"So, what do I do?" I asked, immediately regretting my question. The best tactic would be to follow everyone else's lead.

"We'll have to make drawings and input data into the system," I heard someone reply. "For now, we just need to set up the basement." A lady in her late forties or early fifties was standing next to me. Her name badge read, "Helen Campbell, the University of Chicago."

"Let's get those boxes moving." George gave me a light nudge.

We worked for a few hours, setting up the work area, checking computers and other equipment, and organizing artifacts from oldest to newest. Although the work was relatively easy, I still had no idea how I managed to survive the afternoon without embarrassing myself. I had a tendency to be clumsy when doing something for the first time.

"See you all tomorrow at seven," Helen Campbell announced in the end. I was about to leave when I heard my name called. "Rebecca, can I see you for a moment?" she asked.

"Sure, Dr. Campbell," I said.

"Call me Helen." She smiled. "Is it true that you speak Hebrew?"

"I do." I wondered if she would ask me to put Hebrew labels on the sherds.

"We have an article that needs to be translated into English. Would you be comfortable doing that?"

For a second, I was silent. The task she was offering wouldn't be an easy one. However, I had always wanted to work with a Hebrew text. Back at the U of T, I had even considered taking an independent study course that would involve translating a Hebrew novel into English. Now I had the opportunity to fulfill my wish.

"Sure," I said, without even thinking twice.

"Can you start on it tomorrow?"

"Yes, I can."

"Perfect! See you at dinner then."

The moment she walked away, the reality hit me hard. Okay, perhaps my Hebrew was good enough to ask for directions or order falafel. I could definitely maintain a decent conversation about music and politics. However, I wasn't sure about my ability to understand, let alone translate, a scholarly article. Besides, I only had one week to get it done.

I weighed my options. I could still run after Helen and let her know I'd rather work with the rest of the team on the artifacts. Surely, there would be nothing hard about keying dates and numbers into the system. Or I could give it a shot and decide later if I wanted to continue. I chose the second option.

The best thing to do was to relax for the rest of the day and not dwell on the situation. So I chose to take a short walk around the garden and enjoy the sight of cypress and palm trees surrounding the building. The courtyard had a set of tables and a small pond at the center. After roaming through the garden for a while, I decided to check out the library.

For some odd reason, it reminded me of the Pontifical Institute, a U of T library, which housed a rare collection of books on the medieval studies. Although visitors usually weren't allowed inside, I had managed to get in once by claiming I needed to consult a book for an essay. I could still remember the excitement I had felt from holding an oversized, two-hundred-year-old book in my hands.

Having browsed through different documents, I found a publication on Ekron, another Philistine site. I was casually flipping through the pages when I heard a familiar voice. I turned around to find George standing next to me and peering into my book.

"I passed this site a few times when I was working in Tell es-Safi," he said. "I was also part of the team that worked on the famous inscription, but only briefly."

"Are you referring to the inscription that supposedly mentioned Goliath's name?" I asked.

"Yes. Although I doubt that it actually mentions him."

"Why not?"

"See, it's actually two words written in proto-Canaanite, and they could be transliterated in several ways. More like 'alwty' or 'alt.' The scholars are still working to determine what these words mean. Of course, the Bible enthusiasts want to believe the inscription is about Goliath, but we have to be careful before jumping to these conclusions."

"Yeah, you're right." I closed the book and put it back on the shelf.

"How do you like it so far?" he asked after I put the book away.

"It's all right, but I'm a bit nervous about tomorrow."

"I hear you, Becky. This week won't be an easy one. I've just talked to Andrew, and it looks like we'll be slaving for a while. Well, the thing is, you'll get used to it."

"At least you won't be translating a Hebrew article into English."

"Did they give you the article?" He looked excited.

"Yes. Wait, was it you?"

"I simply mentioned you know the language when trying to convince them to take you on board. The rest was up to them to decide."

Now I recalled George mentioning the translations yesterday after dinner. Never could I have imagined that I would be actually asked to translate something.

"Well, thank you, George," I said with sarcasm.

"What's the matter, Becky? I thought it would be a good way for you to build your CV."

"And what makes you think I'm applying anywhere?"

"Just in case you decide to apply to a grad school, I mean. Plus, you can always count on me for help."

"How are you planning to help?"

"Well, I cannot do the actual translation, but I can always help you to put the words together. I've edited articles before."

"I can put those sentences together myself, thanks." I turned away and picked another book—this time on findings from Jaffa.

"Of course, you can! I only wanted to offer my help in case you needed it."

"Excuse me. Can you please keep the volume down?" the librarian asked.

"Sorry! We are leaving now." I put the book back on the shelf and walked toward the exit. George ran after me.

"Becky, wait," he yelled as I was walking through the corridor.

"What?" I turned around. Our eyes met. For a few seconds, we stood there motionless.

"You can totally do it," he finally said. "I believe in you."

"I hope you are right." I sighed. Suddenly, I realized that I had enough strength to overcome my fear.

DURING THE evening, the staff decided to dine in the courtyard, as it was still bright and warm outside. Having grabbed my plate of couscous, I followed George and the rest of the team to a small marble table that had a box of beers waiting for everyone.

I got to meet Caitlin and Megan, two PhD students who were working at the Albright Institute during the summer. Both of them were in their early thirties and had an air of confidence about them. I also exchanged a few words with the new director of the Institute.

Throughout the evening, no one had raised the topic of archaeology, not even once. Instead, people talked about their favorite music bands, most of which were unfamiliar to me, shared concert memories, and discussed their past trips to Europe. Since I didn't have much to contribute, I sat quietly drinking my bottle of Goldstar and listening to everyone else. I doubted my trips to the United States or infatuation with ethnic music would impress anyone. In fact, I had a small fear of not being sophisticated enough for this group. Still, I enjoyed their company.

After dinner, I went to the common room to relax on a couch and watch TV.

"Do you need some help?" a young man asked me as I was flipping through channels. According to his badge, his name was "Avi Elias," and he was a graduate student at the Hebrew University.

"Sure," I replied casually.

"You are probably looking for an English channel, right?"

"Not true," I said, thinking about all the bad news it was probably broadcasting at the moment. I was in no mood to hear about the Gaza conflict or the crisis in Ukraine.

"Okay, so what are you looking for?" he asked, pressing buttons on the remote control.

"Some entertainment channel in Hebrew."

"All right." Avi looked slightly surprised. He played with the remote control for a while until he finally found a music channel with English and Israeli music videos. At the moment, a clip of Aviv Geffen's "Mistovev" was playing. Recognizing the words, I started singing along.

"Do you know him?" Avi asked, eyes blazing with wonder.

"Yes."

"I'm close friends with his family."

"Oh, how nice!" I exclaimed. "Does it mean you get to have free concert tickets?"

"I'm not a big fan of his music. But he's cool."

"I thought you must be into rock." That was my assumption about all the guys besides my husband, who was a country boy at heart.

"Not really," he admitted.

"So which artists do you like?"

"I prefer Sarit Hadad and Zehava Ben."

"Really? I love them too!" I nearly jumped from excitement.

"Shhh, don't tell anyone." Avi looked serious.

"Why not?"

"Mizrahi music isn't well received in academic circles."

"Really? What's wrong with it?" I began to feel indignant.

"It's considered a bit primitive, but I like it anyway."

"Well, I'm offended now." I pouted.

Avi smiled. "No need to be because I'm just the same."

"Fine! So, who's considered refined then?"

"Arik Einstein, Matti Caspi, Chava Alberstein..."

"Oh, I see."

I had tried listening to their music back in high school, but all of their songs sounded the same. Some were a bit too eastern European for my taste. I liked the Ashkenazi culture in general, but when it came to music, I preferred Middle Eastern melodies with a lively beat and simple lyrics celebrating love.

"Your secret is safe with me, Avi. Otherwise, we'll collectively get into trouble with snobs."

He laughed. "You are so funny. May I ask you what's your name?"

"Rebecca. You can call me Becky." I offered a handshake.

"Nice to meet you, Becky. I assume you're part of the Kiryat Adar team."

"Yes. The Gaza conflict forced us to move here, but I don't regret it in the least," I announced jubilantly.

"I know. My brother is fighting in Gaza now. I'm praying for his safe return." Avi looked sad.

"Oh, I'm sorry." I lowered my eyes.

"It's not your fault. I totally understand why you're happy about the way everything turned out. The Albright Institute is an amazing place to work. Great people, great atmosphere."

"In the meantime, what do you do here?"

"I'm working as a lab assistant for the summer. Hey, I heard you'll be translating an article. Am I correct?"

"Yes. Why?"

"I'm usually the one in charge of the translations, but this year, everyone is so busy that any help will be great."

"I'll do my best then."

"I hope you enjoy it too." He smiled. "Gotta go. See you, Becky."

"Bye."

After he left, I watched TV for a little longer. There were a few songs by the Idan Raichel Project, Shiri Maimon, and some other singer I didn't know. At some point, I accidentally hit the wrong button on the remote control and was immediately redirected to the English news channel. I wanted to turn it off, but something urged me to keep it on for a few minutes. Just as I expected, nothing good was being shown.

Kiryat Adar came under fire several times, and one time, a missile hit an empty house. Although its owners were lucky to be away at the moment, the destruction to the property itself was quite severe. I hoped this house didn't belong to Shlomo or someone I knew from the hotel.

In my room, I checked Facebook and found several photos from the Golan Heights tour. I noticed that Janice was online and decided to say hi to her. She immediately responded with questions about the trip to the Institute and about George.

"No need to ask," I typed back. "We're only friends."

"The rest of us think otherwise," she typed back and added a winking emoji.

"I don't know where you are getting this idea from. Anyway, how is Megiddo treating you?"

"Oh, I'm loving it," she replied. "Better weather, better work conditions. But I'm definitely not going into archaeology. I've had enough of slaving under the sun."

"Cool," I typed. *At least you won't be torn between your family life and your expeditions*, I thought.

I exchanged a few words with Karen and Lara, who were also online. Unlike Janice, they didn't bug me about George but simply went on about their final day trip and the following day at the dig. I wanted to stay online a little longer, but it was almost midnight, and I had to be fresh tomorrow morning. So I said goodnight to everyone and logged off. When I was already in bed, my phone rang.

"Hello," I said, feeling a bit frustrated about being forced to get up.

"Hi, Becky! How are you?" Jason asked.

"I'm good. Yourself?"

"Not so bad. Just wanted to make sure you got to Jerusalem okay."

"I thought I sent you the message earlier," I replied, feeling slightly annoyed. After all, he was stealing time from my sleep.

"Yeah, I got it, but I wanted to check on you regardless. I just read about the missiles in Kiryat Adar and everything, so I felt like talking to you."

"No need to worry. I'm fine." I hoped my quick reply would satisfy him.

"So, how was your day?" he asked just as I was about to hang up.

"It was all right. Thanks for asking."

"Anything new? You told me they moved you to the research institute."

"Yes. Jason, I'm sorry, but I really need to sleep right now. Can we talk tomorrow?" My patience was running thin.

"Okay, I understand." He sounded a bit disappointed.

"Bye now."

"Goodnight, love."

I could tell he wanted to talk a little longer. Under different circumstances, I would've told him more about my day and the impending project. Maybe he would've reassured me about my ability to do the job well. Maybe we would've even laughed about it. Yet I simply hung up the phone and collapsed onto my bed.

Fourteen

I couldn't believe I had gotten myself into this mess. In the morning, all I wanted to do was climb back to my bed and hide under a thick blanket for the entire day. There was no way I would succeed at this task.

"Are you ready?" George asked me as we were finishing our coffees at the cafeteria. The breakfast, which mainly consisted of an omelette and toast, was simple and yet very filling.

"Not really," I admitted, putting peanut butter spread on my toast.

"You will be by the end of today," he said reassuringly.

"I don't even know what I'm doing," I complained, secretly hoping for one last encouragement.

"I think we should get going," he said instead and got up from his chair.

"Let's go then." I followed him without uttering another word.

Most people were already downstairs waiting for the workday to begin. Some were still unpacking boxes from yesterday, while others were sitting at the computers and trying to set up the database.

"Good morning," Helen said, eyeing me and George. "Are you ready?"

"Yes." I tried to sound as confident as possible.

"Let's get you started. You probably prefer to work somewhere else, right?"

"Yes, I'd rather find a quieter place." I was glad she asked me this question. Working in a busy lab was another thing I had been dreading since early morning.

"That's what I thought. How about the library?"

"Oh, that would be awesome!"

We quietly proceeded to the library, where I spotted Avi sitting in front of a laptop.

"Avi, can you please show her what needs to be done?" Helen asked.

"Sure," he replied.

"Thank you. Let me know if you need any help. I'll be downstairs."

"Have a great day," I said.

"You too." Helen quickly left the library.

"Here you go." Avi got up and pointed at the laptop.

"Oh, thanks. What do I do?" I asked, peering at the desktop with a photo of the Shrine of the Book set as its background. At the very left side of it rested a folder named "Articles."

Avi clicked on the folder and opened the top document. "Here is your article," he said. "Don't forget to leave it connected to the power." He pointed at the cord hanging from the desk.

"Thanks."

"I'm going to the lab now. I need to finish digitizing some finds from Sha'ar HaGolan. Let me know if you need any help."

"Definitely! When do you need it done?"

"Well, it would be great if you could finish the article by the end of this week, but you don't have to. Just do as much as you can."

"No worries. I'll have it done by Friday." The words just flew out of my mouth before I could stop myself.

After he left, I put my head down and sat motionless for a few minutes until I finally mustered courage to look at the document.

What I saw next was not for the faint-hearted. The article was thirty pages long, single-spaced, and every single word looked unfamiliar.

"Is there, um, a dictionary I could use?" I asked the librarian, a middle-aged lady named Rania.

"Yes, of course!" She disappeared into the stacks and came out holding a large book. "Here it is."

"*Shukran kathiran!*"

For a few seconds, I sat at the table peering into the computer. Agreeing to translate this article was clearly a big mistake. I considered browsing the Internet for a few minutes just to calm down my nerves. However, half the sites were blocked, and the ones available were directly linked to academic research.

Whenever I got stuck with some difficult project, I would find a million ways to distract myself. From Facebook to text messages and even Google news, anything would do. Here, however, there was no room for distractions. I had left my phone upstairs and even warned everyone ahead of time that I would be busy during the day. The only choice I had was to focus on my work and do the best I could.

I looked closer at the title and recognized a few words. I sighed with relief. The rest of them I could look up. Word by word, I managed to get through the title and the first two sentences of the abstract. The article was about the Palaeolithic settlements in the upper Galilee, particularly the Manot Cave. Although I was starting to feel a little bit better, the idea of translating the entire article in five days was still daunting. It would take me ages to get through at least half of it.

I spent the first few hours looking up the words I didn't know and figuring out how to make the English sentences sound coherent. My progress was ridiculously slow, and by noon, I had barely managed to get through half of the abstract, which was only one paragraph long. Then suddenly, my speed picked up.

It turned out the article wasn't that difficult. There were only a few words I didn't know, and those I soon learned. Moreover, the content was fascinating. It was about the identity of humans occupying Palaeolithic sites. Apparently, there was quite a lot of speculation on whether or not those people were the Neanderthals. If scholars could establish their identity, it would be a big achievement in archaeology. By the afternoon, I became so wrapped up in my work that I almost forgot it was time to eat.

Since our lunch wasn't included in our meal plans, I could either use the Institute's kitchen for cooking or find a place to eat nearby. The second option was more appealing, especially since cooking would take more time, and I would still have to go out to get the groceries first.

I quickly saved my work, grabbed my wallet, and proceeded to the lobby. I was about to leave the building when I saw George talking to Caitlin and Megan. The trio looked happy and relaxed. Apparently, they were going to some falafel café located nearby, and he suggested that I join them. I agreed.

We strolled through a busy street until we spotted a small eatery. The entire time, the three of them were chatting. I heard a few jokes from their favorite shows, which I had never seen. In the last few years, I had hardly ever watched TV for the lack of time. I was amazed that those PhD students, who were probably ten times busier than me, were finding ways to have a life outside of academia.

As we were walking through the vibrant Middle Eastern neighborhood, I started to wonder if staying inside one building all the time was a good idea. Although the area had a shady reputation in the media, it looked like a good place to explore. I wanted to check out the stores and maybe sniff a few spices from the grocery shops. Also, here, most people were unlikely to speak English, which would be a big bonus for me.

I ordered chicken shawarma while George asked for rice and meatballs, and the girls ordered falafel wraps. I considered getting one as well, but decided to try something different.

"How is your day going so far?" George finally asked. He probably sensed my uneasiness over being left out of their conversation.

"Oh, it's going great. Better than what I expected."

"You see? I told you it wouldn't be that hard." He winked.

"What are you working on?" Caitlin asked.

"I'm translating a Hebrew article into English."

"Wow, you speak that language!" Megan joined in.

"Yep!" For me, it was not a big deal, especially since no one really cared about my language skills back in Toronto.

We finally found a place to sit and put our food on the table. I took out my hand sanitizer—a routine practice in North America—and passed it around. From the corner of my eye, I noticed a few glances in our direction. Most locals weren't used to carrying bottles of sterile gel around. Half the time, sandwich makers didn't even bother putting on gloves after handling cash.

"So, where are you from?" Megan asked after applying some gel on her hands.

"Toronto, Canada."

"Nice," she replied, passing the bottle to George.

"What do you do for a living?" Caitlin asked.

I thought about a few possible answers, but none seemed appealing. Telling this PhD group about my dead-end job would make me look like a loser. Lying wouldn't be a great idea either because George already knew most of my story from our bus rides. So I told them I had graduated from the U of T a few years ago and was taking a "break" from school.

"Do you think about going to a grad school?" Megan asked.

"Yeah. Maybe someday."

"Tel Aviv University is offering a great program in archaeology. You can even apply for a grant," George said.

"Oh, yeah! That's where we did our master's!" Megan exclaimed, exchanging glances with Caitlin. "The program was awesome."

"Did you excavate in Azekah?" I asked, recalling the site I had looked up back in the winter when looking for an excavation dig.

"Yes, we did," Caitlin replied. "It was a very busy season."

"I'd love to visit it someday and maybe even join the dig," I admitted.

"Then you should go for it," George said, smiling.

I already knew I would never choose to do a master's in Tel Aviv. Not because I didn't want to, but because I had no right to uproot Jason from his current job or give my parents a heart attack.

During our walk to the Institute, I mostly kept quiet, for the feeling of sadness kept coming back. Sure, I had a great time in Kiryat Adar and Megiddo and was slowly managing through the most difficult task I had ever received in my life. Soon everything would be over, and I would go back to my old life in Toronto.

To squelch my melancholy, I threw myself at work during the afternoon. No matter what the outcome of this trip would be, I had to do a good job at the translation. Thus I perused the Hebrew dictionary, solved puzzles from new words, and put my rough translations into neat sentences.

By dinner time, I was completely exhausted. My head was spinning from all the time spent at the computer, and my eyes were red and dry. I absolutely had to get some fresh air.

I had convinced myself and others a hundred times that I would never go anywhere in a foreign city alone. Had Caitlin and Megan been around, I would've asked them to join me. However, the duo quickly disappeared from the cafeteria, and George was nowhere in sight either. In the end, I decided that taking a few steps around the Albright Institute solo wouldn't harm me.

The streets outside were bustling with life. Smells of different spices wafted through the hot, dry air, as most shops were still open. Noisy cars were everywhere, and gigantic tour buses were lined up in a queue. After a while, my ears started hurting from all the honking. I kept walking straight until I saw a small, narrow street and decided to make a turn. That street led me to another one, which, in turn, led to a third one.

All of a sudden, I had no idea where I was. Having looked around, I noticed a few low-rise buildings clustered together. I took a few more steps forward and saw a parking lot filled with old, rusting cars. Next to the lot was a half-broken fence with heavy graffiti drawn all over the surface. The fence was surrounded by garbage bags and rubble.

Panic hit me as soon as I checked my watch. It was close to nine o'clock, which meant that sunset wasn't far away. I had no clue how I got there in the first place. Nor did I know how to find my way home. I should've asked for a map at the hostel lobby, but thought it was unnecessary. I didn't plan to go this far. Somehow, I had lost track of time and ended up in this creepy area.

I tried using the navigator feature on my cell phone, but the satellites refused to work. It took the system forever to recognize the street and to come up with directions. As soon as the system started working, the battery went dead. I considered getting a map at the closest shop, but most of them were already closed. Moreover, it would hardly be useful since I couldn't read Arabic.

Think hard, Becky, I told myself while trying to recall the last street name I saw. *There must be a way back.*

However, my memory wasn't much help because all the streets looked the same. Gripped by fear, I started running fast from one narrow, crooked street to another until it became completely dark and quiet. At last, the feeling of frustration took over. I sat down on the pavement and began to cry. It was the first time during the trip that I felt utterly helpless.

"Rebecca! What are you doing here?" I heard someone ask angrily. I lifted up my head and saw George rushing toward me.

"George! How did you find me?" I was beyond relieved to see him.

"I asked you a question first!"

"What's wrong?" I hadn't seen him that angry before.

"And you have the nerve to ask? The entire Institute has been looking for you since dinner. We were even thinking about calling the police. Do you know what type of neighborhood this is?"

"Of course, I know! I just went for a quick walk to unwind after a long day and took a wrong turn."

"You should've asked me or someone else to join you! Do you understand what could've happened? Jeez, Rebecca! I always knew you're a bit dreamy, but not to this point!"

"You know nothing about me!" I snapped. "Look, I'm lost and tired. And instead of showing me the way home, you keep on grilling me for leaving alone. Just for your information, I'm over eighteen and have every right to do whatever the hell I want!"

I knew that every argument I brought up was lame, and perhaps he was right about my dreamy quality. I could be easily swayed and often in the wrong direction. But my sense of pride wouldn't give way. So we stood there arguing back and forth until I finally broke into loud sobs.

Startled by what he had done, he tried to console me. "Becky, I'm sorry for screaming at you," he said, hugging me close. "I got scared and overreacted. Please don't cry."

"Get off, George!" I started walking again.

"Where are you going now?"

"Ah, I don't know."

He ran after me and grabbed my hand. Even during such a stressful time, his touch felt electrifying. I looked at him, tears running in streams.

"Hold on, let me get you a tissue." He fished out a Kleenex from his pocket and passed it to me.

I probably looked like a big mess by now. He came closer and touched my face, gently wiping away a tear.

"How about we go home and forget about everything that happened?" he suggested.

"I'm sorry," I said after having calmed down for a bit.

"It'll be all right. Let's go find a cab."

Much to our luck, a taxi car was passing by, and a driver asked if we needed help. George quickly instructed him to take us to the Albright Institute

The ride wasn't very long. Feeling embarrassed by the scene I had caused, I kept quiet. I had never expected myself to have a meltdown right in the middle of a street. I worked in customer service, for goodness' sake! Okay, maybe I'd cried at work once or twice, but I had been in a bathroom, so that doesn't count. In the meantime, George sat very close to me and tried to provide as much comfort as possible. Somehow, I felt protected with him.

"DO YOU want some tea?" George asked me.

I was sitting cross-legged on his bed, still trying to recuperate from everything.

"Sure," I replied. "Earl Grey would be great."

"I'll be back in a minute."

After he left, I looked around the room, which was a copy of my own. It had two bunk beds across from a small table, a chair filled with clothes, and a sink. Two contemporary paintings were decorating the walls. While looking around, I noticed a few drawings lying on the table. I walked closer and took a better look. These were images of the pottery finds and hand-drawn maps of Kiryat Adar. While leafing casually through the papers, I realized how much more I still had to learn about archaeology. Even after all the time I'd spent with the Kiryat Adar Expedition, my hands-on experience was still lacking.

"Here you are." George reappeared with a tray of two cups and a plate of halva.

"Oh, thank you." I took one bite and moved back to the bed.

He put the tray down and sat next to me. For a moment, we sat quietly drinking our tea and munching on the halva treats.

"By the way, thank you for finding me," I said at last. "I just wanted some fresh air. I had no idea how easy it is to get lost in Jerusalem. I should've taken a map or something."

"You're most welcome, Becky. Just please don't scare me again."

Suddenly, it occurred to me that he truly cared about me. First, he'd helped me to get into the Albright Institute and had then saved me from getting lost.

"George, why are you helping me?" I asked.

"What do you mean, Becky? I had to come after you. What would you do if I weren't around?"

"I have no clue. Maybe I would've died."

"Don't say that please."

Our eyes met again, and our lips came close. I felt passion stir inside me. I was completely alone with a man who had rescued me from danger.

"You are right," I said. "I do have my head up in the clouds sometimes, but not always." I trailed my fingers down through the collar of his shirt.

"At least, you're admitting the truth, Rebecca."

For a second, I considered having that last, long-overdue fling. Those eyes were telling me that he was more than willing.

"I have to go now." I pulled myself away from him. "I have to be up early tomorrow."

"See you then." Traces of disappointment showed up on his face.

"Goodnight, George."

"Sweet dreams, Becky."

That night, I tossed and turned, unable to stop thinking about George. No longer could I lie to myself about us being friends. I wanted all of him, and thinking about that rescue scene from a few hours ago only intensified my desire. Even the way he got angry about my carelessness made me drawn to him more.

The intellectual side of our budding relationship was just as fascinating as the physical. All the time we had spent together was amazing, and the conversations we'd had were incredibly fulfilling. I recalled the reassuring words he said to me when I was feeling nervous about my project. I even wondered if, under different circumstances, he and I would stand a chance. "I believe in you" resonated in my ears.

The next morning, I walked into the cafeteria half expecting everyone to turn my way. I was glad when no one showed the slightest interest in my crazy story from the last night.

"How are you finding the translation?" Avi asked me while making a toast.

"A bit tough, but it's fine," I replied, pouring my coffee.

"Yesterday, we were cataloging the artifacts, and they mentioned the one you had found."

"Oh really? That's great!" I was already feeling ten times better.

"Yes. They are thinking about publishing an article about the figurine."

"That's amazing! I hope it makes to the *BAR*."

"I'm not a big fan of it, but that would be nice."

I took my tray and moved toward a table. Avi followed me.

"Really? How come?" I couldn't imagine anyone from the scholarly world not enjoying this magazine.

"It's mostly for lay readers, not scholars. I mean, it's cool and everything, but I prefer ASOR's journals."

"Makes sense. I tried their subscription once but found the articles a bit too dry." In truth, I still had my last issue lying around unfinished.

"So, what's your area of focus, Rebecca?" he asked, taking a bite from his toast.

"I don't have one. I only did an undergrad in anthropology and Near Eastern studies."

"Really? I assumed you were a grad student."

"Taking one step at a time." I smiled. "By the way, you still haven't told me your area of focus."

"I'm focusing on the Upper Palaeolithic era. My thesis is on the Cave of Kebara at Mount Carmel."

"Not my strongest side," I admitted, recalling one time I had completely flunked a test on the prehistoric Levant. Luckily, I made up for the low mark later when we moved on to the Bronze and Iron Ages.

"Lots of people in the field say that. Nevertheless, the Palaeolithic and Neolithic are my favorite periods."

"Why?" Although the breakfast was coming to an end, I didn't feel like leaving yet. I wanted to know what made Avi drawn to such a daunting area. I mean, just look at those tools. They hardly look different from rocks or from each other.

"People underestimate the importance of the earlier periods," he replied. "In reality, those were the times when the human civilizations started forming."

"I see."

"Becky, if you are having any troubles with the translation, please let me know," he suddenly added. "I'll come over and help you."

"It's all right, thanks. I'll manage."

Through the morning, I completely dedicated myself to the article. As I became more efficient with the dictionary and online translation programs, the work became easier. No longer was I spending an hour on a single sentence, and by eleven o'clock, I was already halfway through the translation. Suddenly, my computer froze. I tried restarting it, but the button refused to work.

"Shoot!" I screamed.

"Do you need some help?" the librarian asked politely. This time, it was a young man named Ehud.

"Yes, I think my computer is down." He walked over to my side and tried moving the mouse across the screen. Everything was still frozen. In a few seconds, the screen went completely black.

"Wait a minute." He quickly walked to his desk and phoned someone. "The tech support is coming over."

I let the dread settle into the pit of my stomach as I waited for any news on the fate of this laptop. A few minutes later, a group of young men showed up. They examined the laptop and tried restarting it a few times.

"I'm sorry, but it looks like the disk has crashed," one of them told me. It took me a few seconds to process the news. My worst fear, my greatest dread, just came true.

"Any chance it could be fixed?" I mustered the courage to ask.

"We'll try our best, but we can't promise anything. I'm afraid it has to go to the computer shop."

"When can I expect any news?" I asked, trying to hide my panic.

"The waiting time is usually very long. It could be anytime between tomorrow and the next few weeks."

I couldn't believe my ears. I had less than three days to finish the translation, and I still hadn't gotten to the footnotes and bibliography, which would take quite a lot of time. If the data wasn't salvaged by the next day, my entire effort would go to waste.

"All right, thanks." I walked away without letting anyone see my tears. Having reached my room, I sat down on the bed and spent the next hour or so staring at the ceiling and wondering how much of my work was lost. Surely, I saved it shortly before the system went down, and perhaps some parts of it were saved automatically.

Still, I had no idea if the technicians would be able to retrieve my document at all.

"REBECCA, ARE you okay?" Megan asked me while we were making our lunch in the kitchen. "You look like you've been crying."

"I'm fine," I said, tears rising in my eyes.

"Look, you're crying!" Caitlin exclaimed. "Let me get you a tissue." She fished one out from her pocket.

"Thank you." I looked away.

"What's wrong, honey?" she asked.

"Well, the laptop I was working on crashed," I mumbled. "My article is lost now." I began sobbing.

"Oh, no!" Caitlin exclaimed.

"It's okay, honey. Don't cry." Megan came to my side and hugged me.

"And I promised to finish it by Friday." I couldn't stop crying.

"Wait, did you save it?" Caitlin asked.

"Does it matter now?" I shrugged. "The technicians said it might take several weeks to fix the hard drive."

"How far did you get?"

"Only through half of it."

"Which means the staff can still use it after you're gone," Megan noted.

"If they manage to recover the disk at all."

"They will," she reassured me.

"I wanted to finish everything by Friday." I put my hands over my face.

"I'm pretty sure everyone will understand. Besides, you're not even getting a credit or anything, as far as we know."

Megan was right. The whole expedition wasn't meant to be anything more than a summer adventure. So why was I even here, at the Albright Institute, sweating over some scholarly article on the Neanderthals when I was supposed to be in Kiryat Adar or Megiddo enjoying the sunshine?

"Maybe you're right." I sighed.

"Don't be so discouraged," Caitlin said, patting me on the shoulder. "If you want, we'll take you out tonight so that you feel a bit better."

"No, thanks. I'm not going anywhere again." First, I got lost in a foreign city, and then my article disappeared. What else could I expect to happen?

"We'll go together this time. We'll take a cab and ride to the western side of the city. What do you think?"

"I don't know yet. But thanks for offering." I faked a smile.

"No problem. We all need a little outing. So think about it."

After lunch, we proceeded to the basement, where I was supposed to help the rest of the team with the lab work. I suddenly remembered how I initially preferred this work over the article. Now I was getting my wish but at a high price.

I spent the afternoon entering information about the findings into the database. Countless artifacts had to be documented, and the amount of paperwork linked to the finds was unbelievable. I carefully filled up all the documents and keyed in the numbers. Although the work wasn't as challenging as the translation, it was still quite interesting. Maybe if I wasn't having such a terrible day, I would be enjoying it.

"Don't worry about the project," Avi told me at the end of the workday. "If you don't get to finish the article, I'll take over after you leave."

"Thanks, Avi, but I still can't believe it happened."

"It happens to almost everyone." He smiled.

Throughout my university years, I had always backed up my work on USBs and in email drafts. Sometimes, I went a bit overboard with saving work. Not once had my computer crashed. The moment I decided to skip multiple saves, I got into trouble.

During dinner, I was still in a foul mood. For the first time during my stay in Israel, I had zero appetite for food. So I sat quietly by myself pushing kabob around the plate with my fork and trying to fight back my tears. As soon as the dinner ended, I wanted to leave and huddle in the farthest corner of my room.

"Hey, Becky! Wait!" Avi yelled.

"What?" Was he going to tell me not to worry again and make me feel even worse?

"I brought something to cheer you up." He lifted a bunch of disks in the air. "Want to listen to the music together? I've got a CD player and everything."

"I'm not in the mood today. Sorry."

"That's why I brought the disks in the first place. I want you to feel better, Becky."

"Wait! You brought them for me?" Somehow, this piece of information had slipped away from my ears.

"Yes! I drove all the way to Ein Kerem to my apartment to get the disks especially for you."

"Oh, my goodness! I feel so bad now."

"It's not a big deal at all. If you don't feel like listening to the music, I'll just go home, and we'll meet tomorrow at the lab. I was thinking about taking a little break from the academic stuff and just relaxing."

"All right, you win." I couldn't let him down after all the effort he had made.

Initially, we wanted to go to the common room, but someone else was watching TV, so we ended up in my room instead.

"So tell me, Rebecca. What draws you to Israeli music?" he asked while putting a disk into the player.

"Hmm, good question, Avi. Maybe I just like the beat."

"I could see that. But why did you choose to learn Hebrew in the first place?"

I thought for a bit. "Well, my field is obviously one thing," I began. "I had majored in Near Eastern archaeology and studied Hebrew and Aramaic as the primary source languages."

"That would make sense. I've taken Aramaic too."

"You see? I'm not that weird," I joked, hoping he wouldn't continue asking.

"But how did you find out about all the artists?" he pressed on. "You aren't Jewish, are you?"

"No, I'm not. That's a long story."

"So tell me."

I took a deep breath. "I was in high school going through a tough stage," I started slowly. "I had no friends and was on the brink of failing all my classes."

"Sorry to hear that." He looked at me with sympathy.

I wasn't sure if I was supposed to pour my heart out to Avi. Technically, he was my boss. Moreover, he belonged to the culture that prized achievement above everything else. Yet I kept talking.

"When it came to music, I wanted something different, something that would take me away from the everyday reality. One day, I went to a library and stumbled upon a collection of disks in a foreign language. It was the language of the people I've been fascinated with since the age of twelve. I tried out one recording, and it made me forget all my troubles. Then it kind of meshed up together, and I ended up majoring in biblical archaeology, learning Hebrew, and going crazy about Sarit Hadad."

Avi kept quiet. He probably didn't expect his fellow worker at the Albright Institute to have such a challenging past.

"I'm glad it all ended well for you," he remarked.

"I think it all comes down to going after something that's hard to get," I suddenly said.

"What do you mean, Becky?" He looked perplexed.

"Well, it would be much easier for me to like music from my country or to choose a major with more job prospects. My sister and I are exact opposites in that respect. She'd chosen a very practical program, and she's using her degree at work, while I'm using mine on a vacation."

Avi laughed. "I wouldn't call what you're doing here 'a vacation.'"

"As for the music, she'll like anything that's in trend. As a kid, she was a fan of the Spice Girls and Britney. When we moved to a new school, where most of the kids were rock lovers, she suddenly started cranking up Rush and Queen. I bet if she ever moved to Israel, she would either start admiring Arik Einstein or Omer Adam, depending on the circle she was in. I often wish I could be like her."

"No offense to your sister, Becky, but why would you want to follow the crowd?"

"Then I wouldn't have to feel embarrassed about my playlist or answer annoying questions on how I plan to use my anthropology degree in the real life. But this is who I am, and I'm happy about it."

As I was saying these words, I was finally admitting the truth to myself. All the struggles and all the challenges I'd endured were only part of my life because I wanted them on one level or another.

"*At ben adam miuhad. Bli gvulot,*" Avi said, smiling. He just told me that I was a special person with no borders.

"Really? You mean I've got no boundaries?" I smiled back.

"You are special, Rebecca." He gently pressed his palm against mine. "As for the real life part, you and I are real. The Albright Institute is real. What we do here is real."

"Hmm, I've never thought about it this way."

"I get annoying questions about my field too, but I don't pay much attention to them. So please don't let anyone make you think you're living in some fantasy world simply because you care about learning."

"I'm hungry," I suddenly said.

"No wonder, Becky. From what I remember, you hadn't touched your dinner at all."

"I was upset over the computer crash, but you made me feel better."

"You see? That was my goal for the evening."

"And you did a great job cheering me up with the music."

"So, what should we do foodwise?"

"No idea. I think most of the restaurants are closed already."

"And the ones that are open are far away."

"I don't feel like leaving the building at this hour, especially after everything that happened yesterday."

"I see. It must've been hard for you to get lost in a place like this."

"I got really scared at first, but it's all right now. You don't have to feel sorry for me, Avi."

"Well, we can order a takeout because I'm hungry too."

"Is it possible?" The prospect of eating quietly in my room looked good.

"Wait a second." Avi fished out an iPhone and started typing something on a screen. "What would you like?"

"It doesn't really matter. Whatever is available will do." My stomach was rumbling.

"Then I'm ordering two burgers with fries."

"Sounds like a plan."

He quickly dialed the restaurant's number and placed an order. I offered paying for my portion, but he flat out refused. "That's my treat for you," he said. "I hope it's the last time you decide to skip a meal."

After the food arrived, we ate in silence with Kobi Aflalo crooning in the background. By the time we finished our meals, I was feeling cheerful again.

"Thank you for everything, Avi," I said in the end. "You shouldn't have gone to all this trouble."

"Anytime, Becky. I'm glad it worked for you."

"I think you should get going." I glanced at my watch, which was showing ten-thirty.

"Yes! I'll see you tomorrow at the lab. Have a great night."

Avi grabbed the CD player and walked out of the door. As soon as he left, I realized he had forgotten his CDs. I tried calling after him, but he was already gone. I plopped on my bed and opened the booklet of "Eliko's Golden Collection." I ran my fingers through the lyrics and sniffed the glossy paper. The other disks were hit collections from the Israeli mainstream.

That evening was amazing. We talked like good friends. I learned a few things about myself. There was nothing to be unhappy about. As for the computer incident, I decided not to dwell on it, no matter how hard it seemed. If the laptop wouldn't be fixed on time, I would make the best of the lab work.

Sixteen

"You forgot the CDs yesterday," I told Avi during breakfast.
"Oh, those are for you," he replied.

"What? No! I can't take them."

"It's okay. No biggie." He shrugged.

Before I could say anything else in protest, someone called my name. One of the computer technicians from yesterday was standing by the entrance looking for me. I immediately braced myself for the worst. He was likely to tell me the disk was irreparable, or the information had been lost, or the waitlist in the computer shop was much longer than expected.

"I have some good news for you," he said instead.

Part of me felt relieved. Yet I didn't want to place my hopes too high.

"I found a place where they were able to fix the laptop immediately," he continued.

I sighed deeply. "Did they retrieve the data?"

"Yes, they did."

"So, when can I have it back?"

"It's in the library."

"Yay!" I screamed, unable to contain my excitement. Everyone turned in my direction. "My laptop has been repaired!"

"Congratulations!" Megan and Caitlin exclaimed in unison. I walked to their table and hugged each of them.

"Now I'll finish your translation on time." I turned to Avi.

"Just do as much as you can, Becky."

"You just don't know me well." I smirked.

"HEY, WE should go out like we've planned," Megan announced during dinner.

"I thought the whole thing was meant to make me feel better."

"And now, we can do this to celebrate," Caitlin added. "I mean, it's Wednesday, which is almost Friday."

"Exactly! So let's do this!" Megan exclaimed.

"Fine," I said. "Maybe we should go. We all need a break sometimes."

"I'm still recovering from your last one," George remarked.

I didn't say anything in reply, but simply pretended to get up for a water refill. I hadn't seen him too much ever since our encounter in his bedroom. I ran into a him a few times in the lab and the cafeteria, but we hadn't exchanged too many words other than formal "hellos" and "how are yous." To tell the truth, I felt a bit awkward around him, and I suspected he felt the same.

"Hey, why don't you join us?" Caitlin suggested.

"Nah, I have to finish my pottery drawings," he replied.

"Here is another workaholic," Megan joked.

"Who else is a workaholic?" I asked, feeling curious.

"You, of course!" She pointed at me.

"Me? A workaholic? I've always considered myself a lazy type."

"We all become workaholics after staying at the Albright for a while," Caitlin noted.

"It's all right. Maybe another time," George said. "Have fun without me."

We agreed to meet in the lobby in twenty minutes. For the night, I chose to wear a pair of dark blue capris and a silky top. I also applied extra mascara and lip gloss to look good and let my hair, which I usually wore in a ponytail, hang down past my shoulders. Since I didn't bring any heels on the trip, I had to go with my regular sandals.

I met Megan and Caitlin in the lobby as planned. Both of them were wearing skinny jeans, tube tank tops, and stilettos. Megan also had long, dangle earrings. We complimented each other on our outfits and got in the first available taxi.

"Where should we go?" Caitlin asked, looking at the city map.

"There are quite a few bars along Jaffa Street," Megan replied. "We could go there and walk around."

"Sure, let's do that," I said.

We drove past the walls secluding the Old City, enjoying the view from the window.

"Isn't it Amr Diab?" I asked the driver, referring to the music that was playing on his stereo.

"*Ken*," he replied.

I went to see Amr Diab, the star of Egyptian pop music, when I was in grade eleven. Since I had no one to accompany me, I dragged Erin along. Although the show was amazing, Erin absolutely hated it because (1) she wasn't accustomed to such music and (2) we were the only non-Arabs in the entire hall.

"How do you know him?" the driver asked.

"Great research skills come in handy," I joked as our taxi entered the modern area of the city.

Caitlin and Megan listened to our conversation without uttering a single word.

"You're lucky to live here," I told the girls later.

"Oh, we love this place. Maybe you could join us someday," Megan suggested.

"Maybe," I said, trying to imagine what would it be like to live in Jerusalem.

Jaffa Street turned out to be pretty busy. Couples and families were walking everywhere. Streetcars filled with passengers kept coming from both directions. Some shops were still open, blasting the latest hits from Iggy Azalea and Katy Perry.

The taxi dropped us off in front of a building called Jerusalem Hostel, which I assumed was a motel for tourists. The three of us walked a few blocks before turning onto another street with a long chain of bars and restaurants. The girls asked me if I had any preferences as to where we should stop, and I said that any place they chose would be fine with me. In the end, we all agreed to stop at the bar with the least expensive menu.

"That's the major downside of being in the academia." Caitlin sighed. "You'll always be poor."

Megan laughed, and I said nothing. If only I could have all the opportunities they had. Then nothing else would matter.

A waitress quickly escorted us to a table for three and asked what we wanted to drink. We ended up ordering three glasses of red wine and a plate of cookies with soft cheese.

"Are you married?" Megan asked, eyeing my ring.

"Four years now," I replied proudly.

"Wow, you look so young!" Caitlin commented.

I definitely saw it coming.

"Well, I'm twenty-six," I replied, taking a sip from my glass.

"I'm thirty-two," Caitlin said, passing around the plate. "Quite honestly, I don't think I'm getting married anytime soon."

"Me neither," Megan said. "Right now, I'm too busy with my dissertation and fieldwork."

"Don't you want kids someday?" I asked.

"I'd love to, but I'm afraid of running out of time," she admitted. "I want to finish my program first, get a postdoc, and only then will I think about having a baby. Right now, I can't afford to have a child anyway. Besides, with this crazy lifestyle of ours, I doubt we'll be good moms." She turned to Caitlin.

"That's true." Caitlin laughed. "I'd have to hire a full-time nanny, as my parents are too old to look after a baby."

"Same here," Megan added. "Mine are in their sixties already. They'll be around seventy by then."

A tiny part of me felt happy that my parents were still young enough to help out with my would-be child. Except I was not sure how my marriage and children would fit into a bigger picture, considering all the things I'd discovered about myself very recently. I hadn't experienced that much intellectual satisfaction in ages from all the challenging tasks I'd done and all the conversation I'd had with people at the Institute. Had the circumstances been different, I could see myself living here, doing academic research, and translating Hebrew articles for the rest of my life. Most likely, I would end up aging alone in a tiny apartment by the Old City, surrounded by several cats and maybe a dog. Which was not something I wanted for myself either. I'd longed for companionship since my early teenage years, and I knew I was supposed to be grateful for the amazing marriage back home.

After the baby talk, we discussed life in Israel, particularly in the academic circles. The girls shared their stories about all-nighters, piles of essays they had to mark for undergraduates, and a few computer-related incidents they had encountered along the way. After a second round of drinks, we loosened up so much that we even managed to laugh at my story about getting lost in East Jerusalem.

"You should've seen George's face when he finally found me!" I exclaimed, half laughing. "He was so mad!"

"Really?" Megan asked. "He was mad at you for being lost? That's outrageous!"

"Well, it was kind of my fault."

"No, it wasn't!" Caitlin protested. "It happens to the best of us."

"Did he say anything mean?" Megan added.

"He said that I'm a dreamer with my head up in the clouds. I mean, he didn't say these words exactly, but it was pretty much implied."

"He had no right to act like that!" Megan exclaimed indignantly.

"He later told me he was sorry for reacting that way." I tried defending him without even knowing why. Despite our rare and clumsy encounters over the last couple days, I still held on to the tiny spark that existed between us.

"But still. It was wrong on his part," she insisted.

"Did he tell you about his story in Jericho?" Caitlin asked.

"No! What story?"

"The epic one," Megan replied.

"You should tell me."

The girls exchanged a look, and then Caitlin began. "A few years ago, his group was staying in Jerusalem at the end of the dig in Tell es-Safi. Apparently, he decided to drive to Jericho by himself."

"Okay, this is getting interesting," I said. "I mean, Jericho is in the West Bank."

"On his way back, he stopped in some Arab town to get gas and snacks, and his GPS broke."

"Really? So what happened in the end?"

"The IDF had to rescue him because he drove in the opposite direction," Megan said. "And he's definitely not a dreamer."

"All right, I'm going to confront him tomorrow," I said, half joking.

"No need to," Caitlin said. "Just don't let anyone bring you down next time you're in trouble."

"Well, hopefully, it was the last time I'll have gotten into something that serious."

"You never know," Megan said. "Shit happens all the time. Something similar happened to me when I was in the second year of my MA program."

I probed her for more details, and she told the entire story. Some girls from her class decided to take a day trip to Ein Gedi to celebrate the end of the school year. They agreed to stick together, but Megan got distracted by an ibex and decided to take a few photos of the creature. After she finished posting them on Instagram (she had portable wireless Internet like me), she turned around and found everyone gone. Worst of all, one of the students had her bag, so the poor girl didn't even have water, and it was about forty-five degrees Celsius.

"When I finally found my group, they were so happy I didn't get attacked by a caracal!"

"True," I remarked. "After all, I head caracals are very dangerous despite looking really cute." I recalled a few images of a wild cat with black tufts on its ears. It was a type of lynx that inhabited African and Middle Eastern regions.

"Not just dangerous," Caitlin said. "They're deadly! Although I do agree they look beautiful."

"Yeah, they're pretty and cute and everything until you meet one." Megan rolled her eyes. "The point is, nobody got mad at me for getting distracted. In these situations, you'll be happy to see the other person alive and well."

"Why would they be mad at you?" I noted.

"Exactly! Anyway, we just laugh about it now."

"That's your favorite story," Caitlin said, taking a few sips of her martini. "You always bring it up when we get together."

"It was also one of the best memories from grad school," Megan admitted. "Ein Gedi is totally worth visiting." She turned to me. "Just make sure you stick with your group in case an ibex or a caracal shows up."

"I'll remember your advice." I smiled at the memory of the Ramon Crater. Apparently, Megan and I shared fascination with ibexes.

"By the way, George is a really nice guy, but he is a bit obnoxious," Caitlin said later.

"How do you know him?" I finally asked, realizing they must've known him for quite a while.

"We took the same class as undergrads," Megan replied.

"Where did you study?"

"We went to New York University. Then we kind of lost touch until we ran into each other here a year ago and became friends again."

"Some say his ex-girlfriend is trying to get him back," Caitlin added. "According to the rumors, she's somewhere in Israel right now."

"Have you seen her?" I asked, imagining some skinny Harvard graduate with a trowel in her hands. I could bet she was an archaeology whiz.

"No. We aren't even sure she exists. George hardly ever mentions her."

"Hmm, that's interesting. Anyway, he's fun to talk to."

"But don't let him be mean to you again," Megan warned me.

"Don't worry, I won't."

Three guys walked into the bar. As they came closer to the order stand, I recognized one of them. It was Avi, and he looked completely different from the way he looked at the Institute. Normally, he wore plain, casual clothes that made him look nice and professional. This time, he was wearing trendy jeans, a Hawaiian shirt, and some jewelry. Apparently, he had an ear piercing like Kobi Peretz, but I hadn't noticed it before. The moment he saw us, his eyes lit up.

"Becky, *ma inyanim*?"

"*Hakol beseder, mami.*" I smiled.

"Hey, *motek*! How did you find us?" Caitlin exclaimed.

"It was easy. You always go to this bar, don't you?"

"Kind of. But this time, we did consider going somewhere else."

"Anyway, I just didn't feel like sleeping yet, so I decided to go for a drink. By the way, let me introduce you to my buddies, Eitan and Aron."

"Nice to meet you," I replied, exchanging glances with Caitlin and Megan, who were smiling at the two guys.

"Do you mind if I buy you a drink?" Avi asked me.

"Sure. I'll have another margarita."

"Way to go, girl!" Megan gave me a nudge.

Someone turned the music on. The moment I heard the Oriental groove, I felt like getting up and dancing.

"Shall we dance?" I asked, unable to sit still on my chair.

"Sure, let's go for it!" Megan exclaimed.

The six of us moved from the table and began swinging our hips to the music. The rest of the bar followed our lead and started moving.

"Look how you can lighten up the crowd," Avi told me while dancing along. He had one of the warmest smiles I'd ever seen.

"It isn't me; it's the music," I replied.

"Would you mind sharing a dance?" he asked, moving closer.

At first, I considered declining the offer but went along with it in the end. After all, it was just a dance. So I grooved together with Avi, while Caitlin and Megan ended up dancing with his friends.

Long before we knew it, it was already past midnight. Normally, my tolerance for alcohol was very low, and I could pass out after anything heavier than light beer. Tonight, I was feeling better than ever.

"Should we get going?" I suggested at one-thirty.

"Definitely," Avi replied. "We've got a busy day tomorrow."

His friends, however, decided to stay longer. By the time we were ready to head out, they were already checking out some other girls. The four of us went outside to look for a cab.

"I'm cold," I admitted, as the air was a bit chilly. The desert climate made afternoons unbearably hot, while nights were often colder than expected.

"Let me warm you up," Avi said and started rubbing my hands.

"Are we going to Ein Kerem first?"

"By all means no! I'll wait for the driver to drop you off first."

"Why don't you stay at the Institute for the summer?" I found myself asking. "Wouldn't it make things much easier for you?"

"Trust me, I'd thought about it in the past but decided that staying at the hostel while renting wasn't going to make sense financially."

"Ah, I see."

When we got back, I considered calling Jason and sharing my story about the broken hard drive with him but felt too exhausted to talk. Instead, I typed a quick message and fell asleep almost immediately.

Seventeen

I hurried to the computer as soon as I finished my breakfast the next morning. I typed relentlessly until four in the afternoon, completely forgetting to take lunch. The longer I worked, the easier and more interesting my project became.

Suddenly, I noticed my stomach was churning with hunger. I went to the kitchen in hopes of finding leftovers. Megan was standing by the countertop making a cup of coffee.

"Hey, Rebecca! How are you feeling today?" she asked.

"I'm great, thanks," I replied. "Although I do wish we didn't drink so much last night."

"It was totally worth it. We had lots of fun." She poured coffee into a big cup.

"Is there anything to eat here?" I asked, opening the fridge. To my disappointment, it was completely empty.

"Where have you been today? You should've gone with us. We went to that falafel place we had visited a few days ago."

"I became so wrapped up in my work that I forgot to take lunch."

"Ah, I see. Very typical for grad students."

"And I'm not even one of you guys."

"Well, you act like you are. You seem so committed to your work."

"I'll take it as a compliment."

"So, what are you up to?"

"I have no idea. I'm so hungry now. I kind of want to go to the falafel place."

"Do you remember where it is? 'Cause if you don't, I could walk with you."

"No, it's okay. You probably have your own work to do."

"Are you sure?"

"Yes, I promise not to get lost this time."

"All right, see you at dinner then. And please don't skip it. Most cafés close early, and you don't want to be out after sunset."

"I'll try."

I walked out of the kitchen and proceeded to the lobby. This time, I took a map with me to be on the safe side. Then I ran straight to the eatery, where I ordered a small plate of hummus. Since dinner was only a few hours away, I didn't want to get stuffed. After finishing my snack, I ran straight to the Albright Institute without even looking back. Then I threw myself at work for another hour and a half.

During dinner, Caitlin asked me if I wanted to go for a short walk together. I told her that I still had some work to finish.

"I thought the day was over!" she exclaimed. "I can't believe they make you work after regular hours!"

"No one forces me to stay late. I just have to finish the article by Friday, and I lost too much time after the laptop crashed."

"Well, don't overstrain yourself," Caitlin said.

"I'll try not to. Anyway, thanks for offering the walk. See you all tomorrow."

On my way to the library, I wondered how I had managed to make friends at least three times in less than three weeks. Ever since we had left Oakville, I had never had a proper social life. I was lonely through my high school years and never befriended anyone besides a girl named Dalia at the U of T. Born in post-Soviet Russia, she had spent her childhood in Israel before moving to Canada with her parents. We hit it off almost right after we met at Tim Hortons on a busy, rainy afternoon, and she offered me a seat at her table. We had gone to many Israeli concerts over the years, but we hadn't been very close. Most of my current friends were from Jason's side. Lack of girlfriends never bothered me that much since I truly enjoyed my own company. Besides, having Erin in my life always compensated for the lack of female friendships. Nevertheless, the ability to sit with a group of girls and chat about random topics, like we did last night, felt good.

Needless to say, nothing ever felt better than working on a challenging project for several hours and days. The rest of the week was dedicated solely to finishing the translation. I stopped caring about regular hours and just sat at the library most of the time, except for the short breaks I allowed myself every now and then.

I never forgot to stay in touch with Jason and my parents, calling and texting them almost every night and sharing a few insights into my life at the Albright Institute. I obviously chose to forego the story about getting lost in East Jerusalem, although I did plan on sharing it with Jason at some point.

"THANK YOU so much for your help," Helen said after I showed her the finalized copy, which had the footnotes and bibliography formatted nicely in the SAA style.

"It was my pleasure," I replied. "I learned a lot by working on this article," I added, recalling all the information I had gained about the prehistoric settlements. The Manot Cave was definitely on my travel list.

"Rebecca, I was truly impressed by your level of commitment," she added. "I've never met a volunteer who worked so hard on a task."

"It's just the way I am. Once I'm on to something, I just cannot stop until it's done."

"I'm sure you'll make a great scholar someday."

"Thanks, I'm flattered."

"If you ever need a recommendation letter, you can count on me."

Having looked around, I saw our field directors walk into the library.

"Hi, Rebecca! How did you find this week?" Andrew asked.

"It was tough, but also rewarding."

"Well, we're glad to hear that."

"I have an idea you may like," Jayden said.

"What is it?" I hoped he wasn't going to ask me to translate another article.

"Each year, we have a speaker at the final dinner, and we were wondering if you could become one tomorrow."

"Okay. What do I need to do?"

"You'll talk about your experience in the field and in the lab," he explained.

"Would I have to prepare anything?"

"Just a brief speech. We can provide you with the background info about the sites and the Institute."

Before I could stop myself, I said, "Yes."

"Here you go." He passed me a USB stick. "You'll find all the information about Kiryat Adar and the Albright Institute here. Please remember that we want you to focus more on your experience than on the factual information."

"Okay, thanks." I reluctantly took a USB from him.

"I'll see you tomorrow." Jayden smiled.

On my way to the room, I bumped into Avi.

"Hey, Becky! I heard you're leaving tomorrow," he began.

"That's right. I'm going to Tel Aviv."

"Well, we'll miss you over here. So what are your plans for the next week?"

"I'll meet my husband over there, and then we'll have a week off to relax and recharge."

For a moment, he looked a bit baffled. Then he picked up with our conversation. "Relaxing is good. I just—" I sensed a feeling of embarrassment in his voice.

"What?"

"I was going to ask you out. I didn't realize you were taken."

"Shut up!" I laughed. "How could we possibly date if we are miles apart?"

"You would come back to Israel to get your master's degree, and we would end up working in the same lab."

"And you would take me to Caesarea to see Moshe Peretz, right?"

"We could run off to Eilat to party with Eliko." Avi looked amused.

"Or we could be more cultured and see the Israel Philharmonic Orchestra."

"Or go to Arik Einstein's concert if he were still alive," he suggested.

"Sorry to disappoint you, *motek*, but it ain't gonna happen."

Avi looked a bit sad. "Can we be friends, though?"

"Aren't we friends already?" I smiled.

"You helped me so much during this week, Becky. I don't know how I would've pulled it through if it weren't for all your hard work."

"And you helped me to survive the laptop crash."

"It was no biggie for me."

"I still have your CDs in my room."

"I told you, they were a gift."

"Come on, Avi. I'll bring them over. Wait a second." I was about to walk away, but he grabbed my hand.

"Rebecca, I want those recordings to be the token of our friendship." He looked directly into my eyes. "Next time you're going through a rough patch, whatever it may be, you'll put on one my CDs and feel happier."

"I don't even know what to say." I began to feel uncomfortable. No one had ever done something that nice for me.

"Don't say anything. Just enjoy the melody and the beat."

"I'll miss you, Avi."

"Me too."

As soon as I reached my room, I phoned Jason and told him all about the reunion. I should've mentioned it way back in Megiddo, but the busy week had made me completely forget about it.

"That's great!" he exclaimed. "Now you can arrive at our hotel one night earlier."

I had initially planned to stay at the Albright Institute for an extra night. Jason would drive over to pick me up at the hostel, and we would go back to Tel Aviv together. The reunion only meant that we could avoid all the driving back and forth and meet right at our hotel apartment.

"My bag is almost packed, and I can't wait to see you again." He sounded excited.

"Don't forget swimwear. I can't wait to hit the beach."

"Glad to hear that."

"You won't believe how much I've been working these past few days. But it was a great week."

"I know, and I'm proud of you, Becky."

"Thank you, Jason. Those words mean a lot to me." And they did, at least on some level.

"You're welcome, anytime." I could almost see his smile through the words.

After our short, but sweet conversation, I hung up the phone and dropped on my bed. Eyes transfixed on the ceiling, I thought about Helen's proposition. What seemed like a dream less than a month ago was close to becoming real. Maybe applying to a grad school wouldn't be a bad idea. I could either apply to the U of T or one of the American universities. With my experience at Kiryat Adar and the Albright Institute, I had a good chance of getting in.

But what would happen after I graduated? Would I be able to find a stable job? Judging from the unemployment rates, chances of getting an academic role were slim. Would Jason even want to move elsewhere if I chose to pursue a degree abroad? How would our parents, who were eager to hold a grandchild, feel about all of this? The questions lingered in my head. What I couldn't deny was that the article had made me proud of myself for the first time in the longest while.

I heard a knock on the door. "Who is there?" I yelled, feeling too lazy to get up.

"It's me, George. Can I come in?"

"All right, coming." I walked over to the door and opened it for him. "How did you find me?" I asked when he was inside.

"Very easy. The concierge told me your room number."

"Hmm, I thought they weren't supposed to."

"Anyway, I just came by to apologize for not having talked to you lately. I know you had a few rough days with the computer and stuff. I've been just too wrapped up in my work."

"No worries, George. No need to apologize." I felt myself grow tense as he walked closer to me. Yet my tension dissipated as soon as reached for my hand. Something about his touch made me grow mellow.

"I came by to ask if you would be interested in going to the Old City tomorrow."

"With everyone?" I asked, hoping he would say "yes."

"No, just you and me." He winked.

"What is everyone else doing?"

"Caitlin and Megan will be going back to their residences, and the professors will be working for most of the day."

"How about Avi? Will he come with us?"

"I've no clue what he's up to."

"I have to work on my speech for tomorrow. I'll be speaking at the reunion."

"Come on, Becky. I've seen those speeches before. It's only a five-minute talk. There's hardly anything to prepare."

"Will we make it on time?" I asked, trying to find one last excuse to back out.

"Look, we'll have the entire morning and the afternoon free. It would be lame to waste it by staying inside."

"Hmm, I'll think about it." The idea looked too tempting to ignore.

"See you at seven-thirty."

Eighteen

I t's hard to describe how I was feeling on my last morning at the Albright Institute. I was feeling happy, sad, excited, and a bit teary. The three amazing weeks would end tonight, and I would probably never see anyone from the expedition again. I would miss Kiryat Adar with its sun and dirt. I would miss the greenery of the Golan Heights. Above all, I would miss spending long hours working on a puzzle made up of foreign words. I decided not to dwell on these complex feelings and to make the best of my last outing with George.

I chose to wear a knee-length skirt and a blouse I had packed specifically for religious sites. I also took the white scarf that had come with my purchase at Majdal al-Shams and put it into my purse. I would use it to cover my head at the Western Wall.

When I entered the cafeteria, I was quite surprised to discover that George wasn't there. It was highly unlikely that he had forgotten about our plans for the day, as we had spoken right before going to sleep. I eyed Caitlin and Megan, who were carrying trays with coffee and muffins, and quickly joined them.

"We're leaving today," Megan declared, putting her tray on the table. "We'll be going back to our residences on campus."

"And tomorrow, we are flying back to the States to see our families," Caitlin added.

"How nice!" I exclaimed, feeling a bit saddened by our parting. "Are you both from the same city?"

"No. Megan is from Boston, and my parents live in Manchester, which is only an hour's drive from Boston," Caitlin explained. "But since we're going in the same direction, we decided to fly together."

"Well, have a safe trip home, and I hope to see you again," I said, already knowing that meeting them again was highly unlikely.

"You should come to Boston someday," Megan said. "We'll show you around."

"Well, I really hope to see the Semitic Museum at Harvard."

"We'll visit that one as well," Caitlin promised.

I walked with them to the lobby, where we said our goodbyes. After they hopped in a cab and disappeared, I returned to the cafeteria, where I allowed myself another cup of coffee. Since George was still nowhere in sight, I began to feel a bit annoyed.

"Everything all right?" one of the waiters asked me. I noticed he had a strong Arab accent. According to a name badge, he was called "Ibrahim."

"*Ha kolbeseder, toda,*" I replied, meaning that everything was fine.

"*Eich at mozaat at haohel?*" he asked, wanting to know how the food was.

"*Sababa!*" It meant the food was great.

"You student?"

"Not anymore. I'm spending a month here learning about archaeology."

"Nice. What you do?"

"Well, I initially came to Kiryat Adar to dig for artifacts but ended up here." I tried speaking as slowly as possible. Then I decided to switch into Hebrew because it was much easier for both of us.

Ibrahim was a middle-aged man with an unforgettable aura of friendliness. I told him all about my plans to stay in Tel Aviv with Jason. For some reason, I mentioned my fascination with Zohar Argov.

"My youngest daughter loves his disks," he said, suddenly switching back to English. "Her name is Zeinab."

"Really? How old is she?"

Ibrahim struggled to understand my words.

"*Bat cama he?*" I repeated the question in Hebrew.

He told me she was seventeen.

"I'd love to meet her." I tried picturing a young girl, perhaps in *hijab* or perhaps not, cranking "Elinor" and "Kmo Shikor" while going about her day. Maybe she listened to "Yam Shel Dmaot" when she was feeling sad the same way I did back in high school.

"Then you come to our house," he said, looking earnest.

"Where do you live?" I asked.

"Nablus."

Nablus. Or better yet, Neapolis, the city founded by Vespasian in 72 AD, the home of the Samaritan community. It was also the hometown to someone who liked my favorite music. For a moment, I pictured myself and Zeinab climbing together to Mount Gerizim and singing along.

"Do you commute?" I asked Ibrahim.

"What is commute?" He looked confused.

"Going from one town to another for work," I explained.

"*Ken. Kol yom.*"

"I see. It must be tough." For some reason, my mind trailed back to my work supervisor who drove to our office from Oshawa every day.

"Will you come to our house?"

"Thanks, but we might not have enough time." I tried to sound as polite as possible. "We're only here for one week."

"No let news fool you," he said, sensing my slight uneasiness. "Nablus is safe."

"That's not the issue." I tried reassuring him, wondering if he had just read my mind. "We might simply run out of time."

At last, I saw George dash into the cafeteria, looking all dishevelled and distressed.

"I have to go now," I said. "It was nice talking to you, Ibrahim."

"Have good day," he replied and retreated back to the food stand.

"Hey, is everything okay?" I asked George as he poured his coffee.

"Sorry, I got delayed at the lab," he muttered. "There was a glitch in the system, and we had to reboot everything."

"I thought it's a weekend for everyone."

"Yeah, but we were having issues with the database, so I had to come downstairs and help. Anyway, I'm sorry for keeping you waiting."

"No worries. I had a good time here while waiting for you."

"Yeah, I see."

George quickly finished his breakfast and suggested we get going.

"Where should we go first?" I asked after we exited the building.

"Since I messed up the morning, you get to decide," he replied teasingly.

"Rockefeller is the closest, but I'm not sure you want to go there."

"It sounds like a plan to me."

We walked through the streets of East Jerusalem, taking time to enjoy the morning sunshine. Even with all the delays in our plan, it was still barely eight-thirty. Life around the city was going on as usual. All the shops and cafés were already open, and a few security officers were idling casually by one of the stores. A group of women in *hijabs* passed us. Luckily, no one was hurling stones or burning cars like you'd see in the news.

A few blocks later, we were standing in front of a grand limestone edifice known as the Rockefeller Archaeological Museum. It houses one of the finest collections of Holy Land artifacts, most of which had been unearthed during the British Mandate.

The line wasn't very long, and we quickly made our way to the first gallery, which contained findings from the prehistoric times. A small group of children dressed in identical uniforms passed by with their group leader. One boy started jumping around and singing, and the rest began to misbehave. A museum staff member, who was guarding the gallery, politely asked them to be quiet. The kids obliged, but only for a few seconds. Soon they were laughing and horsing around again.

"And this is exactly why I'm never having kids," George declared.

"Really?" I was taken aback. Technically, I had nothing against people who chose to stay childfree. Sometimes, I even wondered if motherhood was right for me. However, I didn't expect to hear these words from George.

"What if you change your mind later?" I asked, thinking about his future partner who would have to accept his decision.

"That's what everybody says, but you can be certain I won't change my mind."

"All right, that's your choice." I decided to drop the subject. Yet at the back of my mind, I wondered if I truly knew the boy walking beside me.

The next galleries were arranged chronologically, starting with the Bronze Age and ending with the Ottoman Period. Among some of the most-prized artifacts were wooden panels from Al Aqsa mosque, marble lintels from the Church of the Holy Sepulchre, and a Byzantine mosaic floor from Ein Gedi. There were also a few Dead Sea Scrolls on display. George and I were thrilled to spot a few artifacts from Kiryat Adar. Participation in this dig had given us a sense of belonging to something bigger.

"Maybe my figurine will be on display as well," I said, recalling my sensational find from the second day of the dig.

"Maybe." George grinned.

After the museum, we decided to stop at a shawarma place nearby. Since the time was already close to the noon, both of us began to feel hungry.

"I still can't believe how much we saw this month!" I exclaimed while getting seated at a small table and laying down our foods.

"I know," George said, taking a bite from his shawarma wrap. "Shame that we didn't get to see Beit Guvrin."

"At least we're in a safer place now." I took a gulp from my soda can.

"I agree."

Both of us turned our heads to the TV that was hanging on the wall, broadcasting the latest world news.

"By the way, have you been following the news lately?" he asked halfway through the meal.

"Not really," I admitted.

Ever since my first encounter with Avi, I hadn't visited the common room. I wanted to avoid the English channels like the plague, and I was too busy with my work to care about anything else.

"I've been watching the news closely," George continued. "It turns out they've discovered several terrorist tunnels. Can you believe it?"

"Does that mean Hamas militants can sneak into Israeli territory?" I asked, shocked.

"Of course, they can! Luckily, IDF is working on destroying them."

"I still can't believe the number of casualties in Gaza. I heard it's over a thousand now." Even though I strongly supported Israel, I couldn't help but sympathize with those innocent children whose homes were being destroyed and lives taken away.

"That's because Hamas uses its own people as human shields!" Suddenly, he was fuming. "They store weapons in schools and hospitals and then blame this shit on Israel. It's a smart propaganda move."

"That's so horrible! I really wish it would be over by tonight. I mean, I still have a week to spend here, and I want to be safe."

"Nothing can happen to us. We're protected by the Iron Dome." He put his hand over mine as if to make me feel safe.

"What about the tunnels? What if someone manages to use them for kidnappings? It sounds so scary."

"The Israelis won't let them. Besides, the tunnels are almost destroyed."

"Well, I hope so." I sighed and continued working on my meal.

"Want to continue to the Old City?" George asked later, after we were done eating.

"Most definitely!" I replied, taking the trays over to the garbage bin.

The Damascus Gate was only a few steps away from the eatery. The moment I saw the glorious walled structure, I wanted to pull out my camera and take as many photos as possible. George offered to snap a few pictures of me in front of the entrance, and I returned the favour by taking a picture of him on his camera.

Behind the gate was a colorful souk which looked like an inviting place to make more photos. We stopped by a few stores, including a jewellery shop, where George bought a pair of Bedouin earrings for his sister.

"I had no idea you have a sister," I said while he was paying at the cashier. It occurred to me that he rarely mentioned his family.

"Yes, I do. She'll be starting university this year."

"Which one?"

"University of Chicago. She'll be studying communications."

"How nice! I have a sister too. An older one. She's working as an aesthetician in a fancy spa center."

"What is she like?" He appeared intrigued.

"Beautiful, confident, and successful." I sighed.

"You sound like you're a bit jealous," George remarked.

"Maybe a teeny bit," I admitted. "But not that much. We're actually best friends."

"Becky, do you ever regret choosing archaeology as your major?" he asked as we passed a rug shop.

"Not at all." I turned to examine one of the rugs that were hanging from the shop's door. "I love the path I've chosen even with all its challenges and drawbacks. After all, it has brought me here, to this day, to this place." I smiled.

"I can say the same." He smiled back.

We proceeded to a food shop, where I bought some halva candies for my coworkers. Although my return to work was still far away, getting ahead with souvenir shopping wasn't a bad idea. I also bought small souvenirs for everyone in my family, including a few fridge magnets for Mom and Dad and a colorful plate for Grandma who still lived in Oakville. I kept Erin's request in mind but hadn't spotted any stores carrying Dead Sea products yet.

In the meantime, I was seizing the moment and enjoying the Oriental market, which looked much friendlier than East Jerusalem. There were no graffiti walls, no rubble, and no fast cars racing around, just a chain of boutiques with colorful beads and Oriental rugs hanging everywhere. I couldn't remember how many turns we took through the small streets until we found ourselves in front of the Church of the Holy Sepulchre.

"Want to go inside?" George asked.

"Definitely!" I replied. There was no way I would miss out on this beautiful and powerful place.

"I'll wait for you here then."

"Why don't you come in as well?"

"I don't do churches."

"Are you sure? It's a very important place. Probably the most important one in Christianity."

"Nah, I'll pass." He waved his hand dismissively.

"Okay, then I'll go on my own." I proceeded inside.

Having bought several candles at the entrance, I put on the headscarf and joined the line leading to the sacred vault. Tourist groups thronged the building. Most women had their heads covered with headscarves while almost all the men were wearing long pants. I wondered if George refused to come in because of his shorts. If I were in his shoes, I would still try sneaking in.

After the line, I lit a few candles and said a quick prayer for the well-being of everyone in my family and for peace in the Middle East. Then I snapped a few pictures of the dome, the altars, and the Byzantine mosaics. I could spend forever admiring all the art, but my time was limited. A few minutes later, I was back on the streets walking with George.

"Tell me, why don't you do churches?" I finally asked.

"I don't like religion as a social institution," he told me. "It's meant to manipulate the masses, and I don't want to be brainwashed."

"Really?" I was a bit shocked by George's revelation. Jason never showed any animosity toward religion. During our last visit, he willingly joined me at all the churches and even bought a *kippah* as a souvenir. "Are you going to skip the Western Wall as well?" I asked.

"Maybe I'll go there for the sake of pictures."

"So, are you an atheist?"

"More of an agnostic, I'd say."

Although I had nothing against his views, his words brought me out of my comfort zone and made me question everything I'd known about George up to this point. We walked in silence for a while until we reached the Western Wall. We split at the entrance, and after a mandatory security check, I was admitted into the women's section.

On the Shabbat afternoon, the energy around the Western Wall was special. Dozens of Orthodox Jews in black suits flocked to the site. Some were holding holy books while others were simply carrying their notes. I joined the women's section where I wrote a small note of gratitude for the last three weeks. I took time to touch the sacred stones and take it all in.

"Do you think the City of David is open now?" I asked after rejoining George. I was eager to visit this site because it was thought to be the birthplace of biblical Jerusalem.

"I believe so," he said, eying his watch, which was showing two-thirty. "We still have some time left, so let's just go and check."

What I really liked about Jerusalem was the proximity of all the sites to each other. Even if the City of David was closed, we could still benefit from a nice walk. Fortunately, the site was open.

"By the way, the Hezekiah's tunnel is very close," George noted, referring to the strategic tunnel built in the eight century BC by King Hezekiah to defend Jerusalem from the Assyrians.

"Then we should check if it's open. Although I've never been there, I heard it's worth visiting."

"It definitely is, but you might need water shoes." He looked down at my sandals. "It can get very wet over there."

"Oops! I don't want to trip and fall again."

"This time, no one will see us."

"Or force us to wear *abayas*." I giggled.

Much to our dismay, the tunnel was closed. However, we still had the entire City of David to ourselves. A small underground entrance led us to the site. From the corner of my eye, I noticed a few black creatures flying in the dark and immediately recognized them as bats.

"Ouch!" I exclaimed, feeling a shiver travel down my spine. I'd never seen a real bat before.

"Is everything okay, Becky?" George asked.

"I just don't like the bats," I said, pointing at the tunnel behind us.

"Don't worry," George said. "After everything that has happened already, they're just harmless creatures."

"You're right. The missile alarm on our first field trip gave me real creeps."

"And so did the solo walk in East Jerusalem, right?"

"Says who?" I laughed. On the morning after my outing with Caitlin and Megan, I had truly planned to confront him about his Jericho incident, but somehow I had forgotten all about it.

"What do you mean, Rebecca?" He was clearly clueless about my knowledge of his escapade.

"Whoever got lost in the West Bank a few years ago is definitely not a clueless dreamer."

"Oh, you know the story." George smiled.

"Megan and Caitlin told me when we went out for a drink."

"What did they say?"

"They said you had no right to be angry at me."

"I wasn't angry at you, Rebecca! Okay, maybe I overreacted a bit, and I admit it. But the real reason why I acted that way is because I've been in your shoes and I know how scary it can be."

"You made me feel like some misbehaving kid. You said I'm a dreamer living in denial."

"I'm sorry if I made you feel that way." He put his arms around my waist.

"I forgive you," I said playfully.

We were now standing in front of the famous stepped-stone structure commonly believed to have been built way before King David's rule. Next to the ruins was a small garden with flowers and trees. Sacks and shovels lay on the ground, hinting at some sort of an archaeological activity. Classical music was playing from the ground speakers. From afar, a muezzin was calling up for an afternoon prayer.

I drew myself closer to George. His hands started moving upward, sending chills through my spine. He gently touched my shoulders and moved his hands to the nape of my neck. The moment I felt his lips on mine, I wanted the time to stop. At the back of my mind, I knew that what we were doing was wrong in every sense. Before coming here, I could never picture myself in the cheater's role. In fact, I always abhorred that some people did such things. Yet here I was, with another soul, a man who had so much in common with me and yet who still appeared a mystery. He fascinated me, but also left me perplexed.

"*At matrifa oti*," he said, after I broke away from him to catch my breath.

"Since when did you start using Hebrew?" I asked, feeling warmth of the afternoon sun on my face.

"I learned it from the song you showed me the other day."

"I thought you are too cool for love songs."

"Who told you that?" He smiled.

"I just assumed. Anyway, it doesn't matter."

Soon, we were in for another long, passionate kiss. At some point, we fell on the ground, completely oblivious to the surroundings. Never mind we were out in a tourist site in the broad daylight. Never mind an Orthodox Jewish family could walk in any moment and see us. All I wanted was to make the best of the moment.

Then my phone rang.

Nineteen

"Ignore it," George said, while working down my neck.

The phone began ringing louder. It occurred to me that the call could be something important. No, I couldn't ignore it.

"I should probably take it." I pulled myself from underneath him and began fumbling through my purse. Fortunately, the ringing hadn't ended yet, and so I was able to pick it up right on time. "Hello?" I asked.

"Hey, it's me, Jason." My husband's voice resonated through my ears. In an instant, whatever I was having with George was ruined. All the feelings and passions dissipated like a morning fog.

"Just letting you know that I'm at the airport right now, looking for the car," he continued.

"Oh, nice," I replied, trying to play along. "I'm still in Jerusalem, though, and our group is meeting for the reunion dinner tonight. After that, I'm heading to the hotel." I glanced at George, who was standing uncomfortably at the side.

"What's the name of the restaurant? You know I could pick you up."

"Actually, I'll take a taxi tonight. You must be very tired after the flight." For whatever reason, I didn't want my husband to show up at our reunion.

"Are you sure? It's not a problem for me at all."

"I am, Jason."

"Is everything okay? You don't sound too excited to hear from me."

"No, everything's fine. It's just that we're in the middle of a tour right now." I looked at George again, noting the signs of annoyance on his face.

"All right then. I'll be waiting for you at the hotel if that's what you prefer."

"Wonderful! See you later."

"Bye, Becky."

I hastily put the phone away, sincerely hoping that Jason wasn't suspecting anything. In the meantime, I still had the mess to clear up with George.

"I think we should go now," I told him matter-of-factly and started walking toward the entrance.

For a while, we walked with silence hanging above us like a black cloud. There was no need to mention how awkward this whole situation felt. In the morning, I was still a good person, and now, I was officially a cheater and a liar capable of hurting two people at once. Just the mere thought of having to lie to Jason about this afternoon for the rest of my life made me feel sick to my stomach.

"Becky, I think we need to talk," George finally said.

"What's there to talk about?" I shrugged. "We've clearly made a mistake, putting each other into this situation. I should've never gone on this walk," I added, although I wasn't sure if I completely regretted the walking part. The sightseeing tour had been amazing. It was only the last part that brought me regret.

"Can we stop for a sec? I can't walk that fast and talk."

"Sure," I said, my heart pounding from all the pacing. "Although we might want to continue walking," I added, glancing at my watch.

"Fine, we'll walk and talk."

"So, what do you want to talk about?"

He fell silent. "Becky, I know that you are married and every-thing, and I fully respect that," he began.

"Okay."

"Although I do think you were a bit young to do that. And I'm not a big fan of marriage as an institution, to be honest. I think it's a bit outdated."

"And?"

"The truth is, I really like you, Rebecca." He sounded sincere. "I've never met a girl that passionate about archaeology."

"Not even in grad school?" I was flattered by his confession.

"Never! I like everything about you, from the way you bright-en up when you see an artifact to the way you get scared so easily. You are both vulnerable and strong."

"What do you mean, George?" Now, I was learning something new about myself.

"You're not afraid of challenges. I mean, the Albright Institute is a tough place to be, but you don't seem to be intimidated in the least."

"I was a bit intimidated in the beginning, but then I found out that everyone is so nice and friendly and—"

"Don't be fooled by appearances, Rebecca. The level of com-mitment required there is unbelievable. They'll make you sweat like crazy."

"I know, George. But I loved living here, and I'll always be grateful to you for bringing me to this place." He took my hand and smiled.

I glanced at the panorama to my right and at the wall to my left. For a moment, I felt happy again. Each of us would move on. This afternoon's incident would be forgotten. The memories, however, would remain. That feeling of joy didn't last any longer than a few seconds.

"You know that it wouldn't work out," I said at last.

"Maybe it would, if you wanted to," he insisted.

"It just wouldn't. We're two different people coming from two different worlds. You have your views on religion, and you don't want kids. Which is totally fine."

"Maybe we could learn to respect our differences."

"Not when we have different goals. I mean, I want kids someday, and you obviously don't."

"Ah, I should've never said that at the museum." He waved his hand like it was no big deal.

"Even if you didn't, it wouldn't change anything. Whoever you'll end up with will find it out eventually. So I'm kind of happy you told me the truth from the start."

"Maybe you would realize that you don't want kids either, and we would pursue archaeology together."

The idea of giving up my hopes for a family in favor of archaeology sounded utterly cruel and unfair.

"I'm not leaving Jason," I said decisively. "Not in a million years."

"I know, and I respect you even more for that."

Tears rose in my eyes. He turned to me and took my face into his hands. "Please don't cry, Becky. You must promise to think about your future."

"Yes, I will," I said, after recomposing myself. "In fact, I'm thinking about going back to school. It won't be easy now that I've got so many other responsibilities, but maybe taking a plunge will be worth it."

"That's why I think you should've held off on the whole marriage thing. But I'm not going to pressure you into anything. In fact, I promise to never touch you again if that's what you want. However, you must promise me to seriously reconsider your priorities. A brilliant girl like you shouldn't feel trapped."

"I'm not trapped by anything!" I retorted.

"Whatever you choose, I only wish you the best. So if you decide that grad school isn't for you, it's all right."

"I know. I know."

I looked into his eyes. For a moment, I considered sharing one last kiss before we went separate ways. It was unlikely this kiss would lead to anything more, considering how close it was to the bus pickup time and our rooms had already been checked out. *Just another peck*, I thought before turning away to another side.

By the time we reached the Albright Institute, all the staff people were already gathered in the lobby, and the bus was waiting to be boarded. I quickly ran upstairs and grabbed the suitcase I had packed last night. Then I ran straight to the bus to find most people already seated inside.

Twenty

I tried rehearsing my speech on the bus. Guilt raged inside me like a sea storm while I was sitting quietly by myself and clutching the USB in my pocket.

Last night, I had quickly skimmed through the PowerPoint presentations on Kiryat Adar and the Albright Institute and discovered that most of the information wasn't new to me. So I fell asleep shortly afterward. Now, I could do little other than watch the green hill country transform into yellow plains.

About an hour into the bus ride, I saw skyscrapers on the horizon and realized we were approaching Tel Aviv. We drove through busy suburbs and finally stopped in front of a chain of restaurants located close to the beach area.

"Do you need some help?" George asked me as I was trying to haul my suitcase out of the bus.

"No thanks." I pulled the suitcase a bit harder until it finally fell out of the compartment and onto the ground. Then I took the handle and proceeded into the restaurant.

"What do I do with my baggage?" I asked one of the waiters in Hebrew.

"You can leave it here." He pointed at a corner that was already piled with suitcases and duffel bags. "We'll watch it for you."

The waiter quickly led us to the restaurant room, which had full-length windows that showcased a garden located behind the building. Some of the volunteers from Kiryat Adar were already seated at wooden tables that had been pushed together to make one long table. I recognized my three former roommates, who were chatting together, and quickly joined them.

"Oh, hi, Becky!" Madeline exclaimed. I moved closer, choosing an empty seat next to her.

"How was your stay at the Albright?" Janice asked.

"It was amazing. I learned so much during one week."

"I bet you had lots of fun with that hot guy from Wheaton College," she added.

"I worked on translating a Hebrew article about prehistoric settlements," I explained, ignoring her comment.

"Wow! We had no idea your Hebrew is that good!" Madeline exclaimed.

"Me neither. In fact, I was pretty sure I'd bomb the task, but I made it in the end!" From the corner of my eye, I noticed Helen sitting one table away from us. I wondered if she could hear me.

"Anyway, I'm speaking tonight." So far, I still had no clue what my speech would sound like.

"I'm pretty sure you'll do a great job, Rebecca," Madeline said reassuringly.

A waitress arrived with four menus and asked if we'd like something to drink. We ordered four glasses of beer.

"How was Megiddo?" I finally asked.

"Not bad," Janice replied. "We found a few interesting pottery pieces. But like I said, I'm not doing archaeology again. It's too much slaving under the sun."

"I agree," Madeline added. "It was just an elective we decided to take for fun."

"At least, we managed to make it through the program," Janice commented. "I was getting worried the whole thing would get canceled."

"I know," I said, sympathizing. "I'd be worried too if I paid my tuition fee and got nothing in return."

"Why do we have to talk about school now?" Rachel protested. "Let's just choose our meals."

We made our choices quickly. Feeling a bit weary of the local food, we all chose typical western dishes, such as poutine, hamburger, and chicken pot pie. It wasn't until this moment that I realized I was starting to miss American food.

As we were eating, I thought about what I would say when my name got called. Even now, I only had a very faint idea about my speech.

"What are your plans for the summer?" Madeline asked halfway through the meal.

"Huh?"

"I plan to kick off during August," she said, ignoring my silence.

"Say it again?" At this point, I felt too nervous to pay any attention.

"Good evening, everyone," Andrew Logan announced. "Thank you for staying with us until the end of the term. Before we begin our evening, I would like to introduce a special speaker. Everyone, please welcome Rebecca O'Connor-Smith."

Everyone clapped. As soon as I got up from the chair, my knees started shaking. For a few seconds, it felt like I had forgotten everything.

"Here you go." Andrew passed me the microphone as soon as I reached his table.

"Good evening, everyone!" I feigned confidence. "It's a pleasure for me to be here tonight..."

I stumbled for a bit. Then, after a few seconds, my speech started flowing. I talked about the sites of Kiryat Adar and Megiddo, the history of the Albright Institute, and life on a dig versus life in a lab. I even shared some of the insights into the article I had translated and some of the struggles I had encountered along the way. I concluded my talk by emphasizing the role of persistence in academic success. The moment I finished speaking, I was greeted by a big applause.

"Congratulations!" Janice exclaimed after I rejoined the table. "You were amazing!"

Soon, all the volunteers started coming to our table one-by-one and congratulating me on the speech. I received hugs from Karen, Claire, Luke, and a few others whom I had gotten to know on the dig. George stayed at his table, but based on his smile and a wink, I could tell he enjoyed my speech too.

At some point, I became wary of the attention and excused myself to the bathroom to get some quiet time. To my dismay, Rachel followed me.

"So, you're the star of the Orient," she told me while we were fixing our makeup.

For the first time, I noticed how beautiful she looked in her silky red dress, and how elaborate her hair updo was. Although I had a speaker role, I hadn't even bothered to change and was still wearing the same clothes I had worn to the Old City.

"Is it wrong?" I tried ignoring her tone.

"You always get what you want, Rebecca."

"I don't understand."

"Don't you think that someone else might have wanted to speak tonight?"

"Well, I found out I would be speaking at the very last minute. I didn't even want the speech."

"Ha! You think I'll believe you. It was probably a well-calculated plan to get everyone's attention. You wanted to shine, didn't you?"

"Rachel, what's going on?" I was getting tired of her constant bugging.

"What's going on? I'll tell you. I was supposed to be the speaker. I volunteered to speak a long time ago. I had a presentation prepared and everything, and at the last minute, they told me not to bother. Can you imagine how I felt?"

"Oh, I'm really sorry. I swear it wasn't planned by me."

"Why did you have to steal George from me?" she continued on. "Aren't you married?"

"When did I steal him? We just ended up becoming friends. I would've never stolen anyone. He just wasn't interested in you. Sorry, nothing I could do."

"You are such a vixen, Rebecca."

I wasn't sure if I supposed to laugh or cry. Me? A quiet girl from Oakville? I couldn't even stand up for myself at work. How did I turn into a vixen in one day?

"By the way, your outfit looks horrible, and your skirt is soiled."

I looked down and saw a small black stain at the bottom of my skirt. Clearly, fashion wasn't my strongest suit.

"So what?" I asked in an attempt at self-defense. "Everyone still liked my presentation."

"You don't deserve any of the attention everyone gives you."

"Whatever. I'm going back to our table. You are more than welcome to move if you don't like my company."

I stormed out of the bathroom and quickly reached my seat. Janice and Madeline were talking animatedly among themselves. As soon as I sat down, they stopped.

"Is everything all right?" Madeline asked. "Did you two have a fight in a bathroom?"

"Well, Rachel is mad at me for stealing her speech. She planned to be the speaker."

"That's so funny!" Janice exclaimed.

"I kind of feel bad for her because she had her speech and stuff."

"Don't feel bad," Madeline protested. "Look, you did a great job, and she's jealous. Plain and simple."

"Exactly," Janice said. "So don't worry about it."

From the way the two girls were exchanging looks and sharing muffled laughs, I could tell that something wasn't quite right. As for Rachel, she was gone since our argument and hadn't come back. Feeling slightly uneasy with myself, I decided to step outside and get some fresh air. I opened the restaurant door, took a few steps, and froze at the sound of two familiar voices coming from behind the corner of building.

"Tell me what she means to you," I heard Rachel say. Her voice was calm, but not devoid of sadness. I moved closer to hear the rest of their conversation better, but not close enough to be seen. From the corner of my eye, I caught a glimpse of Rachel in her red dress and George, who, like myself, was still wearing the same clothes from the afternoon. Most people at the dinner, including the directors, were dressed pretty casually—shorts, T-shirts, and a few dresses among the female group. In my opinion, Rachel was a bit overdressed for the occasion.

"She's just a friend, Rachel," George replied.

"Don't lie to me. I saw the way you looked at her during the speech. I know she must mean something more to you."

George took her hand said, "Look, I know you're still hurting from our breakup, and I'm really sorry. But you must find a way to move on."

What? I never knew they were an item in the past. He never mentioned it to me, nor did anyone who might have known them. Suddenly, it all made sense. She was trying to win him back, which explained all her attempts to get his attention, her animosity toward me, and the defeated look I saw on her face the morning we moved from Megiddo to the Albright Institute. It was more than just attraction. I should've realized that earlier.

"You didn't answer my question, George. I want to know exactly what she means to you."

"Does it matter now?" He sounded too composed for the situation. It was one of the qualities that made me drawn to him in the first place. He always remained calm, no matter how hard the situation got. Even when we had a missile threat back in Kiryat Adar, he would simply get himself to the bomb shelter or the ground without showing any signs of panic.

"It does, George. We were together for five whole years. I put up with your late arrivals, our canceled dates, your all-nighters at my place, and now you're saying you're ready to move on to the next available chick that comes your way."

"Look, Rach. You were the first one to break up with me. I know it was partly my fault, and I know you're hurting at the moment, but—"

"But what?"

"I don't feel ready for a relationship. Not with you or Becky or anyone else for that matter." I bolted back at the mentioning of my name. Luckily, I was still in a place where they couldn't see me. "And just so that you know, Becky isn't available. She's married."

Rachel stared at him, her mouth agape. "I...I can't believe this," she said. "Are you telling me that our five years together meant nothing to you?"

"I know I should've told you this earlier, when we were still together. Maybe it would've stopped you from flying here because I can tell you don't enjoy archaeology even when you try. When you told me back in the spring you wanted to call it quits, I felt relieved. Relieved that I didn't have to be the bad guy because it was clear we were both dragging ourselves through something that was over a long time ago. Relieved that I could just focus on work without worrying that I'm being too insensitive or unavailable to someone. Now it appears that I'm still being the bad guy."

"But you did fall for this girl," she muttered through tears.

"I don't know what made you believe I fell for Becky. She's definitely pretty and smart, and she's cool to hang around with. But like I said, I'm not ready for anything serious at the moment. Maybe I will be ready someday, in a couple of years from now."

His words hurt like a knife. I spent so much time obsessing over him, torturing myself with guilt, when, in reality, I hardly meant anything to him. I was just a hookup, a nice girl to talk to. Why hadn't I realized that earlier? He never bothered asking me about my computer incident or showing on time for our last outing.

"I hate you! I hate you!" Rachel started attacking George with her clutch bag. "I came all the way over here to show you how much I care. I sweated for three whole weeks to prove that I've changed. I put my life in danger." Her high pitches pierced the warm, musty air of evening Tel Aviv.

"Chill out, Rach. We were over long before this trip." George tried acting cool. "And no one asked you to come to Kiryat Adar."

"I don't want to talk to you again. You understand? I hate you!" She shot him one last look before storming off into the darkness. I expected him to run after her, to check if she was okay. At least, this is what I would do if I were a guy in his shoes. To me, she always seemed a bit crazy, and who knew what she had on her mind in these moments of despair? Instead, he calmly walked back into the building, bumping into me.

"Wow, Becky! You scared me." His eyes tripled at the sight of me.

"You should go after her," I said calmly, despite falling apart on the inside. "She's not in a good state right now. I think she needs help to get to the airport or wherever she's going after this dinner."

"You're worried about Rachel?" he asked, looking genuinely surprised. "She'll be fine, Becky. She's always been tad bit dramatic."

"Still, I think you should try to find her. She couldn't have run off too far."

"I doubt I can do anything to help her at this moment. If you heard us talk, which I assume you did, she's totally bananas at the moment. If I go after her, she'll tell me to fuck off, and she'll be absolutely right. She needs to be left alone for a while until the storm passes."

"Aren't you worried she'll do something stupid in her fit of anger?"

"Like run into a road with cars or something? Nah, she's not that type, Becky. Trust me, she'll be fine. I think it's better that we go back inside and enjoy the rest of this dinner."

"I can't believe you're being so casual about it!"

"Just forget about it, okay? By the way, I forgot to tell you your speech was awesome tonight."

"Thanks, George." I rolled my eyes, opening the door of the restaurant.

As soon as we were inside, I wanted to get away from him, as far as possible. Everyone in the room was eating and talking avidly. I quietly walked over to my table, still in shock from everything I just saw and heard. Janice and Madeline were laughing hysterically. As soon as I showed up at our table, they stopped.

"What's going on?" I asked. "Something funny?"

"We should ask you the same question," Janice said, clearly trying to suppress the giggles.

"Wait, did you know?"

"You mean Rachel and George?"

"Yes, them."

"Well, most volunteers know the story," Madeline admitted. "She's trying to win him back."

"I know that already," I admitted calmly. "I just don't understand how come no one warned me."

"Wasn't it you who said George and you were just friends?" Janice shrugged.

"It was entertaining to see you two interact while she was seething quietly by herself," Madeline added.

At this moment, any feelings of shock or sadness became replaced with pure anger. I'd been let down many times, but not by people I'd considered my friends. I came to this dinner hoping that we would sit together, discuss our best impressions of the expedition, and perhaps share a few good laughs. Instead, I discovered that my former roommates had been conspiring against me.

"Goodnight, everyone." I got up from the table and paced to the front.

"Wait, Becky! Where are you going?" Madeline yelled after me. "Please come back."

I quickly paid my bill and was about to grab my luggage when someone called my name.

"Rebecca, you're leaving already." I turned back to find Helen and Andrew standing a few steps away from me.

"Yes, I am," I replied matter-of-factly. In that moment, I realized it would be a good idea to say goodbye to Helen and to the rest of the field team. After all, they had given me an amazing opportunity to work at the Albright Institute and to give this talk.

"You did an amazing job tonight!" Helen remarked.

"We were happy to have you work with us," Jayden added. "We hope to see you again next year. Let me know if you ever need a recommendation letter."

"You can also count on me," Andrew added, walking over from his table.

"And me," Helen said.

"Well, it was a big honor for me to work with every one of you."

"Thank you, Rebecca. You've been a tremendous help to our team."

After saying goodbye to everyone, I grabbed my suitcase and left the building. By now, all I wanted was to find the hotel where Jason and I would be staying and forget about this entire nightmare.

"Hey, Becky, where are you going?" George yelled after me when I was already outside.

"To my hotel," I replied, wheeling the suitcase behind me.

"I'm about to leave too. Want to share a taxi?"

"No, thanks." I continued walking, while he paced after me.

"Rebecca, I'm sorry for not telling you earlier. I should've—"

"George, I don't want to talk about it." I shot him a sharp look.

"Fine. Look, there's a taxi. Let's hurry up."

"No, I'll get to the hotel by myself, thanks." I continued walking away from him, but he quickly caught up with me.

"Becky, don't be stupid. Your baggage must weigh more than a ton, and you don't even know where you're going. Do you want to get lost for the second time or something?"

"Fine, I'll get in that taxi if that's what you want." In truth, my baggage did feel heavy, even with the wheels, and getting in a taxi seemed like the most reasonable thing to do, even if it meant being in the same confined space with him.

The ride to the hotel was very quick, but to me it felt torturously long. Not long ago, riding anywhere with him was filled with a sense of newness and excitement. But now, all I wanted was to go back to Jason, my sweet and loyal Jason, whom I mistreated so badly. After passing a few busy streets, the cab turned to a quiet residential area and stopped in front of a medium-rise building. I quickly paid my share and was about to leave when George stopped me.

"Wait, I'll walk you to the entrance."

"Don't you need to go?" I asked, looking for an excuse to get away from him faster.

"For the money we've paid, the taxi will wait. Where's your hotel?"

"I'll find it." I took out the printout of the hotel's map.

"Becky, are you mad at me or something?" he finally asked.

"Not really," I lied. "I just wish I knew then what I know about you now."

"Look, I don't know how much you heard from my conversation with Rachel, but I don't want you to think that I'm some kind of a heartless prick."

"That's not what I think of you, George. And I don't have anything against you choosing work over a relationship. After all, it's your life and your choices. I just don't understand why you would say the things you said this afternoon—like pursuing archaeology together and finding ways to figure out our differences—if I'm no more than a fling." I knew I probably sounded pitiful and needy, but for some reason, I wanted to know the truth.

"I just wanted to help you, Becky. I wanted you to believe that you're capable of pursuing your dreams no matter what your circumstances are. I wanted you to envision a different type of life."

"Well, it doesn't change much. I need to go now."

"Are you even sure we are in the right place?" George asked, staring at one of the residential buildings.

"I'm positive it is. It's supposed to be a hotel apartment." I looked at the printout again.

"Well, I guess it's time to say goodbye." He smiled. "I hope you'll still end up at least with good memories of this trip."

"I will."

He came closer and embraced me. I didn't resist this time. His touch was still sizzling, but I was ready to put the feeling behind. Especially after everything I learned tonight.

"You should go. Your cab is waiting," I repeated myself.

"I hope to see you again, and I really hope you continue with archaeology."

"Goodbye, George."

I watched his car disappear in the distance while preparing myself for whatever was yet to come.

Twenty-One

Indeed, the building in front of me didn't look like a hotel. I looked at the printout map twice just to find out that the address was right. I opened the door and walked inside, hoping to find at least a sign leading to the lobby. Inside was a staircase leading to different stories and a small floor flanked by a door on one side. The door had a metal lock with numbers.

Could I've made a mistake? I thought for a minute. However, the door next to me had the same unit number as the one indicated on the sheet. I knocked lightly. No response. I knocked again. The second time, I heard someone walk over to the door.

I froze. I was going to see him for the first time in three weeks. After everything I've done, the idea felt mortifying.

The door opened slowly. Here he was, my first real love and my spouse, standing a few steps away from me, looking adorable as ever despite being slightly jet-lagged.

"Becky! Finally, you're here," he exclaimed. Judging by the relaxed expression on his face, he wasn't suspecting anything.

"Hi, Jason," I said calmly. I knew I was supposed to jump with joy and wrap my arms around him, but something was stopping me.

"What's wrong, love? You don't look happy," he noted.

"Er, nothing's wrong. Just a bit tired from the night."

"Ah, I see. Too much partying, right?"

"Not really. I hardly drank anything today. It was just...er...a bit emotional. I was the night's speaker."

"You were?" His eyes sparkled with amazement.

"Yes, I spoke about my experience as a dig volunteer."

"Well, congratulations! Come in." He took my suitcase away from me and placed it together with his.

I looked around the apartment unit just to realize how lucky we were with our accommodation choice. The place looked more like a luxury condo rather than an apartment hotel.

At the time Jason was booking the trip, this apartment unit was available for a reduced price, so we went for it. Now, we would have a large living room, a fully equipped kitchenette, a spacious bedroom, and another room with a spare bed, all to ourselves.

I came closer and wrapped my hands around him. The familiar feeling of warmth filled me. Maybe I could move past this one mistake and enjoy the rest of the vacation. And the rest of our life together.

"I missed you, Becky," he whispered.

"Me too," I replied, knowing that the statement wasn't completely true. There'd been moments during the trip when I had been too preoccupied with my work to even think about him. Terrible truth that I wasn't ready to admit.

He began kissing me slowly, just the way I used to love it, but as much as I tried to relax and enjoy our time together, my mind kept going back to the City of David.

"Jason, I'm not in the mood right now." I pulled away from him.

"Becky, what's wrong?" He looked mildly disappointed.

"I'm really sorry, but I'd rather take a shower first."

"Ah, I'm sorry if I'm being too rash."

"It's okay, baby. I promise to make it up to you." I moved away from him and began unpacking the suitcase. He moved toward the couch, looking slightly disappointed but still unsuspecting of anything. Having found the shampoo and a change of clothes, I walked to the bathroom, where I let cold water run over me.

I still wasn't sure how I would approach the topic of my future or my lingering doubts. Yet I knew that this past afternoon with George would change us forever. By the time I came out, Jason was dozing on the couch. The sight of my husband being so innocently asleep made my heart melt. I gathered the hem of my bathrobe and sat beside him.

"Hey," I whispered gently. He didn't flinch. I figured he must've been very tired after the flight. So I took a blanket from the other bedroom and covered him. Only then did he move a little. "Good night, Jason," I said before turning off the lights.

I tried hard to fall asleep, but simply couldn't. Too many thoughts raced through my mind. I still couldn't believe I had allowed all the drama to happen to me. Falling for someone's ex, cheating on my husband, and being ridiculed by former roommates—that was too much for me to handle at once. What was worse, I still couldn't forget George's words.

I had to talk to someone and to let everything out. After my fourth attempt to lie still, I took out my cell phone and stepped outside. The apartment unit had a small patio behind the area that joined the living room with the guest bedroom. Having made sure I was out of Jason's earshot, I pulled out the cell phone and dialed Erin's number.

"Hello." She sounded a bit too formal for her usual self.

"Hi, Erin. How are you?"

"Uh, hi, Becky! I'm okay. Yourself?" Although her voice softened a bit, I could tell something wasn't quite right with her.

"I'm fine. Anything new?" I didn't want to jump into my story without first asking my sister about her life.

"Well, I'm taking a vacation in a few months," she declared. "I don't where I'm going yet, but all I know is that I need a break from all this bullshit."

I was a bit surprised by the news. Erin always planned her time off way in advance.

"What happened?" I became alarmed. Maybe her problems were worse than mine.

"Nothing. I'm just tired, and I need a break."

"Busy?"

"Yeah. Plus all the dating crap. I need to get away, Becky. I can't stand it here anymore."

"Another bad date?"

"Long story. Don't want to talk about it now. Just tell me about yourself. How was your last week in Jerusalem? Did you have a good time at all?"

"I did, but there's something I need to talk to you about." I looked around to make sure nobody could hear me. Jason was still sleeping on the couch, separated by the soundproof patio door.

"So tell me." There was an undeniable sense of worry in her voice.

I took a deep breath before starting my story. "It has to do with George again," I said.

"Please don't tell me you made out with him."

"I did, actually."

"Becky! How could you?"

"I know, Erin. I feel awful right now."

"Okay, tell me how it happened. Start from the beginning."

"Today, George and I went out for a walk. We were having a nice time talking, exploring the Old City. Then one thing led to another, and we kissed." I glanced around again, prepared to hide lest Jason woke up.

For a moment, Erin kept silent. I knew she disapproved of me. I would disapprove of this, too, had the roles been reversed. Yet at this moment, I craved support, not judgement.

"So what happened after?" she asked calmly.

"Jason called and interrupted us."

"Good for you. Where is he, anyway?"

"We're at hotel now. He's asleep."

"Aren't you worried he might overhear you?"

"No, I'm outside, on the patio."

"Okay, be careful, Becky. That's all I can say for now."

"You know what's the worst thing? One of my former roommates turned out to be his ex-girlfriend, and now she thinks I stole him from her."

"What? You stealing someone's boyfriend?" Erin laughed.

Although I felt annoyed by her reaction, a tiny part of me was glad the tension between us finally eased.

"I'm serious, Erin. She also thinks I'm a goal-oriented bitch who is capable of cutting throats and stepping on others' heads."

Erin laughed again. "Becky, as far as I know, you hadn't haven't even caught a fly in your life. All right, maybe once, you tried to catch a bee when you were five, but it stung you."

"To be honest, I feel like crap right now. I never intended to deceive anyone, and now, I feel like I'm lying every single moment of my life."

"Tell me one thing, Becky. Just please be honest. Are you in love with George? If yes, are you willing to do what it takes to be happy?"

"Okay, I might've fallen in love with him at some point during the trip, but now I realize it was a big mistake. I think what we had was more about the newness than anything else."

"Then you have your answer here. You need to get back to your normal life and try forgetting about this guy as fast as possible."

"What's worse, I don't know how to approach Jason about it."

"Are you serious, Becky? You shouldn't tell him under any circumstances. Look, you got lost in the heat of the moment and made a dumb choice, but that doesn't mean that the entire world should now revolve around this tiny mistake. Unless you want your marriage to end, of course."

"By all means, no. I want us to stay together."

"Then you should keep your mouth shut." I wasn't sure how I felt about her suggestion. She did have a valid point. I doubted Jason would take the news well. But carrying this secret for the rest of my life would be even more challenging.

"Anyway, tell me something good," Erin suggested as if to make me feel a bit better.

"Well, all I can say that the whole experience at Kiryat Adar and the Albright Institute changed me. I loved the work so much that I'm considering going to grad school now."

"Well, if you believe it's right for you, then you should go for it." Her voice immediately lightened up. Maybe we both needed to discuss something else to feel a bit better.

"I just can't imagine how it can happen now that Jason and I are married and planning to have kids."

"You know what, Becky?" Her voice went back to being tense. "No offense to Jason, 'cause he's definitely a good catch, but I do think you were a bit hot-headed four years ago."

"What do you mean?"

"I think you should've hung in there for a few more years and figured out what you truly wanted in your life. Instead, you jumped at the first chance to tie the knot. It wasn't the wisest thing to do in your situation."

"Erin, are you telling me my marriage was a mistake?" I asked in horror.

"Not necessarily. I still think you could make it work if you started making the right decisions from now on. I just believe you could've waited longer. That's all."

"But what do I do now? I want to be truthful, you know."

"Then it's up to you, Becky. I would keep quiet if I were in your shoes. But if you want to tell him, be prepared for anything."

I sighed. "You're right. I should probably keep quiet."

"It'll get easier with time. Just take it step by step and decide what to do next with your career."

"I hope so." Deep inside, I already knew that forgetting about Jason's call I received in the City of David wouldn't be easy. All the emotions I felt at the moment—the forbidden passion, the waking jolt, and the shame—would remain in my memory for quite a long time.

"Anyway, I need to go now," she said. "I'm running late for work."

"Sorry for delaying you."

"No worries. Sometimes, it's good to just talk to someone."

"Bye now."

Having put down the phone, I turned around and froze. Jason was standing by the patio door looking directly at me.

"Wow, you scared me!" I exclaimed upon entering inside.

"Who were you talking to?" he asked.

"Erin, my sister," I replied wondering if he heard any part of our conversation.

"You should've waked me up from the couch." He put his hands around my waist.

"I tried to, but you were sleeping so soundly that I decided not to disturb you."

"Anyway, let's go back to bed now."

"Let's go." I sighed with relief. Judging by his relaxed behavior, he hadn't heard much of my conversation with Erin. Once we were in bed, I nuzzled my face into his neck that I'd been used to and closed my eyes.

Everything will be all right, I told myself.

Jason and I would get back to normal eventually. Or so I hoped.

Twenty-Two

J ason tried initiating things with me the next morning, but once again, I turned him down. I didn't even know what had gotten to me. I perfectly understood that the faster I began acting as my old self, the sooner everything would return to normal. Yet I simply couldn't fathom getting close to him just yet. Instead, I suggested going outside for breakfast, to which he heartily agreed since we were both hungry.

We walked down Ben Yehuda Street until we spotted a small eatery, where a woman in a long skirt with a scarf around her head welcomed us. My attention was caught by her dark eye shadow and long earrings. It often amazed me how Jewish observant women could beat Carrie Bradshaw with their sense of style. Having looked at the menu, we quickly decided to go with two falafel plates. Although it wasn't a typical dish for the morning meal, we decided to order it anyway since we both knew how amazing the local falafel was.

During our first stay in Israel, it had been virtually impossible to convince Jason to try this dish, for he could not believe that anything that wasn't meat could taste good. One time, I offered him some of my falafel, and he reluctantly took it from me. Then he completely fell in love with the taste. He even tried to coax me into making it at home, but our first and also last attempt turned into a complete disaster. After the fire alarm went off from the foul smell of burnt chickpeas, we resolved to keep relying on Sha-warma King.

"So, tell me more about your excavation adventure," Jason suggested.

"Oh, it was amazing!" I replied. "I learned so much during the last three weeks, especially at the Albright Institute." I was already getting into a better mood.

"I was so worried about you when you were in Kiryat Adar. I was happy to find out they'd evacuated you."

I recalled the times I'd found his constant calls and messages annoying, and the overbearing feeling of guilt returned.

"I was worried, too, but everything turned in our favor. We got to visit many sites in the Golan Heights, including the Banias Springs. Remember that place?"

"Of course, I do!"

"I had a funny incident there."

"You tripped and fell in the Jordan River, right? I remember you sending me a message."

"And I had to wear an *abaya* with a scarf for the rest of the day trip because my clothes were wet, and the driver didn't want me to ruin the seat." I omitted the part about George tripping with me.

We laughed. Jason raised his arm and ran his fingers through my hair—a gesture that used to drive me crazy during our early days. This time, it made me feel safe and warm.

"So, what are we doing tomorrow?" I asked.

"How about driving to Jerusalem? I really want to see it again."

"Really? I thought you would be keener on hitting the beach." In truth, I was a bit surprised by his unexpected suggestion.

"Yes, but I also want to see the Old City. I kind of miss it."

"I see. Well, we'll visit it, then."

We spent most of the morning lying on the beach and enjoying fruit punches. Afterward, we returned to our hotel, where we spent a lazy afternoon lying on the couch and watching TV channels that weren't broadcasting the news. I told him more about my trip, including the week at the Albright, how I had gotten lost in the east end and how my computer had crashed the very next day. Jason, in turn, told me a little bit about his visit to his parents and his last week at work, including a few mishaps with servers, which had to be fixed before he left.

"You won't believe how many friends I've made while being here," I told him at some point.

"I hope you didn't befriend anyone from the West Bank. Knowing you, I can expect almost anything."

"Actually, I did. And we are invited to Nablus to meet his family."

"You gotta be kidding me," Jason said.

"He was our waiter at the Institute, and he's really nice." I felt the urge to defend Ibrahim, especially because of his daughter.

"I believe you. I just don't want you to be in danger anymore."

"Well, the worst is over." I smiled.

On the outside, everything looked good. We were reunited and happy to see each other. However, I couldn't shake off the feeling that our perfect world could crash at any moment.

At one point, I pulled myself away from him and went to grab my phone to check Facebook. There were a few friend requests, including those from Janice, Madeline, Caitlin, and Megan. I considered rejecting the first two, as I was still angry at them. However, I was eager to see the photos they had taken during our sightseeing tours. So I accepted everyone. I also discovered a few messages in my mailbox.

Hi, Becky,

I'm sorry about our last phone conversation. I didn't mean it when I said your marriage was a mistake. I'm just stressed out and tired at the moment, and I need a break.

Have a great vacation with your husband and don't worry about anything. Remember, we all make mistakes.

Erin

Having scrolled down, I also discovered a message from George.

Hi, Becky,

I just arrived safely in Chicago. I hope you enjoyed our excavation season with all of its twists and turns. Best of luck with your life, and I hope to see you again someday.

George

I was glad he didn't mention our kiss or his crazy ex. The faster we both forgot about everything, the better it would be for everyone.

"Hey, what are you looking at?" Jason asked, moving next to me.

"Um, nothing." I quickly hid my phone. I knew it wasn't the best thing to do when you wanted someone's trust, but the move came almost reflexively.

"Are you hiding something from me?" He didn't look terribly suspicious of me, and his question sounded more like a joke rather than an accusation.

"Nope. I was just catching up with my former roommates. You can use my phone for Internet if you like."

"Thanks, Becky. I want to check my emails." He opened the browser and went straight to his Gmail account while I got up and went to the kitchen to reheat the leftovers we had brought from the food place we had visited earlier.

AT NIGHT, I had a dream of falling, gravity pulling me inexorably to the ground. I woke up panting in cold sweat.

"Is everything okay?" Jason asked, hearing me get up.

"I had a bad dream about falling into an abyss," I admitted, shaking.

"Don't worry. It was just a dream." He pulled me closer.

"I have a strange feeling that something bad is going to happen." I started shaking even harder.

He moved closer to my side and hugged me. "Look, you had three intense weeks, as far as I know. It's normal for you to be a bit apprehensive right now. But remember, as long as we are together, nothing can happen to us."

"And what if we aren't?" A huge lump rose in my throat.

"What are you talking about, Becky?"

"Nothing, really. Let's go back to sleep. I'm sure everything will be better in the morning."

He was right. When we woke up at seven, I was feeling rested and refreshed. Part of me even felt embarrassed about what had happened earlier.

"I'm sorry for that nightmare scene," I told Jason as he stepped out of the shower.

"No worries, babe. I hope you're feeling better now." He smiled.

After browsing through my clothes, I was disappointed to find out that I didn't have anything appropriate for the Old City except for that long skirt and the blouse I had worn a day ago.

"Look, you've got a stain on your skirt," Jason remarked while searching for his trousers.

"Oh, maybe I should choose something else," I said, blushing. Not about the stain of course.

"It's all right, Becky. No one knows us here."

"True, but I don't feel like wearing it, anyway." I quickly removed my outfit and tossed it away. "Do you think they'll let me wear pants to the Western Wall? All my dresses are too short for the occasion."

"I don't think it should be a problem." He shrugged

In the end, I chose to wear green cargo pants and the Kiryat Adar Expedition T-shirt, which I had bought shortly before leaving for Megiddo.

We found a small coffee shop a few blocks from our hotel, where we ordered two cappuccinos with muffins. Although we had chosen the hotel apartment with a kitchen on purpose, neither of us was in the mood for cooking yet. I promised Jason and myself that I would make something extra special tonight.

THE DRIVE to Jerusalem lasted no longer than an hour. The hardest part of the journey was navigating through busy streets all the way to the Old City and finding parking at a decent price. As it was still morning, everyone was rushing to work, and drivers kept honking for no particular reason. At last, we found a spot near the Mamilla Mall and began searching for Jaffa Gate.

"Remember this place?" Jason asked me as we were climbing up the stairs.

"Of course, I do!" I exclaimed, feeling grateful to have found a place in the Old City unmarred by the memories of George.

We walked through the Armenian and Arab Quarters all the way to the Western Wall. I must admit that my second walk through the Old City was far from enjoyable. Throughout the entire time we were there, I couldn't shake off memories of me and George strolling through the same streets, checking out the same sites, and even taking photos in the same spots.

Besides, being in the Old City with my husband was less exciting than being with someone from the dig. Whereas my talk with George was full of mind-provoking conversations, the talk with Jason mostly consisted of map reading and figuring out where to go. Sometimes, I would mention a fact or two about the Old City, but Jason would just nod and smile. The intellectual challenge just wasn't there.

"Jason, do you ever feel bored with me?" I asked while checking out a Bedouin necklace. What if he was feeling the same way about my lack of interest in his hobbies? Perhaps he, too, longed to discuss computers or business affairs with someone.

"What do you mean, Becky?" He looked surprised.

"We're so different! You are into business and informatics, and I'm into archaeology. Does it ever bother you?"

"Of course not!" he exclaimed. "No two people can be the same."

"So you don't think I'm boring?"

"Becky, I think you are fascinating! With you, I get to learn something new every day." He looked directly into my eyes, making me feel a bit relieved. "Please don't have these thoughts. You are the best thing I have in my life."

Once again, I became plagued by guilt. I tried my best to push the feeling aside and to enjoy the sunny walk through Jerusalem, but that nagging sensation in my chest refused to leave me alone. I felt like a total hypocrite at the Western Wall and the Church of the Holy Sepulchre. I couldn't pray or think about anything spiritual. So I kept walking around and snapping photos of lamps and Byzantine mosaics for the hundredth time.

Just as we were leaving the sacred vault, the security officers appeared out of nowhere and urged everyone to leave the church. Apparently, someone had left a bag inside, which meant that the entire building had to be evacuated. As we walked away, I could only hope that the bag didn't have a bomb, and if it did, that the security would have enough time to disarm it. I couldn't imagine this beautiful place sharing its fate with St. Jonah's Tomb.

"Want to check out the Jewish Quarter?" I suggested later. It was the only place George and I didn't get to see.

"Sure," Jason replied.

The Cardo had a chain of jewellery shops and small boutiques selling artwork. As soon as I walked inside an art shop, my mood improved. Even though I had never owned a professional painting, I loved window shopping for art. I particularly liked a picture of a tuxedo cat, the live version of which was idling nearby. A few pictures of Jerusalem's panorama also caught my eye. We later found a few shops selling Dead Sea products, where I finally bought a present for Erin.

"I haven't had pizza for ages," I declared at the end of the walk through the Cardo.

"I wouldn't mind pizza either, especially if it has some pepperoni and mushrooms."

We found a small pizzeria in the Jewish Quarter, but, to our disappointment, there was no pepperoni option available. I had completely forgotten that kosher food precluded mixing dairy and meat. It was the main reason why all my Israeli breakfasts had been strictly vegetarian. We decided to go for pizza regardless, and to our pleasant surprise, it tasted good.

"Do you want to go home afterward?" Jason asked, looking at his watch. It was already three-thirty, and in a few hours, the traffic would become impossible.

"Sure. I kind of feel tired."

Having left a sizable tip to the owner, we went back to the Mamilla Mall parking, where our car was waiting for us.

The journey home wasn't a smooth one. In spite of our attempt to leave and arrive earlier, we still got stuck in a huge traffic jam. Halfway through the traffic, we saw a group of soldiers stop cars and interrogate drivers. One of them fired a gun into the air, making me feel a bit uneasy. Although these kids in uniforms were unlikely to harm us, I could tell something wasn't quite right.

We turned on the radio in hopes of finding more information, but all we could hear was a few announcements about upcoming shows in Caesarea and Eilat. The announcement was followed by a lengthy chain of Middle Eastern songs and later by the news hour. I was beyond relieved to learn that nothing bad happened to the Church of the Holy Sepulchre. Two hours later, the traffic finally cleared up, and we were able to reach Tel Aviv.

"THAT'S IT! Tomorrow's a beach day," Jason declared as we were standing in the kitchen unpacking groceries we'd bought on the way home.

"Really? Wasn't it you who suggested visiting the Old City?" I said, half laughing.

"I did. But still, we need a break from all the sightseeing."

"We only spent half a day doing it."

"That was more than enough. The heat is just ridiculous!"

"You won't believe how hot it was in Eilat, or how much walking we did during our mini tour in the Golan Heights."

"Then you might need a little rest as well. You can't be constantly up and running."

"I agree. Nevertheless, I did enjoy all our day trips."

"Now you'll enjoy some beach time." He came over and embraced me. "By the way, you don't have to cook today if you don't feel like it," he said. "We can go out today. We have an entire week left."

"No, I want to make you happy," I said.

"Rebecca, you're amazing!" he exclaimed. "I missed your meals so much!"

"That's why I'm cooking tonight." I winked.

Having unpacked the groceries, I immediately put on an apron and started working. I was planning to make a steak that Jason loved. So I seasoned a piece of raw meat with salt, pepper, and mushrooms, and added some vinegar. While it was grilling, I carefully peeled potatoes and placed them in a large saucepan. An hour later, we were having mashed potatoes with a steak and a Greek salad.

"Cheers." Jason raised a glass of wine.

"To us!" I said in return.

After we finished eating, he walked over to my side of the table and gently took my hand. "I think it's time to make up for all those weeks spent apart," he whispered in my ear before leading me into the bedroom. I didn't resist him this time.

His touch felt familiar and warm, but I could hardly feel anything. No sizzle or passion. I just kept going through the motions of lovemaking, hoping he would not notice the change in me. Once we were done, I ran into the shower and cried for several minutes. No longer could I deny that an invisible wall had been planted between us. The wall I created myself with my mistakes.

Twenty-Three

"Becky, is everything all right?" Jason asked me as we were walking back from the beach the next day.

Although I kept pretending to be happy, I couldn't let go of the heaviness that was weighing down on my chest. Especially since the last night.

"Yes, I'm okay," I replied, fighting back my tears.

"You haven't been acting yourself lately. I can tell something is wrong."

"Maybe I'm just wary of the war threat," I lied.

"I can imagine. It's a bit hard to relax when your favorite vacation spot is in the headlines every day."

I would have broken down right at this moment if it weren't for Shlomo, the guy from Kiryat Adar, standing at a small booth and selling fresh juice.

"Shlomo! Good to see you!" I was a bit surprised to find him there.

"Rebecca! *Ma nishma*?"

"*Ani beseder, toda.* This is Jason, my husband. This is Shlomo. We met in Kiryat Adar."

"Nice to meet you." Jason offered him a handshake.

"So, what brings you to Tel Aviv?" I asked.

"Our house came under direct fire, and we had to be evacuated. That's why I'm here now."

I gasped. Indeed, it was his house I'd seen in the news way back at the Albright Institute. He must've been exiled from his home for quite a while.

"I'm sorry to hear that. How are you coping?" I asked.

"It hasn't been easy. Our house was renovated just before the war started, and now we'll have to redo everything when we come back. My wife's really upset over the whole thing. Our kids want to go home. But what can I do?" He shrugged.

"Where are you staying now?"

"At a friend's place. It's a bit small for two families, but it'll be all right."

"Well, I really hope it ends soon."

"Me too." He smiled.

Suddenly, it occurred to me that all my problems were trivial compared to what his family was going through. I had no right to be sad, given that both Jason and I were safe and sound and our home in Toronto was not under any sort of threat. Still, how could I ignore my feelings?

"It was nice seeing you again," I said.

"Would you like something?" he suggested.

I looked at Jason, who just threw away his finished cup of apple juice.

"Let's go for it," he said.

"I'll have an orange juice," I said. "How about you, Jason?"

"The same," he replied.

BY THE end of the day, I made a decision to talk to my husband. The sooner I let the words out, the better it would be for both of us. I wasn't sure how much I would tell him, but at least, I would try explaining the confusion about my career. Jason would surely understand. He had known about my fascination with archaeology for quite a while.

For dinner, I heated the leftover steak and the purée from last night and cut some fresh tomatoes. I also poured us two glasses of wine.

"Jason, there is something I need to tell you," I began after we sat down for a meal.

"Sure," he replied, completely oblivious to what I was going to confess.

"I...I don't know where to start." My nerves started giving way.

"Just tell me what it is." He looked up from his plate, smiling.

"My stay in Israel made me realize how unhappy I am with my current job."

"I've known that for a while. It's very hard not to notice."

"You know that, right?" I cleared my throat.

"Of course, I do. After all, you'd spent four years studying something you're not using. Anyone would be unhappy in your shoes."

"Right." I gulped.

"But you don't have to stay in your job forever," he continued. "I'm sure something great will turn up after you finish your copy-writing program."

"The problem is, I don't want to hold a nine-to-five job anymore. It's just not for me. I need something bigger."

"What is it that you want?"

"I want to go to a grad school."

"Okay." He looked a bit baffled.

"It could involve moving around."

"Like where?"

"The States, Israel, wherever new opportunities arise."

"Hmm, that would be a bit challenging."

"I know. That's why it bothers me so much. I also know how much you want us to have kids."

He got up and walked toward me. "Look, we can come up with something. We can hold off having kids for a while, and you can apply to schools in Canada. It's not the end of the world, Rebecca."

"We can try." I sighed. So now he was accepting my new plan as long as it didn't involve moving around. That was some progress.

"Is it why you've been a bit sad lately?"

"Yes."

"Don't worry. We can make it happen. First, you need to send applications. The rest we'll figure out." He gave me a gentle hug.

"There is another thing I need to tell you." I pulled myself away from him. "I know you'll be mad." I gently moved his right hand away.

"Nothing can make me mad, love."

For a second, I considered salvaging the situation by changing the topic or turning on the TV. Perhaps I could even suggest going out for another drink or hitting a dance club. And yet, I knew there was no backing out.

"There is this guy named George. I met him back in Kiryat Adar."

"Okay." Even up until this moment he still looked unsuspecting.

"He is a PhD student from Wheaton College. We first started as friends who had a lot in common. We talked about archeology and academic life. We rode buses and ran to bomb shelters together. Then we both ended up working at the Albright Institute. It was completely unplanned."

By the time I finished my speech, I was hyperventilating. I looked up at Jason, trying to find traces of jealousy on his face. His expression was blank.

"When I said we went for a walk to the Old City as a group, I lied. It was only me and George."

"Why did you do that? Why would you lie to me?" He sounded more sad than angry.

"I didn't want you to get mad. I...I kissed him during that walk. It was a terrible mistake, and I promise it will never happen again."

Jason kept quiet. He probably hadn't seen it coming.

"Please say something!" I exclaimed in panic.

"And you brought me all the way here to tell me this?" He stared at me with that blank expression that showed both sadness and a bit of anger.

"Look, I'm really sorry. It's not what you think. I...I'm just confused about my life...and about us."

He stayed silent. Maybe Erin was right, and I shouldn't have said anything to him.

"Is there anything else I need to know?" he asked coldly.

"I often feel like I've missed out on a lot of things in my early twenties. You know I always wanted to travel and to live somewhere else besides Canada. I don't want you to think that I wasn't happy with you. I just...I just...I'm so confused. I don't even know if I can handle it anymore." I started crying.

Looking utterly defeated, Jason moved to the couch. I sat next to him and took his hand.

"I still love you, though, and I really want us to work it out."

"I need time to process everything you just told me."

"Take as much time as you need. I just want you to know that I'm terribly sorry over everything, and it hurts me to tell the truth."

"Good night, Rebecca." He bolted up and walked toward the small room. I heard the door slam behind him. Tears rising in my eyes, I went back to the dining table and quietly cleared our plates of unfinished food.

I wanted to talk longer. I would've preferred that we have a proper fight, throw things around, and call each other names. At least, I would know what was going through his mind. I wondered if there was a tiny chance he would forgive me, but I wouldn't know until we spoke again. For the rest of the evening, I lay down on a large, empty bed and stared into space, unable to believe our marriage had arrived at this point.

I recalled all the happy moments Jason and I had shared together, from our first walk in a park to our first renovation project. I recalled the morning before our wedding, when I was standing in front of a mirror in a beautiful white dress, full of hopes, while Mom and Erin were fixing my hair and makeup.

I couldn't say I'd had no reservations about marrying so early in my life. The spring of that year, our archaeology team from the U of T was planning a trip to Syria, and I was invited along. Since the excavation was to happen in April and my wedding was in June, I could have easily gone. Caught up with the romance and the wedding preparations, I refused.

Halfway into the excavation season, I began to doubt my decision to stay in Toronto. Then I started doubting my decision to commit so fast. The doubts weren't too strong, considering how happy I was feeling, but they were still present. A year later, I learned this opportunity was gone forever along with many others. Maybe if I'd listened to those pesky voices in my head, Jason and I would be in a happier place.

Twenty-four

By midnight, it became clear to me that I wouldn't be able to fall asleep. Although I was no longer crying, the adrenaline was still pumping in my veins. I tiptoed to Jason's room and peeked in. He was lying quietly on the first level of the double bed, eyes closed.

"Go away," he mumbled, without even looking at me.

I put on the first thing I found in the closet, which was the same beaded orange dress I had worn to the beach the morning before leaving Kiryat Adar. Back then, I was still happy and carefree, even with the missile threat looming. I grabbed the car keys from the living room table and left.

Our Ford was parked outside in a reserved spot. I quickly unlocked it and got behind the wheel. As soon as I started the ignition, the GPS turned itself on and asked me where I wanted to go. Without even thinking twice, I typed "Shimoni Hotel, Kiryat Adar."

The streets were still buzzing with nightlife, but the traffic was relatively light. I drove around the city for a bit until I finally exited onto the highway. I had never driven in a foreign country alone. In fact, I hardly ever drove in Toronto. Doing something different for the very first time felt strangely liberating. Moreover, reaching my destination was unbelievably easy. I simply followed the directions and let the highway signs take me to the place. If only everything else in life was that simple!

First, I headed to see my favorite alley leading to the beach. I loved being on the familiar path, embraced by a light breeze. The waves were strong enough to carry me all the way to Cyprus, but I dared to step into the sea and take a couple of steps. The touch of the salty water felt incredibly refreshing.

Then I walked to the bar our group used to visit during the first week and a half. It was the same happy place I'd known earlier. Couples and groups of young people were everywhere enjoying late hours while bartenders were going around and serving everyone.

"Would you like something to drink?" a waiter asked me in Hebrew. I wondered if he remembered me from my previous walk-ins.

I asked if he had any tea, and he quickly disappeared behind the rack. A minute later, he showed up with a box of different tea bags and asked me to choose one. I chose green tea.

"Driving?" he asked, smiling.

"Yes."

"So, what are you doing here at such a late hour?"

"I had a fight with my husband and needed to get away," I blurted.

"Ah, I see."

I half expected him to start making all the stupid comments about me looking young and so forth. Instead, he wished me all the best and disappeared. Before I had a chance to thank him, he was already on to another customer. He probably had tons of visitors like me coming to shake off their problems. As soon as I finished my drink, I went back to my car. I already knew what my next stop would be.

The Kiryat Adar National Park looked even more majestic at night, with the Roman pillars shining under the moonlight glow. I walked around for a bit, inhaling the summer air of the night and taking time to explore each and every grid. During the brief excavation season, I had mostly been confined to one area and never bothered exploring other parts of the site, believing there was still plenty of time left. Having reached my grid, I leaned down and gently touched the ground. This was the earth from which I had pulled out my first treasure—the Canaanite goddess figurine. I let the earth slip through my fingers.

Why did I have to choose between my calling and my marriage? If I sacrificed my dreams for the sake of our relationship, would we be happy twenty years from now? Did I even have to make this sacrifice? Was there any chance that Jason could become part of the world that was so dear to me? Would he even want to take me back after everything I had done to him?

As the time was now way past midnight, I decided to return to the hotel. In the morning, everything would become clearer. I was pretty sure Jason would talk to me by then, for he wasn't the type to hold grudges. Just as I was driving away, my phone rang. I tried ignoring it, but it rang again, this time louder. I had no choice but to pull over and reply.

"Becky, where on earth are you?" my husband yelled on the other line.

"I'm in Kiryat Adar."

"What the hell are you doing there during this hour?"

"You told me to leave, so I went for a quick ride." I rolled my eyes.

"Okay, I'm sorry, Becky. I overreacted."

"Overreacted? I was convinced you wouldn't want to see me again."

"Can you tell me where you are, for goodness' sake?"

"I'm at the Kiryat Adar ruins."

"Just a second...thank you..." I heard him mumble to someone else.

"Hey, where are you? I'm going back to the hotel."

"No! Stay where you are. I'm coming to get you...I'll take this car. Thanks."

"Jason, I'm coming back! Do you hear me?" The phone went silent.

As soon as I started the car, the voice on the GPS asked me about the directions. Feeling certain that I knew my way back well, I turned off the system and turned on the radio instead. I cruised through the highway, Radio Noshmim Mizrahit blasting slow and melancholic love songs from the speakers. It wasn't until I saw signs leading to Sderot that I realized I was in the wrong place. I quickly pulled over to the side and pressed the "start" button on the GPS. My phone rang again.

"Jason, I'm driving back!" I yelled without even bothering to ask who was calling.

"Becky, are you all right? I'm almost in Kiryat Adar."

"No, I'm not. I don't know where I am at the moment. I think I'm close to Sderot."

"You should've stayed at the park."

"Fine! I should've done many things differently." I couldn't believe we were arguing at such a wrong time.

The siren rang on the other line.

"Oh, my God! Get out of the car and lie face down on the ground. Now!" I commanded. The line went dead.

I had to get to him fast. However, I had no idea where I was going. I failed to set up the GPS because it began to glitch. So I continued driving, my hands shaking more with every second. The highway was almost empty. Who would be driving at three in the morning, especially when shelling was happening nearby?

Out of nowhere, some animal jumped on the road. Although it was hard to see in the dark, the creature looked like a goat. I slammed on the brakes with the greatest force possible, but it was too late. The car was a few inches away from what was definitely an ibex and still going forward. In my last attempt to salvage the situation, I sharply turned the wheel to the side of the road and felt my car hit something. Suddenly, I felt immense pain and saw blood splatter on the dashboard. Then everything went blank.

Twenty-five

"Where am I?" I asked upon coming to my senses. Every part of me was in pain. My neck was surrounded by a hideous collar, preventing me from moving, and my entire body was connected to some strange tubes.

"Shhh. It's all right." Jason put his index finger over my mouth.

"I must've had a bad dream."

"You've been in a light car accident," he said. "But you're going to be okay," he added, as if trying to calm me.

As soon as I began to feel a bit better, another awful realization gripped me. If I'd been in an accident, I must've gotten seriously injured, or worse, gotten someone else hurt. After all, I was in great physical pain and hardly able to move.

"Did I lose a limb?" I asked in horror. "Am I disabled?"

"No, Becky," he replied in a soft voice. "You just have lots of cuts from the broken windshield."

I tried wriggling my two legs and felt relieved to find them in place. My right arm was normal; my left one, bandaged. I touched my face with the left hand and, with much relief, discovered that it didn't have any cuts.

"Wait." My memory started returning to me.

Jason and I had a row, which turned nasty. He told me to leave, so I went to drive around the town to calm my nerves. Somehow,

I ended up on a nearly empty highway. What I couldn't remember was how I ended up in the hospital.

A moment later, I remembered everything. Driving in the wrong direction. Getting phone calls from my husband urging me to wait for him. Hearing sirens on the other line. The feeling of panic I couldn't control.

"Was there a missile threat last night?" I asked.

"No, it turned out to be a false alarm," he replied.

"You scared me so much, Jason."

"I'm afraid I have to say the same."

"I'm sorry for everything." That was all I could muster for the moment.

"Me too, Becky. I should've never told you to leave."

"How long am I going to stay here?"

"It's up to the doctors. They told me you sustained multiple cuts from broken glass that had to be surgically removed and a broken arm. They might keep you for a few more days to make sure you're safe to fly home."

"I see. What about the car? What happened to it?"

"The front got completely smashed."

"Oh, no!"

"Don't worry. Our insurance will cover the damage. It was a miracle you survived, considering the seriousness of the accident." He paused for a second and looked to the side. He had heavy bags under his eyes, and his hair was matted. "Look, all that matters is that you're alive despite everything. Now, you need to take good care of yourself to recover." He sat down on the edge of the bed and moved even closer to me. "We'll get through this, Becky. We really will."

"Does it mean that you forgive me?"

"Of course, I do!"

A feeling of relief coursed through my veins. I wanted to continue talking to him, holding his hand, but our conversation got interrupted by a sixty-something-year-old man who walked into the room. He was wearing a lab coat and had a stethoscope around his neck.

"Good afternoon, I'm Dr. Greenberg, your surgeon," he said.

"Hi, Doctor." I tried to sound cheerful despite the excruciating pain in my left arm.

"Is it okay if we talk alone?" He turned to Jason.

"Sure, I'll wait for you outside."

Jason got up and walked over to the door. I noticed that something about the way he acted spoke of sadness. He must've been pretty shaken by the whole accident.

"Okay, where shall we begin?" the doctor said

"How bad is it?" I asked as soon as we were alone in the room.

"Well, you were very lucky considering that you'd hit a sign pole and got several lacerations from the shattered glass."

While I already knew the part about the broken glass, the information about the sign pole was completely new to me—and shocking, indeed.

"Sounds like it was a very dangerous accident," I murmured.

"An understatement of the century," he replied. "Rebecca, if you hadn't slammed on the brakes in time, you could've easily died. But since you braked way before your car hit the pole, the impact was much lighter than it could've been. Luckily, you got away with a broken arm and some cuts which we were able to patch in time."

I lay, my mouth agape, trying to absorb all the new information.

"How long will it take me to get back to normal?" I asked at last.

"Well, the bone will take around six weeks to heal. If all goes well, we'll let you go in a couple of days."

"Can I start walking?" I asked. I knew I had to be grateful for the turn of events, but the idea of spending six weeks in bed still terrified me to no end.

"Absolutely! We encourage our patients to resume normal life as soon as possible."

"Wonderful! Thank you, Doctor."

"No problem, Rebecca. We'll talk to you about managing the broken bone later. For now, I think you need to rest a little. I know it's all new information for you."

"I know. Well, thank you, anyway."

"You're welcome. I'll take off now." He grabbed his bag and walked out of the room.

I sighed with relief. After all, things weren't as bad as they seemed. I was still alive, and Jason had just said that he forgave me. I still had to contact my family about the accident and have that lengthy conversation with my husband about our respective futures, but now that I'd risked losing something greater, all the issues of yesterday appeared manageable. We would work through them, somehow. I knew it now for sure.

Twenty-six

The next few days went by in a blur. There was a constant stream of doctors and nurses coming in, doing tests, and administering medications. Jason mostly stayed by my side, always available whenever I needed help. Despite his presence, we seldom talked, and most of our conversations were curt and formal. Sometimes, he even looked a bit distant and detached. I suspected he needed more time to fully let go of the hurt, but I didn't mind waiting. As long as we were headed into that direction, everything would be fine.

On the day of my discharge from the hospital, his moods seemed to have picked up a little. He even suggested taking me to a falafel place to celebrate my recovery. I reminded him that, technically, I wasn't recovered yet, as my arm was still required to remain in a cast. It was only during our drive back to the hotel that he eased up a little.

"I'm glad to have bought the insurance," I said as our new car cruised the desert highway.

"I agree," he said. "But if I knew how this trip would've turned out, I would've never let you come here in the first place." He briefly looked into my direction before turning back to the road.

"But why?" I felt my defenses rise. Did he no longer trust me enough to let me travel alone?

"Because it obviously did some damage to you and to us."

"But I also learned a lot because of this trip," I retorted. "If I were to go back in time, I would've avoided a lot of mistakes, like hanging out with George alone or driving at night, but I would've still gone to Kiryat Adar. It helped me to realize what I want out of my life."

"Right, it did." He drove into a gas station and stopped the car at the closest parking lot.

"Where are we going?" I asked

"I think we should grab something before we get back to the hotel," he replied. I reluctantly followed him from the car over to the service center.

We stayed in line for the longest time ever to get our coffees and sandwich wraps. I couldn't wait to talk to him again, as his last words before we left the car made me feel perplexed and a bit worried. What if he would never understand my passion for archaeology? Would I have to compromise my dreams to patch things up with him?

"So, I think we need to have a serious talk," he said once we were seated at the table, ready to eat. My broken arm still hurt like crazy, but I was getting used to doing everything with one hand.

"Yes, I'm listening." I took a sip from my coffee.

"I know this world is important to you, Becky."

"If you mean the scholarly world, then the answer is yes." I wasn't sure what he was hinting at. "As a matter of fact, I'm still considering applying to grad schools once we get home."

"I know. But I'm not sure if I can be a part of this."

"W...what?" My stomach dropped.

"Look, you're probably going to move to a different city, meet new and exciting people." He turned away as if trying to hide something. Some difficult emotion.

"Wait, are you telling me we should split?" I asked, my pain rising to the greatest magnitude.

"Exactly." Traces of sadness and regret began to show on his face.

"But, why? I thought we were on the road to making things work between us."

"I'm afraid that if we stay together, it isn't going to work. You want to study and travel the world, which is totally understandable considering that you're still only twenty-six."

"We could do these things together."

"We want different things from life, Becky. You want to go back to school while I want to settle down and have kids. I don't think that staying together would be fair for either of us."

In a moment, my entire world came crashing down. I'd been so desperate for us to get back on track that I'd completely overlooked all the warning signs. The short and stifled conversations that dominated our world in the last few days. The distant look in his eyes. Now all of this made sense. Jason was still hurting from my betrayal.

"So I guess it's over." Tears welled up in my eyes.

"We don't have to cut each other off completely. We can still be friends, if you'd like."

"Well, we still have to make it back to Tel Aviv and to Toronto."

"Exactly. I don't want you hate me for my suggestion. I just feel it'll be the best decision in our case."

"Fine. Let's go back to the car." I carried my tray over to the garbage bin and placed the cup of cold, unfinished coffee on the top. Jason followed my lead.

We drove home in silence. He remained completely focused on the road while I sat quietly by his side and tried to process everything that had transpired between us in the last hour. The logic kept telling me that splitting would be the right thing to do in light of our situation. Yet in my heart, the decision felt wrong. Regardless of how I felt, I knew that if he decided to separate, there would be no point in trying to convince him to stay.

SILENCE PENETRATED the walls of our hotel apartment as we packed our bags for home, each in a separate room. Jason offered his help, but I refused, preferring to do everything with one hand, despite the task being ridiculously difficult. The less I saw of him, I decided, the better. I only asked him for help when I had to carry the suitcase to the entrance, which I wouldn't be able to accomplish alone.

He later offered his help in letting me take a shower and change for the night, but once again, I declined. Letting him see me in that state could create room for crossing the line, which I didn't want to happen now that we were no longer together.

Hence, I manoeuvred out of my Kiriat Adar T-shirt and shorts and slipped into a nightgown alone. He volunteered to sleep in the guest bedroom while I was left alone in the large bedroom with little to do but think everything over.

I still had to decide where I would stay upon returning home. Although he told me several times through the evening that I could get the condo after our separation, I knew I wouldn't be able to stay in the place filled with so many memories.

Shortly before going to bed, I phoned Erin. I stayed in touch with my family back at the hospital, who despite being completely mortified by the news, were also relieved I had survived the accident. Now I had to disclose the news of our separation. As I waited for the phone operator to connect the call, I could almost see her disapproving stare and hear her say, *haven't I told you so?*

"Hello?" she said.

"Hi, Erin. It's Becky."

"Oh, hi! How're you feeling?"

"A bit better. Listen, I need to ask you for a favor."

"Sure."

"Jason and I decided to separate. It's a long story, but the bottom line is, I need your support at the moment, not judgement. So please don't start the whole charade having warned me about marrying young and stuff."

"Oh, no, definitely not. I can be mean sometimes, but I understand what you're going through." Erin's voice sounded much softer than the last time we'd talked.

"Can I stay at your place for a couple of weeks? I'll need time to sort through things."

"By all means, yes. You can stay for as long as you like. I've got a nice sofa bed you can use."

"Thank you, Erin!"

"No worries, Becky."

"Thank you so much, Erin. Will I see you tomorrow?"

"Of course! What time is your plane arriving?"

"Six thirty in the evening. Terminal one."

"Great. I'll be waiting for you at the airport."

"Bye now."

Having propped the broken arm on the pillow just as the doctor instructed, I tried closing my eyes and falling asleep. Yet I simply couldn't. Everything about our separation felt wrong. I wanted to crawl into his room and beg for another chance. I wanted to cry hard until he agreed to take me back and at least try to make it work. Still, there was no backing out of our decision. I would have to relearn to be alone.

Be strong, Becky, I told myself, closing my eyes. *Time will heal all the wounds.*

At least, I was alive and relatively well, which was more than I could ask for. The path to healing would be a difficult one, but with time, I would learn how to cope.

Twenty-seven

I requested to be seated away from him on the plane. He reminded me that we were still friends, still married, to be precise, but I insisted on sitting as far away as possible. Spending time with Jason brought out all of the many happy memories that would make the whole separation much harder. Naturally, this wasn't the way I'd envisioned our week in Tel Aviv—the carefree, fun-filled week I had in mind when planning this trip. The last thing I could ever imagine was that we would be coming home from our vacation barely talking to each other or sitting at the opposite ends of the plane.

I tried reading the latest *BAR* issue just to pass the time, but couldn't concentrate on the words. A few times, I passed his aisle to find him engrossed in a plane magazine or a newspaper. Although he seemed focused on reading, the expression on his face spoke of sadness and detachment. Once again, I wondered how our almost five-year-old marriage had come to this point.

"Hey, Becky. Come and sit here," he said upon noticing me. He patted the empty seat next to him.

"No," I said firmly. If I let myself come even an inch closer to him, I would probably break down into tears. I couldn't let that happen in a place full of people.

We kept our contact to a minimum upon landing in Toronto despite the fact that all I wanted was to throw myself into his arms and cry. By the way he was looking at me, I could tell that he wasn't completely at peace with this decision, either.

Having finished the immigration control, we proceeded to pick up our suitcases and meet our respective families. I knew this mini reunion would not only appear awkward but also painful. I rarely saw his parents, and yet, I knew I would miss them terribly.

"Rebecca!" My sister ran toward me as soon as we walked into the waiting zone. My parents followed her lead.

"Becky, darling! We missed you so much!" My mother literally threw herself at me.

"Ouch. Be careful." I instinctively moved away from her lest she touched the broken arm.

"Oh, I'm sorry, love. How's your hand?" she asked.

"It's a bit better, though the fracture still hurts," I admitted.

"So," Jason's mother interrupted. "I assume the two of you are pretty tired after the flight. We should probably drive you home and leave you alone."

"Yes," Jason said. "Becky needs a lot of rest to recover."

"Come on, I'm not sick anymore," I protested.

"I think your husband has a valid point," my mother said.

"Look," I began. "I know you're all excited to see us back, and I'm happy to see everyone too. I also know that what I'm about to say will shock you."

"Becky, please." My husband tried stopping me.

"Jason and I decided to separate." There, I'd said it. No need to pretend or wait 'til the "right moment" to deliver the news.

My announcement was followed by a pause of silence. Both of our parents looked at me with mouths agape. Just a month ago, we were perfectly happy together, and now, we barely spoke.

"Well, if that's what works best for you, then we ought to respect your decision," Erin said calmly.

I felt a bit annoyed by her cold reaction, but didn't say anything. She never approved of our marriage in the first place, and now she was acting like the separation was no big deal.

"Erin, can you take me to your place?" I asked.

"Definitely. Let's go." She signaled me to keep moving.

"Wait." Jason ran after us. "Are you sure you don't want to stop at our place and pick up your things first?" he asked.

"It's okay. I'll do that tomorrow," I replied, eager to get away from him.

"Remember, we're seeing your family doctor in a few days," he added.

Shoot! I'd completely forgotten about this follow-up appointment we arranged way back in Israel. Since he knew the case with the arm, he wanted to accompany me. As much as I wanted to protest, I knew I needed him for as long as my bone wasn't healed completely.

"We'll talk about that tomorrow, Jason. Bye now," I told him. "Thank you, everyone, for coming down to the airport."

"You're welcome," our mothers said in unison.

"OH, DEAR! You don't look like yourself at all," Erin remarked as I was trying to unpack my suitcase with one hand. "Here, you rest, and I'll unpack your stuff." She helped me to get seated on her couch in a way that made my broken arm comfortable. "You shouldn't be doing anything yourself until you're completely healed. I know that living with a broken arm must be very hard for you. I still remember how horrible it felt when I broke mine during gym class."

I briefly recalled the memory of twelve-year-old Erin coming home with a bandaged hand, her innocent face stricken with pain. The accident that happened when she'd been trying to catch the ball during volleyball practice must've been the greatest shock to her at time. Mom and I did our best to take care of her, but all we could really do was make her as comfortable as possible and wait for the bone to heal itself.

"It's okay, Erin. I'm already used to the new mode of doing things."

"Still, I think you need to rest more, Becky. Look, I'm planning to take off time at work to be with you."

"No, don't do it! I'll be completely fine by myself."

"Too late. I already filed for a temporary leave of absence."

"No way! You should've talked to me first."

"What's done is done, Becky. Now, will you please stop arguing with your older sister and get ready for dinner? I made us lasagna."

"Wow, you're amazing, Erin!"

"Thanks." She smiled. "Now, let's get up and get ready for dinner."

I had little choice in this matter other than to oblige.

Twenty-eight

An oldies song by Shimi Tavori droned in the background as I sat in Erin's home office and worked on the excavation report. It had been three weeks since our return to Toronto, and for the first time, Erin had agreed to let me stay alone.

She hardly ever left my side, except for the short trips to a grocery store and one awful time when Jason had to take me to the doctor. An awkward experience I'd rather forget. To tell the truth, I didn't really want to bring him to the appointment, but he insisted that he should follow me since he knew all about the accident and the fracture. I hadn't seen or spoken to him ever since.

In the meantime, Erin was always by my side, taking care to ensure that I had all my needs met while I adjusted to living with a broken arm. She cooked all the meals and wouldn't even let me go near the kitchen despite the fact that I was perfectly capable of making myself a sandwich or pouring a cup of coffee. She helped with taking showers and getting dressed, which kind of felt embarrassing, but there was little I could do myself until the arm got better. She even made occasional attempts to cheer me up by turning on some funny sitcom I was in no mood to watch. All in all, Erin had been a great sister and a friend, but recently, I've been craving solitude.

Now that she was gone for a considerably long time (I convinced her to return back to work part time), I could finally sit back and play my favorite music without anyone constantly hovering over me. Erin was a ton of fun to hang out with, but Israeli and Middle Eastern music was a big no-no for her. Even now that I was into the second refrain of Shimi's song, I could see Erin's disapproving stare. Back in the days when we were just teenagers, she would lecture me about my tastes being weird and uncool and how no one would want to hang out with me if I didn't change into a normal Maple Leaf-obsessed Canadian girl. Although I knew she cared for me, I often felt frustrated by her inability to fully comprehend my inner world. I now suspected that no one ever would. Not even Jason, whom I once believed to be my soul mate.

My mind trailed back to the sensational find of the second day—the Canaanite goddess figurine. I could still recall the fascination I felt when I held the figurine covered in sand and earth with my bare hands. Asherah, a mother goddess, the queen consort of god El, worshipped throughout Canaan and beyond. Her figurines and cultic stands have been discovered through Israel and Jordan. The one I found was now safely stored at the Israel Antiquities Authority, whose members were still determining its future, and I hoped it would end in one of the museums someday.

I took care to include a detailed description of the find and point at similarities between other figurines discovered in the past—clay objects depicting of a woman in a long skirt supporting her breasts which symbolized fertility. I also mentioned other finds that had been discovered in the adjacent grids, including a piece of Red Slip ware and a handle from a Philistine storage jar. And of course, I mentioned that last-minute changes to the project, including the team's relocation to Megiddo and my move to the Albright Institute. I concluded this report by explaining how this experience helped me grow as an individual.

The typing part was rather challenging, since the movement in my broken arm was still limited. However, I enjoyed creating this draft of the report. It helped take my mind off other things, like the impending divorce, uncertainty over the future, and looming loneliness.

Feeling a bit weary from typing, I decided to check Facebook. Many friend requests were still waiting for me, including those from the former Kiryat Adar participants. As I was going through the list, I saw a familiar face. The girl strongly reminded me of someone I had met at the Albright Institute.

When I looked closer, I realised that without any doubt, Zeinab Assaf was Ibrahim's daughter. She had the same eyes as her father, greenish-brown, sad, but also kind. She was online, and according to her music app, she was listening to "Ruah Yam" by Ofer Levi.

"Hi," I messaged her. "How did you find me?"

"Rebecca! I'm so happy to hear from you! My father has been talking a lot about you lately. Are you feeling better?"

"As a matter of fact, yes. Thanks for asking." Her question caught me a bit off guard. Did she know about my accident?

"We were so worried when your story appeared in the local newspaper. I'm so happy you're doing fine."

"Wow, I didn't know my accident made it into local papers," I wrote back.

"It did, and made us all worried, especially my Dad. We were so happy when your life was declared out of danger."

In truth, I had no idea about the papers. I felt touched by the fact that Ibrahim remembered me from our short encounter at the cafeteria and even told his family about me. Maybe I was wrong to have declined his invitation to visit his family. But what else could I do with all the tourist warnings and stigma associated with the Palestinian people? Seriously, I had to stop believing everything the media said about this world.

"I hope we can be friends," I typed. "I noticed you like *mizrahi* music."

"Yes. I'm in love with Radio Lev Hamedina and Noshmim Mizrahi even though most of their singers support Netanyahu, and we don't like him. He doesn't want us to have our land."

"I understand. It must be a very complicated situation." It dawned on me that I knew so little about the entire conflict despite having been a first-hand witness to a missile threat and the damage it could cause to ordinary lives. Maybe I needed to learn more about the other side.

"Anyway, I have to go now, but let's stay in touch," Zeinab wrote. I wrote back a goodbye before she disconnected from the messenger.

After finishing this short conversation, I decided to go through the letters, most of which were from acquaintances who wanted to offer words of sympathy. One of those was from George who, according to the letter, was very sorry about the accident but, at the same time, relieved that I had survived it and was doing relatively well. Although it'd been a while now, I still felt hurt by his revelation during the reunion dinner. Especially after the damage our encounter had done to my marriage with Jason, and to my life in general. I closed the browser and walked to the kitchen to fix myself a cup of tea. If Erin saw me now, she would've made a big fuss about it, but luckily, she wasn't home yet. Just as I was about to take the first sip, something registered in my mind.

Did I want to bear this grudge for the rest of my life even if I was still a bit hurt by the whole situation? Did I want him to think I was another crazy girl whose world was filled with drama? Even though he played his part in my downfall, it was I who brought all the troubles upon myself. I should've never let his great looks or our similar interests cloud my judgement. I should've never gone out with him knowing my vulnerability to his charms. And he had every right to go on with his life even if it involved only work for now. It was time to own up to my mistakes and find closure. I put the cup on the counter and ran back to the computer, where I typed up a quick reply thanking him for the letter and wishing him all the best. Having hit the "send" button, I sighed with relief. This chapter in my life was closed forever.

I went on to the next message, lest I become consumed with regret again. What I saw next nearly made my heart stop. The letter was from none other than Rachel, my former roommate, AKA the meanest girl on the planet.

> Hi, Rebecca,
>
> I'm so sorry for being so mean to you during our dig. I was simply trying to get my life on track. I'll never forgive myself for the way I acted toward you during the time we shared a room. Seeing you in the news made me realize how stupid I've been. I know you'll probably never forgive me, but I want you to know that I'm sorry. I hope you feel better soon.
>
> Rachel

The letter was so sincere that it almost made me cry. What's more, it'd been sitting in my mailbox for almost a month, and I could only imagine how awful she was feeling about my lack of response. Guilt was the worst feeling in the world, far worse than the feeling of hurt or betrayal. I typed a reply without thinking twice.

> Hi, Rachel,
>
> Thank you for the letter. I should've replied earlier, but I've been too busy getting all the necessary help. I'm back in Toronto and feeling much better. Let's forget about everything that transpired between us.
>
> Rebecca

A minute later, she wrote me back.

Hi, Rebecca,

I'm so happy you're safe and sound! Please tell me you're not disabled! I won't be able to sleep until I get your reply.

Rachel

The situation was far worse than I imagined. Not only had she been waiting for my response for all this time, but she was also worrying about the damage of my accident. Truly, she didn't deserve such pain even if she'd said hurtful things in the past. I typed up a response reassuring her that, despite having to get around with a broken arm, I was doing well. She thanked me profusely for my response before suggesting to stay in touch via Facebook. A huge relief swooshed over me after I typed the last word in our conversation. I hoped it would become an end to our conflict, another closed chapter.

After disconnecting from Facebook, I went on Google and spent the next few minutes researching graduate programs in Near Eastern archaeology.

What have I done? I asked myself in panic while reading admission requirements for one of the international universities. Every single university I was interested in required an expensive fee to apply plus GRE tests, which I knew nothing of. The tuition fees and the living costs for all the universities looked astronomical. To top it off, there were virtually no guarantees that I would get a job after graduating from a masters or PhD program.

The reality hit me. I had traded a good marriage and a stable job for a path of uncertainty. Maybe it was for the best that Jason had walked away.

The sound of a key in the lock interrupted my train of thought. I hastily turned off the music knowing how Erin would react if she heard "that shit" playing in her house. Then I went forth to the living room to greet her.

"Here you are." She put away her purse and ran toward me with open arms.

"What brings you home so early?" I asked.

"Remember I arranged to work part time for the next few days?"

"Still, you could've stayed longer. I'm totally fine getting around by myself."

"Ha, you won't get rid of me that easily." She walked to the kitchen and turned on the kettle. "So, have you thought about your future?" she asked, noting a cup of cooling tea on her countertop.

"Yes. As a matter-of-fact, I'm thinking about applying to a bunch of grad schools," I replied despite being unsure of my decision.

"Great! We all want to succeed, Becky. Me, Mom, Dad. Everyone wants you to be happy."

"Oh, that means the world to me." I walked over to her side and gave her a hug.

"Mom invited us for a dinner tonight. Should've told you earlier."

"Really? That's wonderful." I'd been avoiding my parents since the return to escape any unpleasant questions or conversations, but all that time, I'd also been missing them.

"Let's get ready then."

Twenty-nine

A late summer breeze tangled my hair as we were walking toward Erin's car across the outdoor parking lot. The weather had been just perfect for late August. It was warm but not too hot, with a few clouds here and there. After the longest wait for the summer back in May, this recent weather seemed like a perfect compensation for the fierce winter and the long spring.

The drive to our parents' place had been smooth and quiet. Erin seemed to have been preoccupied with her own thoughts. I couldn't quite tell what she was thinking about at that moment, but judging by the tense expression on her face, she wasn't exactly in a happy mood.

It wasn't until we reached our parents' house in Annex that she spoke, and even then, her comment was about something related to the scarcity of parking spots in the area. The house where our parents lived had been built a long time ago, and like the majority of homes in the area, it didn't have a proper driveway. Hence, most drivers left their cars on side roads wherever they could find space, while homeowners had to register with the city authorities for a reserved parking spot.

"Here you are!" Our mother ran toward us as soon as we got out of the car. "Becky, darling! How are feeling? We've been missing you over here."

"Much better," I replied. "Thanks for asking."

"Let's go inside. Dad made a cake for you."

The smell of our father's signature shepherd's pie tickled our noses as we walked inside. The sight of antique furniture and the unique smell of this old house brought back all those memories of my premarriage years. Back then, my life seemed hard, but recently, I've been doubtful if the small-scale problems of university life could be attributed to hardships at all.

"Hey, girls." Our father was standing by the stove, wearing an apron and a pair of cooking gloves. With his early gray hair and an unforgettable smile, he looked adorable. "Help yourselves with a seat." He pointed at the dining table.

Our mother served us the cake and tea from the antique china set she'd brought all the way from Oakville. Rumor had it that the set had been passed from our great-grandmother on the maternal side.

Throughout the evening, we discussed random topics, including their upcoming trip to California in the fall and my imminent return to work. They took care not to mention my separation from Jason or the accident except for a few questions about my healing bone.

I asked if I could stay over for a night. I did it partly because I wanted to spend some time alone in my former room and because I felt Erin deserved a break. My mother gladly agreed. She'd been offering me a place to stay ever since my arrival, but something kept stopping me. Tonight, I had the chance to revisit all the high school and university memories, good and bad, and perhaps find the answers to the bugging questions about the course of my life.

My mother knocked on the door and asked if I needed any help as I was trying to wriggle out of my shorts and T-shirt into a nightgown she always kept for my rare overnight visits. I told her that I was fine. After all, my broken arm was getting stronger, as my physical exercises prescribed by the doctors were finally doing their job. After I was completely changed and under the covers, I told her to come in.

"How is my girl doing?" She took a seat on my bed.

It was then and there I burst into tears. I'd been managing to hold it together quite well for a while, but at this moment, all the doubts and difficult emotions came on the surface.

"Here, let me hold you." She moved closer and offered me a hug. "Cry, child. Let it all out," she spoke softly as I sobbed into her shoulder.

"Mom, I don't know what I'm doing," I said after breaking away from her. "My marriage has fallen apart practically overnight; I'm about to pursue something that has little-to-no guarantees for success; and all along, I want to do the right thing, at least this time."

"Well, you don't need to have all the answers now." Her voice was smooth and soothing.

"But I want to!" I said, wiping my face with tissue I found in a box resting on the nightstand. "Back in Jerusalem, I thought that going to grad school would be the wisest thing considering how much I love archaeology, but now that I have all the information in front of me, I no longer know what the heck I'm doing. And did I mention that I still miss Jason like crazy?"

"It's understandable, Becky. He was such a good man. I believe he partly did this to give you a fair chance at life. And I think you need to take it with both hands. Have you looked up the applications yet?"

"Yes. I've signed up for night classes in French and German for this fall." Such was a requirement for most of the programs I was interested in—a need to have a reading knowledge of both languages to comprehend foreign scholarly articles.

"That's wonderful, Becky. At least, you have a plan."

"But I don't know if it's worth all the sacrifices. I mean, Jason and I could still be together if it wasn't my quest for a different life."

"Becky, let me tell you something."

"Yes." I looked at her.

"You know I might be a bit old now, but I was once a young girl, too, with dreams and all."

"Well, you don't look old at all." I laughed for the first time since dinner.

"Anyway, I used to have that all-encompassing fascination with geology during junior high. You see, when I was little, your grandfather used to travel a lot. Sometimes, he would bring small boxes of rocks and minerals from his expeditions."

I had faint memories of my grandfather, Brandon Cadwell, a famous geologist who used to spend months in Alberta doing research. Unfortunately, he died when I was still a small child, so I didn't remember much about him.

"At some point, I became obsessed with rocks. I wanted to know more about them, from their composition to opacity. I started asking my father a lot of questions. My parents freaked out, thinking that I would grow up to become a geologist and never get married or have kids. Anything remotely related to this field became forbidden. 'Geology is not for girls,' your grandma would tell me."

"How awful!" I exclaimed. I couldn't imagine archaeology becoming banned in our house.

"I continued sneaking into my father's room and playing with rocks whenever he wasn't around. As I grew older, I started going into my school's library and reading books about mountains and volcanoes. It was a secret I kept during my teen years."

"Did your classmates ever think you were weird?"

"I didn't tell anyone. They would've made fun of me."

"I see."

"Then I met your father and fell in love for the first time. He knew all about my quirky passion and even promised to take me to the Rockies someday. Since we were very young—I was only seventeen, and he was nineteen—we wanted to wait a few years before getting married. We had plans to finish university and travel the world first. Anthony was already in a culinary school, commuting hundreds of kilometers every day, while I was planning to major in environmental sciences either at Western or York. He and I were thinking about having a long-distance relationship."

I listened to her tell my parents' love story, wondering what it felt like to live and breathe at that time.

"So what made you change your mind?" I asked at last.

"I learned that my father had a terminal illness and was unlikely to live past a year, two maximum."

"That's horrible!" Shock ran through my body like an electric current. I knew that my grandfather had been very ill before he died, but hearing it from my mother brought a whole new dimension to this tragedy.

"No one ever told me in person. I overheard my parents' conversation by accident and learned about his desire to see me married with kids before he would die. He told my mother how much he was yearning to hold a baby for the last time. I ran away before they saw me crying. That day, I found Anthony in a park and told him everything. He immediately proposed, and we got married shortly after my eighteenth birthday."

I gasped. I had always romanticized my parents' young marriage and believed it would become a blueprint for mine. Never could I imagine that it had been founded on broken dreams and shattered hopes.

"Erin was our honeymoon baby," my mother continued. "The day she was born, my parents were overjoyed. It was then when my father had told me about his fatal disease in person and thanked me for granting him the very last wish. I smiled and said, 'Dad, I already know.' He lived way longer than the doctors had expected and was even lucky enough to see you turn five."

I smiled, recalling snippets of that unusually warm day in late September, with the sun shining brightly on our backyard and him showing up at the kids' party, looking unusually thin and sad.

"He died on the next Christmas Eve in his sleep. No one is completely sure what happened to him, but the doctors suspect it was a heart attack."

"It was such a sad holiday season!" My memory trailed back to the ickiest December ever.

The rain kept falling for the entire month, and many even began to give up their hopes for a proper white Christmas. Nevertheless, our family was determined to make the best of this time. My parents made the best roasted turkey, apple cider, and Yule log I could ever remember.

Erin and I were opening our presents when the phone rang. Then our father announced that we had to get ready and leave. When Erin asked what was happening, he didn't say anything. Our mother quickly helped us dress up, and we were soon off to the emergency room. There, I saw my grandfather for the last time. He was lying on a bed, motionless, pale, but with a very peaceful smile on his face.

Needless to say, the holidays came to a halt. My mother spent most of the season together with my grandmother arranging for the funeral. When she wasn't busy, she was mostly by herself, most likely crying, although we never knew for sure.

"So you were forced to put dreams on hold for us," I remarked grimly.

"Please don't get me wrong, Becky. You and your sister are the best thing in my life. I wouldn't have done anything differently if I could go back. But sometimes, when I was too caught up with housework, I felt that something was missing from my life. So I began to look for opportunities to read. Whenever I was nursing or one of you was napping, I would pick a random book and start reading. Then I began to collect books. Friends and relatives would donate me books on everything, from fantasy to romance. I just had to keep on reading to prevent my mind from going stale.

"At some point, our house had so many books that we had to do something about them. Anthony and I decided to organize a garage sale. The event was very successful, and by the end of the day, I came up with an idea to open a bookstore. Your father was initially unsure about it, but we decided to give it a try. Soon enough, I had a full-blown business that was providing us with food and a roof over our heads."

"And you felt happier then, right?"

"Much happier, darling. Although I had to close it down eventually, this business lasted for more than a decade, providing me with a sense of satisfaction every day. I think the real reason why your father and I made it this far was because both of us had something we enjoyed doing. I ran a bookstore while he worked at a restaurant and occasionally helped me with finances and paperwork." She put a strand of hair behind her ear. "Anyway, let's not dwell on the past," she continued. "The reason I told you all of this was to let you know that I'd been in your shoes. So I do understand how you feel about archaeology."

"You were fascinated with volcanoes, right?"

"Yes, I was. When you told us you were going to that Israeli town, I recognized my younger self in you."

"I guess the apple doesn't fall too far from the tree." We laughed, and she hugged me close.

"Rebecca, I'm all up for you and Jason to stay together if that's what you both want. But no matter what happens, you have to put yourself first. I don't want you to have the same regrets that I had. That's why I always encouraged you and Erin to get your degrees first and to settle down later."

"So you do support my choice to go to a grad school?"

"Completely."

"Thank you, Mom. It means so much to me!" We shared another heartfelt embrace.

"Goodnight, darling. You need to rest well to recover."

"Thanks, Mom."

She kissed me gently on the forehead before leaving the room, leaving me alone to my thoughts.

thirty

"You've been very quiet this morning," Erin remarked as we were driving home. She came to pick me up around ten in the morning, and now we were stuck in traffic on Dupont.

"Says who?" I asked, half teasing.

"Me? I'm always in the mood for a talk."

"Not yesterday," I noted.

"I was a bit quieter because of some issues at work." Just by the look on her face, I could tell my sister was fibbing, but I let it slide.

"Anyway, I'm a bit quiet this morning because Mom told me some of our family history yesterday. I mean how she and Dad got married, and you and I came into this world."

"She did?" Erin turned toward me for a second, her eyes tripled in size.

"Yeah. I learned how she wanted to study geology at York but had to marry quickly, so that her dying father would get to hold a child."

"This is awful, isn't it? I mean, imagine waking up every morning knowing that you came to this world because someone else felt obliged to 'do the right thing' by having kids."

"Wait, you knew the truth all along and didn't tell me?" I couldn't believe my sister knew something about my parents that I didn't.

"Of course, I did! Mom told me the story many years ago. I'm surprised she held it off from you for so long. Perhaps, they wanted to protect you."

"I could've handled the truth just fine if it came out earlier."

"It wasn't so easy for me, Becky. I was angry. With everyone. With Mom for sacrificing everything to have us. With Grandpa for forcing her to give up her dreams and have babies."

"But you can't be angry with a dying man! Besides, our grandparents would have never pressured her into anything. She simply overheard their conversation and made her decision."

"I couldn't help myself, Becky. I just hated the whole situation. Most of all, I was angry at myself."

"But why? It wasn't your fault."

"I felt that our parents were forced into having me. I'd rather be the product of a drunken one-night stand than be born out of an obligation. It took me a long time to learn how to forgive."

"How come no one ever told me until today?"

"We didn't want to upset you, Becky. You always thought of us as a happy family."

"I still do, Erin."

"Good for you. I always believed we were a bit dysfunctional."

"No way! I don't think you even know what that word means."

"Do you remember the amount of fighting we did after moving to Toronto? It was a nightmare!" By now, the traffic had cleared a little, and we were moving steadily.

"We were going through tough times, Erin. Well, you weren't, of course, but everyone else, including myself, was walking on eggshells."

"What makes you think I wasn't going through tough times as well?" She put her foot on the break lightly as we approached the traffic light on Yonge and Davenport.

"You were always so happy and cheerful. You loved our new school and your new friends. I couldn't blame you for that."

"Me, loving Evergreens? You gotta be kidding me!" She laughed.

"Wait, is there something else I need to know?"

"I probably hated high school more than you did. That mandatory English class and those science courses I had to take were killing me. I still don't know how I pulled through in the end."

"I hear you, Erin. I struggled with classes too. But at least, you had friends and a boyfriend."

"My friends were all fake, and my boyfriend... I don't even want to talk about him."

"Why? I thought you were happy together."

"We had a lot of problems since the first day we'd met. Trust me, I tried hard to make it work, but we were simply not meant to be."

"Why?"

"He thought I wasn't sophisticated enough for his family."

I gazed at my sister. Erin, the social butterfly, the fashionista! The girl everyone admired. How could she possibly not be sophisticated?

"Remember I brought him home once?" she continued.

"Yes."

"The next day, I asked him why he wouldn't do the same for me. I felt I deserved to know his family. He told me his parents wouldn't approve of me since I wasn't of their level. They wanted him to meet someone from higher circles."

"What?" I couldn't believe my ears. How could've her boyfriend turned out to be such a jerk?

"We had a terrible fight but made up a few days later when he took me to see Green Day. But even after that, we continued having our problems."

"And you decided to break up with him."

"It wasn't me, Becky. I was so naive that I believed he loved me in spite of everything. At the heart of it all was the fact that he wanted to study at McGill and to become a lawyer, which was totally cool with me. I wouldn't mind continuing long distance. When I caught him making out with another girl at the prom, he announced we were over. Worst of all, that chick flat out told me that Jake would never feel serious about a college-bound girl like me. I was way out of his league."

Now it made sense why Erin always stayed away from guys that belonged to higher circles. Every time she met someone from a medical or a law school, she would run for the hills without even giving the poor guy a chance.

"I was devastated," she continued as we drove along Yonge Street, "but I tried my best to hold it together for the rest of the night."

"You're so strong, Erin." I would never stop admiring my sister's ability to conceal her emotions.

"I'm simply good at hiding my feelings when I need to."

"I need to practice that." I recalled all the tears I'd shed openly.

"Anyway, men complicate our lives. That's why I decided that I don't need one anymore."

"Well, it's good to take a break from dating and reevaluate things."

"No, I'm not on a break, Becky. I'm done with relationships. Done for good!" She looked dead serious behind the wheel.

"Really? What made you decide?"

"Shortly before you called me from Tel Aviv, I saw Jake walking down the street with some high-profile chick. They looked like a celebrity couple. When I casually said 'hi,' he ignored me. It was the final straw for me."

"Was it the same day I called you?"

"Yes, Becky. I'm sorry for being so insensitive on that day."

"It's okay. I understand now."

"I'm just sick of wasting my time on assholes."

"I'm sure you'll find someone worthwhile in time."

"No more waiting for me, Becky. From now on, I'll focus only on myself."

"That's a pretty drastic decision to make." I felt a bit shocked by her announcement. Was she ready to put off dating for good?

"No, it's not." She sounded determined. "I just woke up the next day, looked in the mirror, and realized that I'm perfectly complete on my own. I know it may sound like a cliché, but it's true. I have you, Mom, Dad, and my friends. We hang out sometimes. I've got a great career I enjoy. I hope you'll also find one someday."

"So do I."

"And I'm glad my younger sister is alive."

"And she's about to embark on a new journey." I smiled as we entered the parking lot of Erin's apartment building.

thirty-One

"Rebecca! Welcome back!" Rosa ran toward me as I entered the office. Dave and Ashley got up from the cubicles and walked toward me.

"Hiya, girl! We missed you," Ashley exclaimed. "How's your hand?"

"As you can see, it's back to normal." I waved with my left arm, which was now perfectly healed. Never could I imagine how nice it would feel to be able to do everything myself and to have complete privacy again.

"Well, we're all glad to see you again," Dave said. We walked together to my cubicle, where he showed me the type of work that needed to be done. Most of it consisted of new orders and invoices—hardly anything special.

I busied myself with orders for the next few hours, taking care to avoid all the little mistakes I was so prone to making. The last thing I wanted was to give the wrong impression to my supervisor after such a lengthy absence.

In the meantime, I noticed that the atmosphere of our company had changed a lot. Although people seemed friendlier and less snappy, something wasn't quite right. It wasn't until the lunch hour that I could figure out what was going on.

"Did you hear what one of the sales reps just said!" Rosa exclaimed while heating her lunch in the microwave.

"No," Ashley replied, pouring herself a cup of coffee. "I didn't hear anything."

"They might sell our company to a bunch of new guys. Can you believe this?" Rosa pulled out her lunchbox and walked over the table.

"Now, ain't that some shit?" Kenyon, our shipping and receiving assistant, exclaimed. "Are they gonna get our asses fired?"

"That's exactly what I'm worried about!" Rosa exclaimed. "What I heard, our company isn't doing great financially."

"What! You never told me." Ashley took out her meal and joined us at the table.

"How was I supposed to know?" Rosa replied defensively. "I just learned this morning by passing the boardroom where they were having a meeting."

"Yo, man. I think we're in trouble," Kenyon remarked.

"Exactly!" Rosa exclaimed. "Ten years of services, and now I'm going to get kicked out."

"Wait, they didn't say they're laying people off," Ashley noted. "What if they'll just sell the company without firing anyone? Maybe we don't need to panic just yet."

"I want to believe you, girl, but quite honestly, I don't know what to think anymore," Rosa said.

I sat at the farthest corner of the lunch table and tried absorbing the new information. If the rumors were true, I could be jobless within a month. I would still get severance pay and benefits, but this money would only take me so far before I would have to start looking for a new job. Which meant another row of interviews at work agencies, another set of tests on Word and Excel, and ultimately, another administrative role. The mere thought of going through the same hell felt more depressing than the layoff itself.

The afternoon dragged slowly. The work was mostly made up of invoices and customer emails. A few times when no one was looking, I went on Facebook and looked over my old albums. I hadn't removed the photos of me and Jason yet, and now I had a chance to look at them and revisit all the happy memories. I found an old photo of us standing in front of the Western Wall, my eyes partly closed from the glaring sun. In another photo, Jason and I were standing in the Dead Sea, in our bathing suits, smeared in mud. For the first time since our return, I thought about all the marriages that actually lasted. I thought about my parents' marriage too. Despite the less-than-perfect circumstances at the time of the wedding, they were still strong as a couple. They must've had something special to last through a lifetime. I wondered if Jason and I were missing that part.

Or maybe not.

I closed Facebook and went back to invoicing. The monotonousness of work left plenty of room for thought. No matter how you put it, leaving Jason felt like a big mistake. Maybe with time, I would learn to live without him, but the pain of losing what we once had would always stay with me. Worst of all, it had been entirely my fault. Had I not kissed George or said all those things to Jason, maybe we would still be together.

Maybe we would even find a way to accommodate my desire to go back to school. People changed careers and moved around all the time. Even people from regular occupations sometimes had to move for work. It wasn't something insurmountable.

Or maybe I would find a way to convince myself that I didn't need a career in archaeology. That I could become happily settled in Toronto suburbs, raising a couple of kids, and commuting daily to a nine-to-five job. The last part seemed less likely, especially now that I was entering a pile of invoices into the system. Luckily, Dave had absolved me from the filing duty for the week, insisting that it would be too much strain on my arm. Still, I wanted to see Jason. Maybe I would call him either today or tomorrow. We needed to have a closure before we could go separate ways.

WHEN I arrived home, Erin was already lounging in the living room. In her baggy T-shirt and with little makeup, she hardly looked like the sister I'd known for my entire life. Something was bothering her lately, for she often acted a bit detached.

"Becky, I think we need to talk." She jumped from the couch the moment I walked in.

"What happened?" I became alarmed by the tone of her voice.

"It's a long story. Sit down. Let me get you coffee." She started walking toward the kitchen, but I stopped her.

"No, you tell me everything now. I can get myself coffee later." She turned around and walked back to the couch.

"I want to know what's been bothering you. 'Cause I can tell something's been going on with you."

"I think you need to see Jason," she said. "I saw him a few days ago. He was in a bar with his friends. You should've seen how awful he looked. Matted hair, sunken eyes. You need to talk to him, Becky."

"But wait, weren't you the one who encouraged me to forget him and move on?" My mind recalled all the times in the past month that she had lectured me about learning to let go and all that stuff.

"I did, but it was a big mistake. I should've never suggested him to split from you."

"W...what are you saying, Erin?"

"I know you're going to be mad, and I can't blame you." She stared guiltily into space the way you do when you're seven and are about to tell your mom that you've spilled hot chocolate on her favorite Persian rug. Or her favorite book. "I was the one who suggested a divorce to him."

"Wait! What?" I looked at her eyes, full of remorse, unable to fully comprehend her words.

"He called me on the morning of the accident, asking for advice. You were probably still unconscious, getting treatment from the doctors. We talked about your confusion over life goals and your crush on George. He told me that he really loved you despite anything, and that he was very worried about your state. We talked a bit longer, and I tried to make him see things from your perspective. I mean, you're still young, undecided about your career, and still interested in meeting new people."

"I'm not interested in meeting anyone!" I snapped.

"I know, Becky. Anyway, he asked what I thought he should do in this situation, and I suggested that he should let you go."

"Wait, so it was you who stood behind his crazy decision."

"Yes, it was me, Becky." She stared into the floor. "Before we ended the call, he told me several times that he didn't truly want to leave you but was willing to do it for your sake. I got a feeling he was very upset, but believed it would be fair for both of you."

"No, no, no!" I screamed, unable to hold my temper. "How could you do this to me?" I put my hands over my head

"I'm really sorry, Becky. I should've never said anything." She tried reaching out to me, but I bolted away.

"That changes everything for us. Goodness, I wish I knew it earlier." I grabbed my purse and began searching for the phone.

"Becky, wait."

"I need to see him now." I hastily found his number in the call log and hit the "dial" button. He picked up after my second attempt.

"Hello?" His deep voice rang on the other line.

"Hi, Jason. I think we need to meet."

"Becky! Great to hear from you! How have you been?"

"I'm fine, thanks. I need see you, like today. Is it okay with you?"

"Of course! You can come over anytime you like."

"I'm driving over, then."

"By all means, come. I'm home now."

After disconnecting from the phone, I slipped into my shoes, threw a jacket over my pencil dress, and informed Erin that I would be using her car.

"No, you can't drive in your current state," she panicked.

"Yes, I can." I took out my pocket mirror and checked and applied some blush.

"I've nothing against you using my car, but don't you remember how it ended the last time when you got all emotional and decided to drive?"

"Rest assured that it won't happen again." I grabbed her car keys and began to leave.

"Be careful!" Erin yelled after I was already in the corridor.

I MUST admit that getting behind the wheel for the first time in two months was more challenging than I expected. Between getting out of the parking area and navigating the rush-hour traffic, all I could hope for was getting to Jason's place in one piece. Luckily, I managed to survive the drive that felt like the longest one in my lifetime. All the emotions—the anger, confusion over next steps, and fear of rejection—floated onto the surface as I sat in traffic, waiting to arrive at the destination.

When I got to his condo—our former condo—I took a deep breath before dialing the unit code. I had to hope for the best. There was no way around it. The ride in the elevator lasted for what seemed like eternity. With every passing second, my heart kept pounding faster, and my palms became clammy. Having gathered all my strength, I walked over to the unit and knocked lightly.

"Becky, where have you been?" Jason exclaimed upon opening the door. "I was getting worried you'd never want to talk to me again."

I surveyed the condo after removing my shoes and walking into the living room. For the most part, it looked the same as it did before my trip—the same off-white walls, Ikea furniture, and an old TV stand. Yet it was different in subtle ways, perhaps emptier and a bit messier. I picked up a pair of socks from the floor before taking a seat on the couch.

"Jason, I'm sorry for all the damage I've done," I finally said. "I should've never gone out with George or said all those things on that night."

"It's okay, Becky." He paused. "I mean, it's not okay that you've kissed another guy, but I've made lots of mistakes too."

He took my hand. The touch of his skin felt fresh and familiar at the same time. The spark we once had wasn't gone after all. Suddenly, it occurred to me that I needed him more than anything else in my life.

"Becky, I know you're young, and you've got your entire life ahead of you. So if you want to leave, I'm not going to hold you back."

"But I don't want to leave. I never did." I looked straight into his eyes that showed signs of weariness.

"That makes me so much happier." He lightened up. "Lord knows how much I didn't want to leave you alone during the time you were still healing from the accident."

"It's okay, Jason. I'm here now." I moved even closer to him. "Erin told me about your conversation at the hospital."

"She did?" He looked a bit surprised.

"Yes, and she said you never really wanted to go through with it."

"I didn't, and I never will. I know it won't be easy, but can we forget everything that went wrong and start over?"

"We can certainly try. Although it might be harder now," I admitted.

No matter how much we wanted to forget everything, the damage was already done, and it would take time to restore the broken side of our relationship. But for now I wanted to hold him close and forget about all the troubles in the world.

His hand ran across the nape of my neck reaching over to the zipper of my dress. His other hand ran along my waist and then my hips. I began working on his shirt as we walked over to our former bedroom. Then we tumbled over to our bedroom, closing the door behind us. There we didn't exchange a word for a long time.

This time, everything felt right, from the way he held me close to the way I responded to his every touch. It was urgent and passionate yet also tender and sweet—just the way it was supposed to be.

"I have a suggestion for you," he said later, as we were lying in bed, entangled in an embrace.

"Tell me what it is." I began to feel intrigued.

"Since our last trip to Israel completely bombed, how about we go on another one?"

"You must be kidding, right?" I trailed my fingers across his chest, thinking about all the places I would gladly revisit. The Gaza conflict was long over, so we could go back anytime and travel safely without worrying about any political threat. Yet the problem of uncertainty with my job was too big to ignore.

"No, I'm not." He smiled.

"But how can we afford it? I just got back to work after a prolonged absence. I'm still getting back into the work routine. And did I mention that our company might go through layoffs in the next few months? I found out over lunch today."

"Well, we do have some savings, so we should manage," he said calmly. "And if the worst happens, you won't need to worry about the vacation requests."

"This is crazy, Jason. What about your job? I don't think they'll let you go so soon."

"I could arrange to work remotely for a week or so. My boss would be totally fine with it."

"Well, I don't even know what to say," I admitted, still taken aback by his crazy yet appealing idea.

"Just say 'yes,' and I'll book the flight to our second honeymoon."

"I'll have to think it through first." I rose up, wrapping a white bedsheet around my chest. "For now, I need to go." I kneeled down to find some of my clothes scattered on the floor.

"Where are you going, Becky?" He rose up, pulling on his boxers, and followed me.

"Home. I mean, my sister's place."

"Why do you need to go back to her place? This your home. Our home." He walked over to my side. "Please stay here tonight. I've missed you." He took my hands, reigniting the spark yet again.

"I've missed you too," I admitted, hugging him close. "And I think I'm getting a bit hungry."

"I'm afraid I have to say the same."

"Let's order pizza," I suggested. "And then we can discuss our holiday plans if you wish."

He gently wrapped his hands around my waist. I, in return, wrapped mine around his. Then we stood there, holding each other tight for the longest time I could remember.

Thirty-Two

One month later

"Look! That's the sign leading to Bethsaida, the site that got mentioned on CNN this year!" I exclaimed, knowing that I absolutely had to see this place. It was the site where a rare coin had been discovered earlier that summer.

"Are you kidding, Becky? It's almost seven in the evening. We have to go back to Tel Aviv before it gets too dark," he said, eyes transfixed on the road.

"Come on, Jason. Just one more stop." I pouted.

"Okay, okay. We'll stop, but only for fifteen minutes." He turned onto the side road leading to the site. "We can't be here much longer."

"*Sababa!*" I exclaimed, feeling all excited about the prospect of seeing this enigmatic site myself.

Despite my initial reluctance to go on this trip, everything worked out perfectly well. Jason worked remotely during the day, and we went out at night when Tel Aviv came to life. We did not have to worry much about the money beyond what was reasonable, as I was still getting my severance pay from the company.

Yes, I did get laid off, but that was one of the best things that ever happened to me. No longer did I have to go through the daily grind of the cubicle work or wonder about my future. I'd already chosen archaeology as my vocation, and I knew that as long as Jason and I were in this together, all difficulties would be manageable.

Despite his job, we still had a lot of time for each other. On the busy days, we would wait until the evening to take a short walk around the beach or Sderot Ben Gurion. We also rented a car for a few days and drove to the south, where we took our time to admire the magic scenery of the Negev Desert. For the second-last day of the trip, we agreed to drive to the Galilee and see all the sites I'd missed when I'd chosen to move from Megiddo to the Albright Institute.

The list of the sites we visited on that day was just unbelievable. We saw everything, from the Arbel Cliffs to Beit Shean and Capernaum. How we did this in one day is still beyond my understanding. We just did. And now that we were exhausted and ready to drive back to the hotel, my natural curiosity wouldn't let me go.

"Here, let's take a photo." I pointed at the large cactus tree standing next to the site entrance. A passerby, who happened to be a middle-aged Israeli man, volunteered to take the photo for us.

"That will become our happy memory," I said as we entered the innermost parts of the site.

We spent a few more hours exploring what used to be the biblical town of Geshur, where King David had met Princess Maacah. The site was later renamed Julias after Roman Empress Julia. As we were trekking down the ancient path and exploring the Iron Age defense wall, the *bit hilani* complex, and the Greco-Roman pillars, the atmosphere felt magical, especially with the sunset flaming on the horizon. By the time we were done with sightseeing, it was already dark.

"What will you suggest now?" Jason asked while starting the car.

"We can go back to our hotel, or—"

"We can stay somewhere closer," he finished my sentence.

I took our GPS and immediately began searching for the closest hotels in the area.

"Here, I think I found one." I showed him the screen with the name Ginosar being written on the top. "It's only fifteen minutes from here."

"THIS IS your key." The guy at the reception gave us a plastic card along with the map. "The unit houses are this way." He showed us to the left.

"*Toda raba,*" Jason said.

"Wow, you're speaking Hebrew," I remarked as we were searching for our unit later.

"Well, with you, anything's possible."

It turned out that the hotel area of Kibbutz Ginosar consisted of small houses, each representing a separate unit—somewhat similar to the kibbutz in Megiddo.

"I'm glad we took a toothbrush and toothpaste," I remarked as he tried opening the door.

"Admit it, Becky. You planned this ahead of time." He winked.

"Not really." Yet the sense of thrill of being somewhere new quickly filled me up. "How about taking a walk along the Sea of Galilee?" I suggested.

"Nah, I'm good here." He took me into his arms and gave me a passionate kiss.

"Me too."

By the look in his eyes, I knew that the night was just starting.

thirty-three

Two Years Later

"Yes, we'll see you all in May," I tell my mother over the phone. "How are the wedding preparations going?" I add.

"Wonderful," she replies. "Erin is glowing. You should've seen them yesterday. They kept chirping about the venue they've just found."

"How nice!" I can't believe my sister, who'd once sworn off dating for good, is finally getting married.

She and Paul met during her trip to Mexico two years ago, which was around the same time Jason and I traveled to Israel. It turned out that Paul is also from Oakville and was on a week-long vacation with his buddies. Who could imagine such a coincidence?

"How is your program, by the way?" my mother asks.

"Oh, I've just met with my supervisor. He wants me to focus on the cultic practices during Iron II for my research." As I'm holding the phone with one hand, my other one moves the cursor across the article about another goddess figurine that was discovered in Kiryat Adar this year.

"Well, it doesn't tell me too much." My mother laughs. "How is Julia?"

"She's great. We've just learned a few new words." I hear my daughter's laughter in the other room.

"Oh, that's wonderful! I can't wait to see her."

"I know, Mom. I'm sure time will fly fast." When Julia was a baby, my parents would visit us every so often. It must be hard for them now that we're miles away.

"Well, Becky, have a great year and keep us posted."

"Thanks, Mom. Say hi to Dad and to Erin. I love you all."

"Bye, sweetheart."

As much as I love Chicago, I can't wait to go back to Toronto and see my entire family. I'm still a bit angry at Erin for her part in my near-divorce with Jason, but I do realize that we all make mistakes. Sometimes, the best you can do is forgive and move on. Everyone, in turn, misses Julia, who will be two years old by the end of this spring. For the past few months, my mother has been extremely excited about Erin's wedding. After all the anguish my family had gone through because of my car accident, we all deserve a little bit of joy in our lives.

I put down the phone and walk toward the nursery room, where I eye Irene, our babysitter, playing with little Julia. She's been such wonderful company for our fifteen-month-old daughter.

"Thank you for all your help," I say while handing her the paycheck.

"Anytime," she replies.

In less than a year, Julia will be starting her daycare. I feel nervous, excited, and dreadful, all at once. Sometimes, it's hard to believe how fast children grow. Yesterday, she was a little baby cooing at me all the time. Today, she's rapidly approaching the toddler stage, ready to run and jump around.

As soon as Irene leaves, I start getting my daughter ready for a walk. It takes a while to get her dressed and strapped into the stroller, for she is constantly restless. In the end, we are out, walking down the street and enjoying a nice September day.

As we stroll through tiny alleys, exploring old buildings, I see a familiar woman walking in our direction.

"Aunt Rachel!" Julia exclaims, kicking her arms and legs inside the stroller.

"Honey, do you want out?" I ask her.

Julia doesn't reply but starts kicking harder. So I let her out of the stroller. She immediately runs toward the woman.

"Rebecca! I'm so happy to see you," she exclaims. "Hi, little one." She waves at Julia.

"Hi, Rachel. How are you doing?"

"I'm great, thanks. Yourself?"

"Oh, I'm great, too. Just met my supervisor this morning. Can't wait for the program to start."

"I'm on lunch right now. Want to grab a coffee?"

"Sure."

It's the same Rachel I lived with on the dig. Except that she's no longer the same person she used to be, but neither am I. A few weeks ago, we ran into each other at a coffee shop by accident and ended up getting two lattes together. I learned that she moved to the city this summer because she was offered a job at the University of Chicago Press. A few days later, she met Greg, who is currently her boyfriend. Rachel and I are best friends now. Whenever I need a break from the busy family life, I call her, and we go out for a short walk. We often laugh at our hostilities from the past.

Two years ago, Rachel was trying hard to fix something that was beyond any repair. Her relationship with George had been stalled for quite a while, but she kept hoping for another chance. Not unlike me, she was a recent graduate who had no idea about her future. She enrolled in the course with the Kiryat Adar Expedition in hopes of winning her ex-boyfriend back just to discover that he had already moved on. Rachel already apologized a hundred times for everything she had said to me during our reunion in Tel Aviv. I forgave her a long time ago, for she is the person who helps me stay sane.

I also ran into George one time when he was walking through the campus with his new girlfriend, Jessica. He spent this summer working at the Oriental Institute and is back at Wheaton College, finalizing his dissertation. I might have developed feelings for him during our stay in Israel. After all, we had so many adventures together that our short friendship began to resemble a summer romance. Yet looking back, I realize how foolish I had been to even think that another man could replace my Jason.

Over last two years, we had grown so much as a couple and a family. The move to Chicago had been challenging, but in a way, it had also brought us closer to each other. We had struggled with selling the condo, putting all the boxes together, finding a decent place to live in a big, new city, and of course, he had to find a new job. It's still hard to believe how far we've come.

I still kept in touch with most of the people I met on the trip, especially Caitlin and Megan. Both of them haven't given up on their promise to take me to the Semitic Museum. I just need to find the right time to visit them in Boston.

I don't talk to Janice and Madeline a lot, but I've forgiven them for their prank. I later learned that the reason they decided to play this nasty joke on me was because they were both feeling old and wanted to be irresponsible for the very last time. Well, I can understand the sentiment, because that's how I often feel when I'm cleaning Julia's highchair for the fifth time in a day. Avi got married a year after I left and moved to California, where he currently teaches prehistoric archaeology. I sincerely hope all the people I'd met are happy wherever they are in their lives.

As Rachel and I sip our lattes and talk, Julia keeps tugging at my leg, saying, "Mama, mama, ma." Like a typical toddler, she's full of energy, always ready for some mischief. The moment I look away, she tries climbing up a stand with mugs and ground coffees.

"Julia! No!" I yell. "Sorry," I later tell the café staff. They reassure me everything is all right.

"So, how was your first meeting?" Rachel asks me. "Did you decide what you'll be focusing on?"

"I plan on researching about the cultic practices in southern Israel dating to the Iron II. I'll be using the evidence from Kiryat Adar as the backup for my research."

"You sound like my ex." She laughs. "No wonder you two almost ended up together."

"No, we wouldn't have. We might be from the same field, but we are two different people with separate journeys."

"Now I can't even believe I used to think we had a future." She sighs. "Sometimes, when I look back, I wish I'd focused more on enjoying myself during that trip. Instead, I spent those three weeks obsessing over him and wondering what he was doing."

"Maybe you should come with me this summer," I suggest. "We could go for a girls' night out in Eilat."

"Are you sure you won't stray this time around?" she half jokes.

"No. My mind and my heart are in the right place."

Just as I say these words, my phone buzzes. It's a message from Jason, asking me about my day. Last week, he started a new job at an IT firm in downtown Chicago. After being out of work for three months, we began worrying that both of us would stay unemployed forever. However, things actually turned in our favor, and he's now earning more than he did back in Toronto. It's not that my husband's salary matters to me. It has more to do with the feeling of achievement, and I can tell Jason feels like he has accomplished something by landing this job.

I BELIEVE it was at Ginosar where I became pregnant with my daughter, whom we decided to name after the beautiful site of Bethsaida Julias. Following our return from Israel, I became fully focused on applying for a PhD program. I must admit that with morning sickness and swollen ankles, taking courses wasn't easy. Many people didn't believe I would make it to a grad school with a baby in tow. To tell the truth, I sometimes didn't believe it, either.

All I did the next year was manage through sleepless nights, endless feedings, and countless diaper changes. Sometimes, I barely even had time to shower or eat. Nevertheless, it was the most amazing year of our lives. The first smile, the first crawl, and ultimately the first walk brought so much joy to us that we would gladly do it all over again. Someday, we might.

When Julia turned six months, I started sending applications to graduate schools across Canada and the United States. I obviously used my experience from the Albright Institute and Kiryat Adar as part of the application, and everyone I worked with was more than happy to provide me with references. The day I learned about my acceptance to the University of Chicago was also the day my daughter stood up for the first time, so it was double excitement.

I still don't know if I'll ever succeed in academia. I plan to specialize in the archaeology of Syria-Palestine, which is a very narrow field with few job prospects.

My program will require me to gain more fieldwork experience, which means I'll be gone for most of the summers. After Erin's wedding, I'm heading to Ashdod Yam to work for three weeks. Jason and Julia will travel with me since I cannot imagine being separated from them for that long. My mother will also come for a week to help with Julia. It won't be easy considering my mother's view of Israel, but I'm sure they'll have a great time in the end. I often feel guilty about choosing this career path with all its challenges. However, I also remind myself that someday, my daughter will grow up to develop her own dreams, and I can only be a better parent by following mine.

AFTER A brief chat with Rachel, I return to our apartment, where I make a meal for Julia. She plays with her toys until I call her for lunchtime. Recently, she started saying small words, delighting us along the way.

"Mommy love!" she exclaims, putting her little hands around my neck.

"Love you too, my little pumpkin." I kiss her on the forehead.

After a long, messy meal, she is exhausted and ready for her afternoon nap. I wash her face, dress her in sleepwear, and gently tuck her into bed. As soon as she is asleep, I retreat to my desk and go over my files. This year, I'll be working as a teaching assistant for an introductory undergraduate course on ancient Near East. As I go through the list of students' names, my jaw drops. Zeinab Assaf is in my class!

I knew that she had moved to the States for studies, but not in a million years could I imagine that our paths would cross again. Although I had never made it to Nablus, we've been talking regularly on social media. In the process, I've learned that we have a lot in common, and it's not just the music we enjoy. We are two small-town girls with big dreams. Zeinab wants to work for UNESCO, while I hope to become a tenured professor. Well, we both have a lot of obstacles along the way, but we'll surely overcome them. I hope that someday, we'll be able to celebrate our successes by climbing Mt. Gerizim and touring Jericho while our husbands watch the kids. Provided that she'll be married by then, of course. I hope she will. Each one of us deserves to experience a happy marriage and parenthood no matter what beliefs we uphold. I bet some would disagree with me.

In the meantime, I look at the books I have just bought for my courses. Those are the books written by the top scholars in my field—Israel Finkelstein, William Dever, Amihai Mazar, and, of course, David Ussishkin. Among the books rests *Encyclopaedia of the Ancient Civilizations*, the book I had gotten as a Christmas gift as a little girl. As soon as I open it, I am flooded with happy memories from Oakville mixed with memories of Kiryat Adar and the Albright Institute. As I flip through its pages, I realize that my long-awaited journey is about to begin.

About the Author

OLGA SUSHINSKY is a freelance editor/busy mom by day and a writer by night. She earned her B.A. in History and French and M.A. in Near Eastern Civilizations from the University of Toronto. She also holds a certificate in Publishing from Ryerson University. Prior to embarking on her writing journey, she worked in a number of fields, including education, office administration, and ultimately publishing. She began writing shortly after graduating from university, but it took her several years to complete the first novel. When she is not writing, Olga enjoys reading light fiction stories with happy endings, visiting local galleries, and spending time with her family. She currently lives in Toronto, Canada.

CPSIA information can be obtained
at www.ICGtesting.com
Printed in the USA
LVHW090843230620
658719LV00003B/345

9 781643 970981